HER
LAST
HOUR

BOOKS BY B.R. SPANGLER

DETECTIVE CASEY WHITE SERIES

Where Lost Girls Go

The Innocent Girls

Saltwater Graves

The Crying House

The Memory Bones

The Lighthouse Girls

Taken Before Dawn

Their Resting Place

Two Little Souls

Our Sister's Grave

B.R. SPANGLER

HER LAST HOUR

bookouture

Published by Bookouture in 2024

An imprint of Storyfire Ltd.
Carmelite House
50 Victoria Embankment
London EC4Y 0DZ

www.bookouture.com

ISBN: 978-1-83525-317-5
eBook ISBN: 978-1-83525-316-8

This book is dedicated to my family, friends, and readers enjoying the Detective Casey White series.
With much love, thank you for your support.

PROLOGUE

A drippy plink. A red bloom opened onto the table. Breathy whispers of courage broke the fusty air as he cut deeper, wincing at the parted tissue. The vacant gap filled instantly, the blade sweeping silently across another vessel. Glorious release made him shudder. This was good. This was how he'd been told it was done. This was how he'd been showed.

He tipped his arm to capture the spill, a warm path weaving over ruptured skin. There wasn't a drop to waste. Not with the number of words that needed to be written. He pinched his wrist to stop the bleed, gauging the amount. This was the first letter and there was no knowing how much was needed. Not yet.

Candle flames flickered in an autumn breeze and carried the smell of freedom. There was purpose in his liberation of her: she was selected. And she would be grateful like he was. More so because he chose her to be first. *That's enough*, fingertips pressing to stave the bleed, a white gauzy bandage circling the wound. The bottom of the small porcelain bowl was covered, the tip of a quill made wet, a sheet of paper centered in wait. The type of paper was selected for her too. The words were for her as well, even the blood used to create the message carried significant weight, telling how she was going to die.

The flame shined against a glass bottle as he tilted it and watched it glimmer. The sparkly dance was simple. They'd called him simple but he wasn't. He was told so and would show them. Impressionable was another word used. It was like the candle's soft wax, which he collected too. It'd be used to seal the message inside after the words were penned.

The bottle chosen had been forged by hand, its shape made to resemble a womb. When his riddles evaded, would the detective smash it in frustration? Absent of fingerprints, of fibers, and hair, the bottle was made sterile and would be planted for the detective to find. Only then would the message get delivered.

He leaned back with a satisfying sigh, a wave of relief breathing through him. Time was short, the gauze already drying and turning sticky, the blood thinners and anticoagulants reserved to make the ink. He'd been shown that too. He regarded his DNA, regarded the obvious clue in the ink. But did it matter? It didn't.

These were the components in planning a perfect murder. The clues accompanying it were for the detective and would establish the game. And what a game it would be. Glorious. Detective Casey White only needed to figure out how to play before it was too late.

ONE

Bright headlights bled into Ruby's eyes, a glaring shine that bounced off the rearview mirror. She flipped the switch beneath it, the wedge moving the way her father showed her it would. It doused the beaming lights while she mumbled a complaint about how newer cars did that automatically. She bit her lips and sighed, guilt surfacing with sweeping sadness. She didn't mean it. She'd do anything to have her dad back. The car she drove was the last thing he'd given her. It was their project.

It wasn't just any car either. It was a muscly '86 Chevy Camaro that he'd hand-picked from a pile of wrecks. The rusty carcasses were parked along the south-side fence at Sea-Junk Auto Recycling, a place he'd said used to be a junkyard and that only the name had changed. It was still a junkyard. They'd gone there on a sunny afternoon to look at another car altogether, and when he saw the Camaro, he'd told her that it was a gem like she was. Ruby didn't see it and wanted to keep looking. She remembered that his coughing was bad that day. His color too. It looked sickly. Mom had warned her about them staying out too long, the worries for him already beginning by then.

Mom was the real challenge, the look on her face priceless that afternoon when they pulled up to the house. The car behind her with the high beams was almost forgotten as the memories returned. Her mom was right though, the Camaro did look like shit, especially that awful factory metallic-blue paint job which had bubbled and turned to rust. How would they fix that? Little did she know, the rust feasting on the metal wasn't the only cancer. There were the tumors in her dad's lungs too. They'd been doing what they do. They'd been doing it for a while.

Maybe he knew, she wondered. *Maybe he knew that he was dying.* That's why he'd insisted she helped him with the car. He'd said that they would put it right. That's how he explained it. That they'd put the car right.

Never in a million years did she think she'd become a mechanic. Truth was, she enjoyed working with the tools and the motor, along with the bodywork. She'd learned everything there was about restoring an eighties muscle car. They'd transformed that car before he became bedridden, before hospice care and the last days of life. The rusty blue was gone. In its place, there was a flashy, bumblebee black and yellow. He'd wanted a shade of red to match her name and hair, but the combination of yellow and black was too good to pass up. She'd picked the yellow because its reflection made him look good. It made him look healthy.

The Bee. That's the name Ruby gave the Camaro. On her father's death bed, he told her that if she could fix The Bee, then there wasn't anything in this world she couldn't do. Tears welled in her eyes and blurred the road, tires rumbling against the roadside's rumble strips. She straightened the wheel and swiped her cheeks, glimpsing the scar between her index finger and thumb. It was the first of a few she'd earn during those late nights and weekends working on the Camaro. She squinted at the bright headlights, the car behind her moving across the lane.

What was the scar from? Ruby tried to remember. *The bumper!* It was from the old bolt holding the front bumper in place. Her wrench had slipped on it, the force pushing her hand into a piece of jagged metal. It was the tetanus shot in the arm that hurt more, the stitches only slowing her down a few days.

Lightning flashed silently in the west, and thick drops ticked against the roof and windshield. Ruby spun the knob to turn on the wipers and said a silent prayer about the electrical relay, the one she'd replaced. *Please work.* It did, old rubber squelching against the glass. Another flash made Ruby duck and search the sky. It wasn't supposed to rain, the weather making her nervous. Her knuckles went white, the steering tight. She went through the list in her head, asking questions like her dad told her. It could be low fluid or air in the line. Eyelids springing open. *A leak?* That was bad if the road got slick, especially on worn tires.

"A little help to get home," she said, gripping the wheel and glancing at the picture of her dad. It'd been there since the funeral, edges frayed, his photograph torn from the program her mom had printed. There were words on the other side, parts of a prayer he used to say. When she needed it, she'd flip the picture sometimes, his voice reciting the words in her head like it was a dream. "Dad, I miss you."

Blue lightning. Ruby squinted to look again. *That can't be right?* It wasn't lightning. It was a light though, the car with the bright headlights was behind her again, blue lights flashing from its roof. Her heart sank. It was the police, a patrol car that had been behind her all this time. This time she heard both her mother's and father's voices telling her what to do. They'd rehearsed this with her, her dad playing the role of the police while her mother gave instructions from the passenger seat. Ruby flipped the turn signal, the tires crossing the rumble strips as she stopped on the side of the road.

The patrol car parked behind her, its headlights continuing

to beam into her car. She couldn't see anything but the white and blue and shielded her eyes. There was a shadow, a silhouette, an officer approaching. He tapped on her door window with the butt end of a flashlight, his face above the car. She rolled down the window enough to hear his instructions, the wind sweeping the rain into the car.

"Ma'am," he asked, turning on a flashlight.

Ruby shrank back, the light enormous and blinding.

"Can you point that thing down?"

"It's for my safety, ma'am," he answered, keeping the head of the light as close as possible. "You've got a nice ride here. I can't say I see cars like this very much."

"I fixed it up with my dad," Ruby told him, handing over her driver's license and the registration. "Can you tell me why you pulled me over?"

"Let's take a look at these first," he said, the flashlight's beaming light finally dropping. The reprieve was short, a green afterimage staining her eyes. The spots moved wherever she looked, impossible to blink away. The light returned, the shine like an attack. "You swerved back there. Off the road and then back."

"I... It wasn't intentional." In her head, she heard the tires rumbling, the gravel spitting and knocking the wheel well. Was it enough to pull her over? "I'm sorry, officer. I'll be more careful."

The man stood in the shadows, his head and shoulder a gray outline that he straightened. He pivoted away from the car, roadside grit beneath his shoes. *Was he leaving?* She watched him in the side mirror, seeing him go to the back and the other side, flashlight shining up and down the car's sides. *What's he doing?* She rubbed the back of her neck and got her phone.

"You won't need that," he said, his voice suddenly booming.

"My mom is going to worry—"

He waved the flashlight again, a brightness so hellish she thought it would burn the skin off her face. "Sorry to be the bearer of bad news. I can't let you drive this car any further."

"Huh? What? I don't understand what you mean?"

The officer didn't answer, tapping his wristwatch instead. Confused, Ruby glanced at the clock on the dash, the old numbers barely visible, the time it told her unreliable. She checked her phone's screen instead. It was a minute past midnight. No more. No less. "Why? Because it's after twelve?"

The officer held up her driver's license, explaining, "You're driving past curfew. You won't be eighteen for another month. That's when you'll have full driving privileges."

"But I'm five minutes from my home," she said, feeling the heat of an argument rising. *Never talk back*, her mother and father told her. *Never to the police.* Deep down she wanted to say fuck it and tell him to go scratch his ass. That she wasn't playing whatever game this was. She forced a breath and wiped the rain dripping into the car. She decided to try and reason instead. "Sir? If you hadn't pulled me over, then I would have been home already. I would have been there before midnight."

He seemed to squirm at the comment, a hope springing forward from wherever it was that hope comes from. Ruby shifted and pinched the lip of the window to take back her license and registration. Leather creaked and the officer leaned closer to the door, close enough she could feel his breath on her fingers. "Honey, I wouldn't have pulled you over if you hadn't swerved back—" He flinched with a start, the flashlight swinging suddenly to point inside the car. He sniffed the air like a dog. "Is that alcohol I smell?"

"What?" she asked, fingers retreating. Her insides turned to jelly when she smelled it too. It *was* alcohol, but it was mixed with lavender and peach. Relief. "I am so sorry, officer, that's just my hand sanitizer. I volunteer at the assisted living place on

Yellowfin Drive. The one with the nursing care unit." No response. No motion. There was only the flashlight staring at her with its blinding dead eye. "Do you know the one? It's a couple miles south—"

"I need you to exit the vehicle," the officer demanded abruptly, his voice booming. He made room, a gloved hand reaching for the door.

Her heart thudded against her chest, the sound of metal latches in motion. The door swung open. Ruby clutched her front, sudden fright gipping her. Her dad said they were never supposed to do that. It was a violation of privacy. Something like that.

"Exit the vehicle!"

"Can I just call my mom?" Ruby pleaded, voice breaking as the rain spilled across her legs. The wet touch was cold and raised goosebumps on her skin. The officer adjusted the flashlight, the beam wide enough to cover all of her. It covered the entire car too. "Sir? I swear to you, it was only hand sanitizer."

He lowered the flashlight enough for her to blink away the burn. Wish it away was more like it, the space where he stood gobbled by glowing orbs.

"Tell you what," he began to say, shoes grating on the blacktop. "We'll call your mother from the station. It's already past my shift and I really don't want to spend the next three hours processing a DUI."

"A DUI? Processing? But officer, I wasn't even drinking," she argued, the heat in her words fleeting, swallowed by emotion. She regarded his offer, quiet descending between them. Finally, she asked, "We can call my mom from the station? No arrest or anything?"

"No arrest tonight. Unless that's what you want," the officer said with a chuckle, a hint of snark. He seemed to relax, the outline of his shoulders slumping. "Listen, I'd really prefer it if we just got you home so I can go home."

Ruby felt the words on her lips, felt the need to ask more questions. The officer swung the flashlight, urging her to follow. The cold was setting in, the rain drenching her clothes and making them cling to her skin. "Would you mind if I asked you to lower that light?"

"Sure thing. In a minute. There's always traffic on Route 12."

A pair of headlights approached; the sight of them supporting the officer's words. She heard a door open on the patrol car, the light preventing her from seeing it. She hesitated, stopping to see the other car pass.

"Come on now, keep moving... I'll tell you what. You mentioned that you live close by? How about I drop you off at your house."

"Home?" Ruby asked, inching forward as the oncoming car grew, her vision returning. She shaded her eyes long enough to see it, to recognize it from school. It was Michael Larson from her homeroom class. She raised a hand to wave, a reflex or instinct. His windshield was dark though, his face hidden. But the car was slowing; she heard the motor, heard it idling. *Michael saw me.* And then she wondered with a hint of embarrassment, *how am I going to explain this?*

She reached the open door and looked inside, her vision restored. The dashboard instruments were the first thing to come into focus, the speedometer and tachometer with their needles sitting on zero. There was an old-style AM and FM radio in the place where there should have been a two-way police radio. Confused, she gripped the car's roof. The radio would have been installed by her father since it was his dealership that outfitted the local police vehicles. He'd sold them all their cars, which included the equipment rigging too. The back seat wasn't right either. It was cushioned instead of that hard plastic with the bucket seating. The fake leather was cracking with foam jutting from a torn seam. The plexiglass partition with the metal screen was also missing, and there was no weapons mount or traffic computer. This wasn't a police car at all.

Panic ran rampant through her insides like wildfire, the hair on her body standing up on end. Ruby felt small and afraid, the man behind her squaring his body to block the road as she locked her arms against the car's roof. If he wasn't a cop, then who was he? Ruby couldn't breathe and dared to turn around and look over her shoulder. Before she could see him, the corner of the door struck. A deadening thwack came with a silvery flash, a distant pain surfacing like a sunrise. It was small in the beginning and then hit her all at once. She sensed falling over, consciousness becoming faint. Thick fingers dug into her sides and hoisted her inside the car, the ringing in her ears needling her mind to stay alert.

"Please..." she groaned and tried to focus through the fuzzy, dim light. Ruby was barely aware of being turned around, her body flopping face down onto the back seat with her mouth and nose smashed against a ripped seat cushion. There was a stink in the foam. Sweat. Or was it urine? Revulsed, she sprang up and was met by another jolt, a star-filled darkness. Ruby fell forward, faintness rolling in like a fog.

Her arms and legs were wrenched, muscles and bone and tendons strained painfully until they were pinned behind her. Cloth ripping pierced her ears and heart, alertness returning like a gunshot. Heart pounding, she squirmed desperately, his grip like metal restraints. It was tape she heard being torn, her ankles and wrists bound together in a way that made every movement hurt.

"Please, sir," she begged. "Sir, please don't do this."

Her lungs were being squeezed of their last breath, the weight on top of her impossible to bear. It was his knees as he drove them into her lower back while pressing on her shoulders. Stars returned for a swim in the pool of darkness that invaded her eyes. She gasped, the pain unbearable, the heaviness crushing. This must be what it feels like to suffocate, she thought errantly, gulping at the stale air. An image of her father rested in her mind. It came to comfort her as the fight to stay awake slipped to a place she'd never return from. She saw his lips moving, his head nodding, his voice telling her, *it's okay, Ruby, we'll put the car right*.

Michael Larson saw The Bee, that shiny yellow and black Camaro he admired in the school parking lot. Ruby got pulled over? That can't be. She'd never do anything wrong. He saw the blue lights too, his foot easing off the gas pedal as he tossed the burning joint from the car window. It was raining, but he lowered all the windows so the gushing air would suck the smell out of the car.

He'd learned the hard way that where there was one cop, there were likely two or three waiting. He slowed to ten below the speed limit, his focus narrowing on Ruby. She wore the paisley scrubs he'd seen her wearing before. It was for that job in the old folks place up the street. He slowed a little more, a nugget of doubt forming deep in his head. It wasn't paranoia either. There was something off about the patrol car. Was it a patrol car? Ruby stood in front of it, the patrol lights flashing the same blue he'd seen in his own rearview mirror. He knew what the unmarked police cars on Route 12 looked like. This wasn't one of them.

His cellphone. *Call Dad!* He snatched it from the front seat and held it sideways to grab a picture, the phone's strobe glinting off the windshield. The guy standing with Ruby saw it, Michael's heart sinking into his gut. That's when the light came, the biggest flashlight he'd ever seen. Not a flashlight. It was a handheld floodlight and it blinded him enough for him to stomp the pedal, the motor revving and tires peeling against the wet asphalt. When the light was gone and the spots in his eyes started to fade, he slowed again, drifting into the parking lot of the Snack Shack. It was closed, the lights turned off. That was not a cop.

"Michael?" a groggy voice spilled from his phone. More alert this time. "Son, are you okay?"

"Yeah, I'm fine, Dad," he managed to say. His voice cracked with the thought of something sinister. The fear of it making him sit up and stare at the dark road behind him. "Dad, do you remember that guy you used to golf with? The one with that car dealership?"

"Yeah, sure. You're talking about Jonathon Evans. He died last year." The sound of blankets rustling, a light switch, and a heavy breath. "Michael, where are you? What's going on?"

"I'm at the Snack Shack off Route 12." Michael braced the steering wheel and revved the motor. In the rearview mirror, the faint glow of headlights brimmed the road. "Listen, Dad, I think something happened to his daughter. I think it's happening right now."

"Wait, son. What do you mean, *is happening*?" There was anger. A familiar frustration in his dad's voice. "Dammit, Michael, have you been drinking?"

"No, Dad, I swear it!" The faint smell of pot had him sniffing his fingers. He tucked his hand beneath his leg thinking it would help. "Dad, there was this guy with blue lights on his car roof. He had Ruby Evans pulled over. Only, I don't think he was a cop."

"Jonathon's daughter?" his dad questioned. Phone moving, a panicked voice returned, "Michael! Son, come home and we'll make some calls."

"But she's—" The glow in the rearview mirror faded. "Shit, Dad. I think it's too late."

"Come home, Michael!" his father demanded, the voice

tinny, his cellphone returned to the passenger seat as Michael spun the wheel. He drove back, flooring it, ignoring the speed limit. He didn't stop until he reached Ruby's car.

"The Bee," he mouthed and searched the darkness with frantic worry, picking up his phone. "Dad, Ruby's gone."

TWO

There's a certain look I've come to know through the years. It comes with a claim by a witness, a testimony given. In it, there'll be a certain quality, a level of sincerity that I can see and hear. Sometimes, I think I can almost smell it too, if that's even a thing. Whatever it is, I've learned to trust it. Grown to use it. And when there's something dire or foreboding, I know to investigate it.

That's what I do. Investigate. My name is Casey White and I am a detective in North Carolina's barrier islands, the Outer Banks. I saw that same disquieted look on the face of a teenage boy this morning while a uniformed patrolman asked him questions. I heard it too, recognizing it immediately in the young man's voice. When we locked eyes, I knew. I saw it and felt the stir in my gut. If I hadn't been there at that moment, I would have certainly missed it. I waved my arm toward a few from my team who were waiting back at their desks. A hand poked up above the heads of passing office traffic, signaling they'd get started without me.

"Morning, officer," I began, and shuffled a cup of coffee with my laptop bag, the strap digging into my shoulder. The officer was a first year, possibly second, every inch of his uniform proper, which was unlike his demeanor. There was frustration on all the faces of the adults with the teen, a temperament reaching a point the officer didn't see coming. I searched for Alice, our office manager, looking to the counter and her computer. She wasn't there.

"What's the issue? Maybe I can help."

"Morning, Detective," the officer said, swallowing dryly. He pawed at his chin which looked baby-soft like the rest of his face. There wasn't a single wrinkle, the rookies joining the force looking younger and younger every year. "Detective, I'm trying to explain that it's a bit too soon for a missing persons report."

"Why's that?" I asked, unintentionally putting him on the spot. He stopped to think, which gave me a moment to size up the couple with the teen. They were early to mid-forties, the man dressed well in denim jeans and a polo shirt; a thin jacket for the cooler weather was draped over his arm. The woman wore an oversized jogging suit, her thin frame swimming in it. She had her hair pinned back as if she'd run from the house. It was the shoes on her feet that were telling: a pair of bedroom slippers, the kind with cottony insoles that were poofy around the opening. I think I once had a pair just like them.

The teenage boy looked like he might have been around the station once or twice. His hair was oily black, slicked back straight with a widow's peak that matched his dad's receding hairline. A few weeks of scruff had grown out and become scraggly on his chin, his sideburns a shadow. There was a faint smell of marijuana, which I had to regard, the teen possibly being under the influence when the subject of the report went missing.

"Missing persons reports are usually taken after twenty-four hours?" the young officer said, asking rather than telling.

"Yes and no. It's not a hard rule like they show on television shows." I took a sip of coffee, the caffeine my drug of choice.

The teen's eyes were clear and alert, albeit with some pouches that said he'd been up late the night before. The man and woman wore the same tired look. Whatever happened must have occurred in the early morning hours. "Most of the time, we discover that there's been a slight miscommunication, a phone call or a text message that was never received."

The woman shook her head, lips disappearing in a bite. "No. Uh-uh. Ma'am, that's not it. That's not it at all."

"Please, my son saw something last night that needs to be looked into," the man said, speaking with his hands on the move, the tension climbing in his voice. When he saw me watching, he lowered his arms, plump cheeks shaking as he continued. "We came here to get help around two thirty this morning and got none. We left to go look for her again. We looked and looked and then came back. But we're still not getting anywhere."

"You were here this morning?" I slipped the laptop bag from my shoulder, hiding my disappointment, thinking there would have been a report. Then again, it wasn't uncommon for the station to get flooded with missing persons reports, parents and siblings and friends coming in at all hours of the day and night. It happened all the time during the summer months when tourism was peaking. It was teens mostly, but not exclusively. However, this wasn't the summer and the tourists exited our islands like birds flying south for the winter. We were deep into autumn months which meant the couple and teen were from here. "You're local?"

"Yes, ma'am. Nags Head. Born and raised," the man answered, puffing his chest proudly.

"Me too. My husband also." The woman slowly nodded. "He passed this past year."

Confusion narrowed my focus. "Could we start at the beginning? Who is it that went missing?"

Whatever frustrations the man held on to drained from his

face. His color followed. "Ma'am, please, my son saw this woman's daughter being taken last night."

This woman's daughter. He passed this past year. This wasn't a married couple. The man was the teen's father, and it was the woman whose daughter was missing. They noticed me staring. "I'm sorry, I am still catching up." I took the woman's hand, asking, "My name is Detective White. You are?"

"Mrs. Evans," she answered in a frail voice. She had weepy eyes that looked sorrowful. "Can you help us?"

"Of course," I said, assuring her.

The officer shuffled his feet, hands on his hips, impatiently waiting.

"Officer, I'll take it from here."

He didn't reply, choosing to walk away, the father of the teen, huffing, "Thank God!"

"Sir," I said, garnering his attention. I turned to the man's son, asking, "And your name is?"

"It's Michael, ma'am," he answered nervously, eyes frozen.

"As mentioned, I'm catching up so if you wouldn't mind, could you tell me exactly what you saw?"

"Around midnight last night, I was on my way home and saw blue flashing. That's when I saw a black and yellow Camaro pulled over on Route 12."

"The Bee. She was coming home from the old folks care facility," the woman interjected. When she saw the look on my face, my questioning the mention of a bee, she moved closer. "That is what my daughter calls her car. It was a restoration project that she did with her father before he passed."

"Jonathon Evans. I golfed regularly with him. He did all the patrol cars for the police, including the unmarked ones," the teen's father said. His brow rose. "Look, we already told the other officers about him. That's why my son—"

"I understand, but really I need to hear it," I said, raising a hand against the growing chatter. I faced the teen. "Please, continue."

"Ruby owns that car. It's the only yellow and black car at our high school. I saw her standing with a man at the other car. You know, like she was going to be arrested. But he wasn't a cop."

"My husband's place, all the police cars come from there," the woman said, reiterating what the boy's father said.

The scent of pot remained, and I had to play devil's advocate, and ask, "How can you be sure it wasn't a police car?"

The teen shook his head, mouth turned down. "There's no way that was a cop car." He pulled a phone from his back pocket. "I knew it didn't look right and got a picture."

"Let's see what you have," I said, unsure of what to expect.

The picture was of a white flash, the phone's light reflected in his windshield. But beyond his car, I recognized Route 12, the ocean's berm further away. There was a vehicle with blue lights along the side of the road, and another vehicle in front of it that was black and yellow. There were two figures, but they were badly blurred, another light washing out much of the bottom third. One figure was short and thin, head barely reaching the car roof. The other figure with the light towered above the car, his face blurred dark and thick like an inky smear. "Hard to make out anything in this."

When I motioned to the washed-out area, the teen said, "The guy was carrying this huge light and flashed it at my car when I slowed down."

"This is her?" I asked, pointing to the lighter colored figure, the smaller one.

"Uh-huh. She's got them paisley scrubs she wears," he answered. There were yellow stains on his fingers which trembled as he moved to point to the taller image. "That's a big dude. It was hard to see his face, but I think he was white. At least six feet too. He had these darker colored clothes that looked like what a cop would wear."

I waved to Sherry Levin, our resident technical investigator, a newer member of the team. She didn't think I noticed, but I saw her peeking over the cubical wall, curiosity goading her. Silence filled the moment as she made her way toward us. Her brown hair was pinned back in a small bun, her slacks swishing as she moved fast while we waited. She was shorter than me, the top of her head reaching my chin, her eyes narrowing on the phone, my asking, "See the people in this picture, and the car behind the black and yellow one?"

"Whoa, that's a hot Camaro," she said, catching her breath. She looked closer, focusing on the second car with the blue lights. "That's not like any of the unmarked cars I've seen."

"Thank you," the teen said, clapping his hands together.

Tracy Fields from the team joined Sherry's side, interest in the picture growing.

Michael's eyes grew hopeful while watching them. "I told the other cop that I didn't think that car was the same sedan like the others."

"You can tell it's a sedan," Tracy said, having driven one for some time. "Even with the picture being washed out, I can make out the four doors and trunk. But it's not one of the patrol cars."

The teen's story was checking out and the direness of what had happened urged me to take action. "Mrs. Evans, this is what we're going to do next." I slowly nodded my head until she was following my words with her attention. "Michael, this is Tracy and Sherry, they work for me. You'll follow them back to their desks so they can get a copy of that picture. I think you'll see some imaging magic as they enhance the blurry figures and identify what kind of car that is."

"Okay." He nodded, fright and concern on his face.

My stomach twisted with worry of someone posing as one

of us. How many young people would pull over at the sight of police lights in the rearview mirror? "We might find out who it was that pulled over your friend."

"Thank God," Michael's father repeated. "Finally, someone is going to help."

"And, Mrs. Evans, you'll come with me so I can get a report started."

She breathed a sigh of relief, her fingers brushing my arm. I still didn't know enough to assess what happened. But if this was a kidnapping, an Amber alert was the first thing to get issued.

"Your daughter's name, ma'am?"

"Ruby," she said. Her lips were thin, the color of them near impossible to recognize. But I saw them quiver as she continued, eyes glistening. "My daughter's name is Ruby Evans."

"Mrs. Evans, you mentioned your daughter works at a nursing home?"

"That's right. She's a volunteer." A slight smile showed pride for her daughter. "Ruby volunteers her time there. Might study in that field at college."

My hand was up again, waving for Tracy to join us again and help with the questions. That's how it began. The questioning. It was the tedious and most critical part of every investigation. Time and time again, I'd heard the first details shift and morph and then change entirely. That's what time did to memories. It changed them. That's why the initial reports were the most reliable. They were critical. Ruby Evans's life might depend on what we heard in the next hour.

THREE

The roads were oily slick, the windshield wipers working double-time to keep pace with a storm that was running up the coast. We were garbed head to toe in thin plastic, a vain attempt to stay dry. The winds were blowing the rain sideways though, ensuring we'd get wet no matter how much cover we wore. Michael Larson sat behind Tracy, one lip tucked between his teeth, eyes wide. The faint odor of pot had been replaced by coffee, steam rising from a cup he held between his fingers. He'd barely touched it, the adrenaline from the night's activities keeping him upright.

I glanced at the clock on my dash, the number one appearing four in a row. The time was eleven after eleven in the morning, which had me thinking it had been more than a full day since Michael last slept. He caught me looking at him through the mirror, spurring me to ask, "Michael, how are you holding up?"

"Honestly?" he asked, gaze drifting to the passenger window, the rain's shadow running down his face. "I'd rather be in school with Ruby and know that she's okay."

"I get that." Deep down, I wanted to tell him that it would

be okay. I couldn't. There was no ignoring the sickening feeling that what he witnessed was a kidnapping. "We've got another mile before the Snack Shack."

He touched the cup to his lips. "It was about a mile or so south of it."

"It's good that you're helping," Tracy said with a spark in her baby-blue eyes. She was young in her career and eager, which meant she was perfectly paired to work with me. She turned around to look at him, wavy brown hair growing long, the summer highlights all but gone. He gave her a shallow nod, the words not helping. "Most people would have driven by without a thought. But you didn't."

"That says a lot," I told the teen. It was guilt he was feeling. It was weighing on him like a heavy blanket. I knew it to be a kind of remorse. The type witnesses can experience when believing there was more they could have or should have done. His eyes returned to the rearview mirror, weepy. "Michael, you did everything you could. This is the part where we take over."

The car went quiet, tires drumming against the road. "The Bee, I can see it," he finally said, face appearing between the front seats. His mouth fell open. "Wow. I'm kinda shocked it's still there."

"You and me both," Tracy commented, fingers dancing across the keys of her laptop. She saw something, clicking through a screen and nodding her head. "Normally it would have been towed by now. But with this storm, there's a lot of cars getting stuck."

"What's that mean? Like, free parking for everyone?" Michael said with a soft chuckle.

"That's one way to look at it," Tracy answered. She swapped the laptop for a camera, fixing a plastic hood to the flash and body. Head cocked to the side, she told me, "This would have been good for Sherry to do. Just saying."

"Yeah, you're right," I said, certain it wasn't helpful. With

Tracy's recent promotion, Sherry was set to take over the task of crime-scene photography. That included all aspects of the digital storage, the indexing and archiving, along with fulfilling requests for any court usages. Transition was a slow process though. I heard the annoyance in her voice, adding, "Thanks for picking up while she works on Michael's picture."

"I understand," she said, sliding a plastic sleeve over the lens. She followed the wipers back and forth, adding, "Hard to think we'll get anything in this."

I flicked on the car's blue lights, an assembly of them hidden in the grill and behind the visors. My car was outfitted like an unmarked patrol car, and I couldn't help but wonder if Ruby Evans's father had worked on it. "I'm going to swing us around and park behind the Evans's car. Safer that way."

"Park ten or fifteen yards away," Michael said, elbows perched, chin cradled atop laced fingers. "Maybe there's a tire impression from the car that was behind The Bee?"

"That's good thinking," I told him, impressed that he knew. The road was asphalt, the sides thick with loose gravel and a rumble strip. If it had been dirt or mud, a tire track was possible. I parked, turning off the motor, the lights whirring with each energized cycle. There could be something between my car and The Bee. Anything out of the normal was apt to be of interest. With the weather, every pair of eyes was helpful. I handed Michael a plastic parka and latex gloves. "We'll walk the ground slow. Call out if you see anything that is suspicious."

"Me too?" he asked, a grin appearing. "You want me to help?"

"You can walk? You can see too?" I asked. He replied with a stern nod. "Then you can help."

"It's gonna be a wet one," Tracy complained, opening the door, the rain pelting against the plastic. "Yech!"

"I put around twenty feet between us and Ruby's car." Cracking the door, fat raindrops bounced up from the road.

"Michael, just don't touch anything. Call us over if you find something."

"Right on," he said, the worry in his face gone for the moment. He slipped into a sheet of plastic, the static making long strands of his brown hair poof uncontrollably. He repeated back to me, "Don't touch anything."

"Ugh," Tracy complained, swiping the rain from her eyes. I lowered the plastic hood closer to my head and searched the road, which was mostly empty in both directions, the traffic light. There was a vacant lot across from us with an abandoned building. Its windows were boarded, and half of the south-facing wall was in a crumbly pile, the insides exposed to the elements. A stirring wind drove against us, Tracy leaning into it while trying to cover her gear.

"You okay over there?" A grunt. A flash followed as she proceeded with the work. I scanned the lot, seeing if anyone could hide in the building. They couldn't. There were also the remains of a parking lot, which nature had taken back, with ground shrubs and holly bushes that had bright red berries.

A berm stood next to where we parked. It was high and deep and threaded with sandy paths to the beach and ocean. Just two lanes wide in most places, Route 12 was the main road linking the barrier islands. Much of it was lined with businesses and homes. This part of the road was empty. It could be that whoever stopped Ruby Evans knew to do it here. For a mile or two in either direction, there was nothing, the road standing alone. Michael was watching me. He was following my lead and staying next to the car until I moved. I pointed toward the south, and spoke over a gale, "You were driving from that direction?"

"From the south," he said, his voice breaking as he forced it. He waved ahead of us. "I live about five miles north of here. I think Ruby lives around here too."

"She does. I confirmed the address," Tracy said with a yell. "Two more miles and she would have been home."

"This spot," I began, pointing at the road. "If you know where someone is going to be and wanted to kidnap them, this is where you'd do it."

"Whoever it was must have known she'd pass through here," Tracy commented, a camera flash swallowed by the gray daylight.

"If that's the case, if someone did take her, then they knew to be here."

"You mean they knew who Ruby was?" Michael asked, a morbid look mixing with the rain on his face. He blinked rapidly, the whites in his eyes glistening. "Ruby was a target?"

"It's likely," I answered, concern growing for what might have occurred. I risked the rain and took my phone from my pocket. The screen got wet before I could cover it, the drops acting like lenses to make the letters in the text bulge. Heart sinking, the Amber alert issued hadn't turned up a single thing. "Michael, how we doing over there?" I asked while making my way closer to the yellow and black Camaro. No answer. "Michael?"

The thin rain parka did little to keep the teen dry. His tall hair was flattened against his head, his shoulders and chest soaked. The gusty winds picked up the plastic, twirling it around his legs as he stood still like a mannequin. There was a grim look on his face, the color of it turning blue in the steady downpour. "I think I found something."

My gaze shot to his shoes, a pair of black Chuck Taylors. *What's old is new.* They were not all that different from the pair I'd worn growing up. His heel shifted and a toe tip rose, but other than that, he kept his feet planted until I got there. "What do you have?"

"Those are Ruby's," he answered and pointed at the side of the road. "I sit near her in homeroom class. They're always in the outside pocket of her backpack."

Beyond the road's white line and before the asphalt

changed to sand and grass, there was a set of keys. "Tracy," I yelled and stretched my arms, blocking the possibility of us touching them. "Let's get some picture of these."

"Is that what I think it is?" Tracy asked, working around the keyring, the metal turning white when the flash bounced. She peered up from the camera. "It's a Smurf."

"A Smurfette," Michael corrected her, the cartoon character made of foam or plastic. "I remember seeing it. It's a floatable kind in case you drop your keys in the water."

"Like a life jacket for your keys," Tracy said, continuing to work toward the car.

"Do you recall Ruby Evans sailing?" I asked, realizing what it was used for. I'd seen them before—my fiancé worked on patrol boats and used one too. But his wasn't shaped like a Smurf. It was a float that looked like a miniature buoy. Michael nodded slightly. "Tracy, let's take a note of it."

"I remember her talking about a boat docked out of Wanchese. She'd take it out on Croatan Sound," Michael said, shaking his head. "That was before her dad died. I remember that too."

"What happened to him?" Tracy asked, her gaze fixed on the road, eyeing it through the camera lens. The parka did nothing to keep her dry either. There were long hairs pasted to her forehead and cheeks, her shoulders and top of her shirt wet. She eased up to force a stretch into her back. "Was it an accident?"

"Cancer, I think I heard," Michael told her and made his way closer to the car. "They were close. Worked on this car together."

"I haven't seen one like it since I was a kid," I said, confessing my age. I saw a sarcastic remark perched on Tracy's lips and added, "Even then, the car wasn't new. It was considered a classic."

"No tire impressions," Tracy said, the grass turning white

with a camera flash. She pointed at the ground. "If they parked here, they didn't leave any evidence of it."

"Just her keys." I opened a bag and picked them up. There was a car key, the square shape with the letters G and M on it. "I forgot the company was General Motors."

"Fingerprints on them?" Tracy asked while shaking her head. She held out her arms and looked at the sky. "Doubt we'd find anything anyway."

"That's my thinking," I said and made my way to the Camaro. The driver-side window was rolled down slightly. It was opened just enough to speak through. Rainwater beaded and ran together down the glass, finding its way over the black and yellow paint, dripping to the street. But at the top of the glass, there was a smudge, one or more partial fingerprints that had survived the rain. "Tracy, we've got fingerprints on the glass."

"Yes we do." Her voice was muffled while focusing on them, a reflection of the flash catching me in the eyes. The camera cycled, sucking juice from the batteries. "Do you see what I see?"

I'd gotten my hopes up until seeing what could be a thumbprint which was on the inside of the glass. "She was holding the top of the window."

"You mean those are Ruby's fingerprints?" Michael asked, rapidly blinking the rain from his eyes.

"With the mention of blue lights, if whoever took Ruby was impersonating an officer, they would have asked for a license and registration." I made a hook with my fingers, explaining, "It looks like Ruby held the window afterward."

Michael put his hand near the glass, using it for scale. "She's petite," he said with emotion. He looked at us over his shoulder. "She's a small girl, ya know?"

"I can lift the prints. Might be able to get enough as is, a picture and then run it," Tracy said, talking aloud as her focus centered on the find.

Disappointment fueled the remainder of our time, the seconds ticking into a minute, the minutes rolling into an hour. We waded through the rains and batted the winds that pushed with each nor'easterly breath. Tracy worked the pictures, digitally preserving the details which would get reviewed later with greater scrutiny. Eventually, Ruby's schoolmate slowly made his way back to my car, hope waning, his head hanging low.

Other than finding the keyring with the Smurfette, there was nothing else on the Camaro considered remarkable. Nothing that would tell us who took her. We knew going in that it wasn't the car they were after. It was Ruby. Whoever it was that took her, they'd made sure not to leave anything behind. Finding Ruby's keys had sparked us to try to find more. Were the keys planted to keep us looking? I couldn't help but think that whoever took her made sure we'd waste the most valuable thing we had in this investigation. Time.

FOUR

We were warm and dry. Almost. The steady rains had finally
lifted to leave behind a light drizzle. The skin on my fingers had
pruned to look like the rind of a fruit. Oranges perhaps. We'd
inspected Ruby Evans's car, which turned up fingerprints and a
keyring. I was certain both were Ruby's and that there wasn't
more to come from them. I also knew that finding them had
come with a high cost. We'd lost time. We lost hours we did not
have. With towels around our necks, our hair and clothes still
damp, the station televisions along the walls were on, screens
filled to show Ruby's face, the speakers cranked up as the chan-
nels continued to broadcast the Amber alert.

It was Michael's father who'd done the most during the time
we spent searching The Bee, Ruby's car. He knew a guy who
knew a guy, one the owner of a newspaper, the other a reporter,
and he wasn't shy about sharing his experience with us when
he'd brought Michael and Ruby's mother to the station. By the
time we were parked, it seemed that all the reporters in the
Outer Banks had made their way to our front doors.

I'd seen them in my walk from the parking lot. There were a
half dozen news vans lining the street with telescoping

antennas raised, the doors ajar slightly to showcase racks of humming electronics, panels blinking. The reporters were inside the station with their crews, bodies gathering at the front with Alice. Their voices clamoring, words competing, they were looking for comments to accompany the news coverage. Tracy helped me pull together the words, stitching them into sentences to craft a statement. It wasn't the first time I'd done a press conference, but it still put nervous jabs in my belly.

Facing the cameras and light was a part of the job. It was also a tool we sometimes used to speak directly to the public. That included reaching the person of interest, the kidnapper. If they were watching, they'd know we were working the case. I eased the wood gate open to leave the quiet of our office space, pinching the slip of paper which contained the vitals of what we could share. When the gate's latch clanked shut, it triggered a rustle. The news crews took position, long camera snouts aiming toward me, reporters competing to move closer. I took a place next to Alice as she began to move away. When I eyed the floor, her brow lifting, she understood and faced the crowd. For a moment I was made blind and deaf by shutter clicks filling my ears and camera flashes putting spots in my eyes.

"Detective, what's the progress on finding Ruby Evans?" a reporter asked, a fuzzy microphone jutting from the pack. "Any indication on what happened?"

The back of my throat itched as I cleared my voice and lowered the statement to look into the lens. "At around midnight last evening, seventeen-year-old Ruby Evans was abducted. A witness has come forward and described seeing Ruby's vehicle along Route 12—" Camera shutters and rising voices interrupted. I waited a moment, the noise waning. "—a second vehicle was seen behind hers. It had flashing blue patrol lights on its roof. However, we've confirmed that it was not a patrol vehicle."

"You're saying she was pulled over by the police?" a reporter asked, her voice scratch.

I shook my head. "That is not what was said. It was *not* a patrol vehicle." Shutter clicks continued as cameras were adjusted. "There are no records of any traffic stops at that time in the area."

"Is there anything about the other car?" asked a new reporter, his shoulder saddled by a battery pack. He flicked the switch on a light which turned my face white. Alice shielded her eyes, turning away. He doused it, saying, "Sorry."

"The witness was able to provide a description: the vehicle is a four-door sedan that is silver, possibly ten years or older. No make or model. Ruby's kidnapper is a white male, light to medium build, and approximately six feet tall."

"How about Ruby's parents?" someone asked.

"Ruby's mother was notified and is being kept informed. That is all we have at this time." I turned to leave, my mind training on the message. I returned to face the lights, the reporters reforming, their camera gear buzzing. "Lastly, we are doing everything in our power to bring her home."

"Detective, one more question... does this remind you of when your daughter was kidnapped?" A reporter called after me. I made like I didn't hear the question and continued forward. I held my tongue and took a deep breath, the wooden gate cool to the touch, the top of it smooth as it slid from my fingers and clapped shut behind me.

Of course, I heard what the reporter asked and instantly saw images of that dreadful morning. I saw my daughter at the open door of a stranger's car, the inside of it an inky black, a fluffy teddy bear used as bait. She was born with the name Hannah and to me she'd always be a Hannah. In every case where a child went missing, I was reminded of my daughter's kidnapping.

"Do you think the kidnapper is watching?" Tracy asked, urging me to sit as she rolled her chair between our cubicles.

"He's watching?" Sherry asked, jarring me, her chair wheels squealing. Her narrow eyes were big with curiosity. Her eyelids lifted briefly like leaves fluttering. "What you said at the end, that wasn't for the reporters, was it?"

"Extra points go to Sherry today." I sat down, the anxiety of the press conference draining out of me. "That was a message to Ruby's kidnapper. I want him to know that he was seen. We've got his picture... bad as it might be."

"Still working to clean it up," Tracy said with an unfocused smile. "I'm hoping it isn't a disaster. That we can make something of it."

"I'm on it," Sherry said, chair on the move again as she returned to her desk.

"You know, guys, one can hope. Sometimes that's all we've got."

———

Tracy's cubicle was littered with the station's camera gear. There were parts of it strewn across her desk and in open desk drawers. The pieces of one camera had been removed, disassembled as though she'd dissected its guts. There were pads beneath the components, the kind made to absorb moisture, their centers wet and raised. The pictures scrolling across one of the monitors told me she'd recovered the photographs first, relief coming with a gentle pat on her shoulder. The camera might not have been salvaged, but at least we had the pictures from it.

A certified criminologist with multiple degrees (it was hard to keep up with the count), officially, Tracy worked as a forensic science technician, a crime scene investigator. It was the crime scenes she liked. She saw them like they were a puzzle for her to solve. She reached for another camera part, her hair brushing against my face, the color and body of it like mine. But it was her father who I saw most when she looked at me, especially in her baby-blue eyes and the dimples on her cheeks.

Tracy sat back with a mystifying grin, asking, "What are you staring at?"

A shrug. I saw Sherry had gone for a break and answered, "Can't a woman look at her daughter now and again?" In addition to being a part of my team, Tracy Fields was also my child. When she was just three years old, she was kidnapped. Our baby girl was stolen from me and my husband, and it was cases like Ruby's that reminded me of how critical every minute was. It was more than fifteen years before I'd see my daughter again. That was fifteen years of firsts I never had with her. First days of school. First sleepover. First crush. First everything. Sad as it made me feel at times, we were lucky.

The report of her kidnapping went viral and blew up online. It went viral. Big. Huge. From the web, it spread like fire with pictures of her on television and milk cartons. Her face was stapled to every telephone pole and blasted across every available billboard in the city. It was the ever-present news vans parked outside our house I remember most, the reporters trampling the grass on our front lawn, standing in wait for any change. Tracy was known from coast to coast.

It didn't last. Soon, the house emptied, and my husband and I were left alone to pick up the broken pieces of our lives. The posters on the telephone poles had become faded in time, paper tattering before the winds finally carried it away. The news reporters were gone too. Even my precinct where I'd been a decorated officer had changed the status of the case to *unsolved*. I never stopped looking though. I couldn't stop searching. I continued working my daughter's case as if the kidnapping had just happened. Years later, after my daughter had grown to become this beautiful young woman, we were reunited.

For much of Tracy's life, she didn't know her true identity.

It was only after she'd joined my team to work an adoption fraud case that we discovered there was a connection to Philadelphia and my daughter's kidnapping. Since the discovery, we'd kept things simple. She grew up in the Outer Banks, where she still had a mother and father, a couple who gave her a terrific life and who were as much a victim of the adoption agency as Tracy. I respected the boundaries but couldn't help wanting more. I couldn't help how I felt.

Her kidnapping wasn't something we talked about. Not sure why that was, other than thinking it was simply because she'd had an amazing life. Her adopted parents were wonderful. Tracy was the woman she was because of them. I'd be lying though if I said it didn't hurt sometimes. I often wondered who she would have become if she hadn't been stolen from me and her father.

Every once in a while, I'd glimpse a ponderous look which ended with a warm smile. Those were the smiles that made my heart swell. They all did, but those were special. Lately, I'd seen other changes. There were words used like *mother* and *daughter*, or a question raised about her father, about who he was. She'd even started asking about the family in Philadelphia, the relatives that she'd never gotten to know. Tracy was becoming curious about who she was and I was eager to tell her more. When she was ready.

Her other computer screens came alive, breaking my empty stare with an array of fingerprint images, the smudges lifted from the driver-side window. On one of the screens, the pixels were dancing, their colors inverted. I saw the ridges that made up the arches which Tracy had isolated and enhanced. What I believed to be the thumbprint on the inside of the window's glass had become our best lift to use for matching. In my heart, I knew it was from Ruby, but we had to process it anyway and confirm it.

"Anything notable?" I asked, nudging the empty camera body, the pad beneath it swollen.

"Help me with this," she said angrily, and handed me a thick plastic bag. I held it open while she poured rice into the bottom, the weight bending my fingers. She was mad. I could feel it coming off her like heat. When the bag was full enough, she added the camera body, dropping it in carelessly. With a disapproving tsk-tsk, she added heatedly, "Welp, we got nothing to lose if this doesn't work."

"It'll be okay. We're budgeted for equipment loss," I assured her, troubled by the annoyance. I leaned forward to find her eyes and stayed there until she saw me. It wasn't the gear that was eating at her. It was something else. The case? "Tracy, what's bugging you? The camera?"

"Yeah, of course it's the gear," she answered. I wasn't buying it and she knew.

"Come on now?"

A sadness appeared in her eyes that I'd never seen before. Working together and becoming closer, I'd seen her through enough ups and downs by now to know what was what. This was different. Seeing her sad like that pinched my heart.

I lowered my voice. "You can tell me."

"Mom," she answered, tears welling.

"Oh, Tracy, I'm sorry, what's wrong with her?" I asked, concern building for the woman who'd raised her. "Is she sick?"

She slowly blinked and took my arm. "You. You are my mom. I remember what happened."

"Huh? Remember?" My heart stopped that moment. She was speaking to me, her mother. I glanced at her laptop, the bag with the rice and camera falling onto the desk. There were pictures of our Philly home, the house we used to live in. There was another picture of the front lawn where she used to play. Another picture with her father and me from twenty years ago. I could feel my hands begin to tremble when I saw the browser's address bar and the crime sleuthing website. I recognized it from when I'd investigated a clue in the Outer Banks, the same clue that brought me to her. "You remember the... your kidnapping?"

When I tried to pick up the bag, she took my hand, fingers weaving with mine. "Casey, I remember some of what happened that morning."

"I didn't think you'd ever remember that day," I said, barely able to whisper. The weakness in my legs caused me to fall back, my weight leaning against the cubicle wall. Tracy had known her true identity for a while now. She'd known it long enough to have picked up the original case file and dig into it. She hadn't though. "Why now?"

"I think it was the car." She squinted and shook her head, the overhead lights shining on her wet cheeks. She let go of my hand to click through some of the photographs. "It's Ruby Evans's car."

"Scroll to the bottom," I instructed. When online sleuthing became popular, my daughter's case was one of the first to be worked. There were hundreds of eyes on it day and night. Thousands possibly. I'd been on there too, her father also. And when her identity was revealed, the site was updated to include the clues discovered in the Outer Banks. "Click on the link with the title, The Barn."

"That's the car I was taken in," Tracy said, words soft.

The folder opened to show the candy-red muscle car driven by her kidnapper. Nearly two decades had passed, the kidnapper's husband hiding the car in a barn where age had found it. The bright red paint was faded, a thin layer of rust pitting the metal. But even in that state, it was still a muscle car from an era like the one Ruby Evans drove.

Tracy's lower lip trembled. "I remember you were running and—"

I shook my head when the memories slammed into my

brain. I wanted to shut my eyelids tight and hide in the dark, but I couldn't look away from my daughter's face. She saw me running after that car. That fucking car. "You saw?!"

"Mom—" she continued, voice breaking on a sob. "I heard you screaming so loud and I remember being afraid and terrified."

I gently touched her hands, cupping them in mine and leaned over to kiss them. "I am so sorry you were frightened like that."

Tracy gripped my hands with a squeeze, urging me to look at her. There was an odd smile on her face. She half nodded as if coming to terms with the memory, saying, "I think it's kinda okay to remember."

"It is okay." It was the only thing I could think to say, the images of that day as fresh as the ones from when Ruby Evans was taken. I rubbed her back, trying to console. "I can help fill in the gaps—"

She closed the laptop abruptly, the smile gone, blinking rapidly. "Oh wow. I'm sorry about that."

"Tracy," I began, confused. "It's okay to remember."

"It was a long time ago." Her expression went cold, her baby-blue eyes like ice. From the kidnapper's husband, I'd learned some of what happened to Tracy after that day. She'd gotten sick. Deathly. Rather than see her die, he took her to a hospital and left her outside where she was found lying in the rain. Little did he know, an extensive fake adoption ring was operating there, using the hospital as a front. What happened to Tracy afterward remained a mystery.

The hot touch of anger burned somewhere deep inside. It was old and familiar and stank like the sour sweat of resentment. There was a gap. It was a block of time that went unaccounted before she was placed with her adopted parents. Only Tracy knows what happened, the memories buried. Maybe she saw a glimpse of one? I glanced at her closed laptop, questioning, maybe she saw them all? I'd thought the memories didn't exist at all, but if she recognized the muscle car and the lawn from that morning, I was wrong. I went to touch the side of her face but she leaned away, saying, "Casey, I don't want to remember any more of it."

I backed away, making space, questions rising. What happened to my daughter after she was kidnapped? It was a question I might never have answered.

FIVE

The Amber alert for Ruby Evans had yet to turn up any sightings. She'd been missing for more than twenty-four hours, the alert circulating less than eighteen hours. Every passing hour meant we were further from finding her. I gripped the steering wheel with a shake, the statistics forever weighing on my heart. I knew to count the seconds, the minutes and the hours. I didn't just know it but felt every bit of angst that came as the hands swept the face of the clock. It wasn't empathy or sympathy for the family either. I knew it because I'd lived it. I'd been a mother who'd lost a child and would never forget what that was like.

As much as I wanted to stay in the Outer Banks and pound the pavement going door to door, there was a place I had to be today. I eased up on the steering wheel and saw daylight rising in the rearview mirror, the morning's darkness chasing us from North Carolina and the Outer Banks. We were only a few hours south of the place I once called home: Philadelphia. The city of brotherly love, the home of Independence Hall, the Rocky steps, and the Liberty Bell. But for this city girl, I knew it for the finer dining which included some of my favorites like scrapple and cheesesteaks, hoagies, and soft pretzels. Only, I didn't have much of an appetite today, and I wasn't feeling any part of the brotherly love thing at all.

Why? His name was Dr. P.W. Boécemo. A sick and dangerous man. I'd put him behind bars in the earlier years of my career when I was a Philly detective. It'd been a long minute since last seeing the doctor or hearing his name read aloud, but I never forgot him. I never forgot what he was capable of. His was the kind of case that left a lifelong impression. It wasn't what he'd done that stuck with me though. It was who we'd saved that night. A twelve-year-old girl named Allison.

A doctor of psychiatry by trade, it was his practice as a child therapist that made him a particularly dire threat. Highly intelligent and formally educated, the doctor was well-spoken; he had an air about him that was personable and deceivingly friendly. That's how he'd gained trust with the children. The parents too. To those who'd never met him before, those who didn't know him like I did, he had an attraction that was charming. But that's where the dangers lived. Where the lies waited. It was why we left the safety of home to journey north.

This morning at exactly ten o'clock, the doctor was going to try and convince a panel of people that he had been fully rehabilitated. He'd explain that during his time in the penitentiary, he recognized what he'd done was wrong and that he was sorry for it too. He would use his skills to please and delight and express his remorsefulness. He would be very convincing. Persuasive even. But not pushy. No. Not pushy. Pushy was beneath the doctor. Still, he was going to do everything in his power to see his sentence paroled and to win his freedom. Just the thought of it made me sick, the hair standing up on the back of my neck. I came here today to make sure the doctor stayed exactly where he was. In prison.

It was near the end of October with clouds hugging the road, the weather cold and wet and raw enough to put an ache in my bones. Warm air pumped futilely from the car vents while I lowered the driver-side window, the brakes squealing as we came to a stop before approaching a guardhouse, the sign on the door reading, Greensboro Correctional Facility. I peered through the prison gates at where the doctor was in his fifth year of an eight-year sentence. That meant with his time served, he was eligible for parole. He'd originally been sentenced to serve his time in a Pennsylvania prison, but after a few years, his lawyer was able to get the doctor transferred south, closer to his ailing mother in the northeast region of North Carolina. It was a shorter drive, not that it mattered. I would have driven across the globe to make certain he remained incarcerated.

Gray mortar stitched large sandstone blocks together, the face dripping wet. The prison walls were thirty yards away and looming tall enough for the top to hide in a low fog. Rows of fences edged the prison property, the barriers crowned with spiraling razor wire, the metal gleaming. A young man wearing a uniform poked an arm out of the gatehouse window, gaze fixed on my front license plate, his lips moving as he read the tag and the state: North Carolina. When he finished, he waved me forward until our windows were level and I could hand him my badge and picture identification.

"Casey White?" he asked, water dripping from his hat which was covered in clear plastic. Recognition came to his eyes when seeing the license plate frame. "OBX. The Outer Banks. That's a drive, isn't it?"

"It's a drive, yes. Detective Casey White," I said, correcting him. "We're here for this morning's parole hearings."

"The prisoner's name?" A gust of wind swept the rain into his face. The guard squinted, eyelids fluttering as he repeated, "The prisoner's name, ma'am. For the hearing?"

"It's Dr. P.W. Boécemo," I answered and began to spell out the last name, stopping when the guard found it.

Headlights flashed behind us, the guard waving them through. I bit my upper lip, the time on the car's radio showing that there was less than thirty minutes before the start of the hearing. "Is there a problem?"

"Not at all, ma'am," the guard answered and wiped his face before handing back my badge along with a prison pass. He looked past me, asking, "I'll need yours as well if you are attending the hearing."

"Yes, sir. Here's my identification," Tracy said from the passenger seat. She stretched across the center console to hand it to the guard. When she caught me staring, she snapped her fingers, face filling with concern.

I couldn't help but smile. "Have I mentioned lately how proud I am of you?"

"Your identification and a pass," the guard said, interrupting.

Tracy reached across to get them, answering, "Only like every other day."

"Well, it's because I am."

"Detective, the parking is to your left." The gate creaked as it rose, metal grating on metal. "Show your pass at the main doors."

"Thanks," I told him, shifting the car into drive. A minute later we were parked. I planted my feet on the asphalt to stand and to stretch, muscles bunching in my legs and back. Tracy's gaze traveled the height of the stone behemoth, its walls windowless save for a few vertical rectangles, the glass darkly tinted. "Thanks for joining. This should be a good experience for you."

"Who is this guy?" she asked, notepad flipped open. Standard procedure had us leaving our phones and any weapons in the car, a gun-safe built into my trunk. That meant notebooks and pencils. "Boécemo? Is that a French name?"

"Must be. He's got a slight accent. Probably from the years he lived with extended family in France."

"Why are you dead set on being here? Especially when we're in the middle of a case," she asked, continuing to write.

"Because he's a monster."

SIX

We entered the prison, wet footsteps squelching, tiny puddles left behind on the tiled floor. The dampness carried as we presented the passes, the guard directing us to the hearing room. There were three corridors, each with a bend, the navigation like a serpentine. We'd gone deep enough into the prison to hear the clamor of metal doors shutting and see prisoners being escorted, including Dr. P.W. Boécemo. He entered the room after us, his stare fixed on me, eyelids rising slightly when remembering who I was, his seeing me here a surprise.

"He's kinda handsome," Tracy whispered, the fold-out chairs sitting perpendicular to the parole board panel. The people were already seated, waiting to hear the doctor's plea. "I mean for an older guy."

"He's a predator."

The doctor was staring at Tracy, a coy smile showing faintly. Did he see it? Did he see a resemblance? Maybe he knew we were related. He raised an eyebrow, the curiousness building.

I pressed a hand against Tracy's thigh to steer her attention toward the panel as they got started. "He's one of the most dangerous I've ever come across."

"If he's that dangerous, then how is he up for parole after only five years?" she asked, tipping her head to whisper. "What did he do?"

I motioned to the panel, answering, "They'll cover the original charges."

The doctor continued to stare. Had he blinked once? It was his eyes that made me uncomfortable. They had that kind of look you instinctively turned away from. I didn't though because that's what he wanted.

For the next thirty minutes, the panel of men and women reviewed the doctor's charges, taking turns to ask questions and field his answers. It was just over six years ago when it all happened. I was living in Philadelphia and had taken a leave from working homicide cases, switching gears to work in our sex crimes division. There'd been a rash of maternity leaves and retirements and some poor resource planning that left our staff of detectives anemic and stretched thin. The move was my captain's insistence. To be honest, I needed a break from the murder mayhem that had become my every day. Only, at the time, I didn't know that I was trading one horror for another. I'd thought I'd seen the worst in people. I was wrong.

We were working an operation alongside the FBI who'd built a case the last year. They were going to arrest the main players in a nationwide child pornography ring, the hub of activity found to be centered in the northeast part of Philadelphia. There was one building in particular which had come up time and time again. The building was owned by Dr. P.W. Boécemo. When we searched the place, a room was discovered which no single, adult male who lived alone would ever have. It was a dream room that had been decorated for a young girl. There were locks on the outside of the door, the intentions obvious to everyone there. While we knew the doctor's plan, it was fortunate for him that there was no evidence supporting a committed crime. As his lawyers addressed when it was brought up, there was no crime against what they called *the doctor's artistic expression*, an interior design hobby of his. We knew what the room was. It wasn't art. It was a cage.

It was the child pornography on the doctor's computers that would send him to prison. He wasn't the ringleader the FBI were after, but his computers were being used as a hub in the distribution of the illegal content. His lawyers argued that their client had been hacked and that he had no knowledge of the pornography found or the issuance of it. Everyone knew the doctor was guilty. Even his lawyers knew it. But they were paid well and negotiated a good plea deal that any client in the doctor's position would be happy with. The doctor would serve time with an opportunity for parole. There was some good news in all this. In addition to the time behind bars, the doctor had also lost his practice, his license and would be a registered sex offender the rest of his life.

The doctor wasn't home when we searched his place. He was at work. And it was there I saw what would stay with me forever. It was the scene before the crime, the intent horrific. On the floor of his office, sitting across from the doctor, there was a girl named Allison. She was twelve years old at the time. A young, twelve-year-old, pre-adolescent and could have passed for an age closer to nine or ten. Doe-eyed and looking uncertain, the doctor's fingers were woven through her brown hair, the other hand on her shoulder. She'd later tell me in private that the doctor said it was a game of trust and that he wanted to teach it using touch. In my gut, I will forever believe we interrupted a crime before it happened. I also believe that the timing of the FBI child pornography case saved Allison.

"Casey?" Tracy said, nudging my arm. When I looked up, the door we'd entered through was opening, a woman standing in it. I didn't know who it was until I saw the same doe-eyed look on her face and the long brunette hair. It was Allison.

I went to her, the difference of six years seeming like magic. She was a grown up and even had an engagement ring on her finger, the small stone throwing sparks. "I wasn't sure if you'd come."

She cocked her head shyly and spoke softly, "I wasn't sure I'd come either." The room had gone silent, the parole hearing panel staring. Dr. P.W. Boécemo was staring too. There was a look on his face, a mix of delight and horror, if that was even possible.

"Detective Casey White?" a panel member asked.

"A moment please," I replied, voice soft.

A man entered behind Allison. He was tall and had the shoulders of a football player. He stood close enough to Allison to leave no question who he was. She leaned in, continuing to speak softly, "My parents thought this was a bad idea." She looked over her shoulder briefly, a smile in her eyes. When her focus returned, she said, "I've got Chuck with me though. I'm good."

"Detective, you requested attendance to this hearing," the panel member said. "Having completed the questioning, we are inclined to close the hearing."

"Thank you for allowing us to attend. I have a few more questions."

I went to the doctor, a folder in my hand. He dabbed his cheeks, wiping the tears of remorse he'd produced for the parole board. When I stood between him and the panel, the coy smile returned briefly, his dark eyes following the folder I carried. He'd lost weight and aged since I'd seen him last, his jet-black hair salted by long strands of white. His skin had turned pale, unavoidable due to the lack of sunshine or tanning salons. The yellow jumpsuit he wore was a dramatic difference from the expensive suit I'd seen him in at his arraignment and trial. It was the chiseled features that had changed most. There was a lump on the bridge of his nose, which told me it had been broken once or twice during his incarceration. His eyes were edged by wrinkles, the matching pair joined by deep creases across his forehead. His jawline, once firm and straight, now pooched out with the slightest showing of jowls.

"Detective," the doctor said, greeting me, his accent ticking against the syllables.

I pinched the folder and kept it closed for now. "Would you tell us about your practice?"

He put on a professional smile and squared his shoulders, his hands clasped on his lap. "I am a doctor of psychiatry, specializing in child and adolescent therapy, as well as a leading member of the American Board of Psychiatry and Neurology—"

"You mean *was*," I interrupted. I moved enough to ensure the parole board could see his reaction, and asked again, "Don't you mean *was,* as in, *I was* a child psychiatrist and a member of the American Board of Psychiatry and Neurology?"

"Doctor. My title remains doctor," he said with a flinch. It was subtle. Too subtle. "But yes, of course. Detective, you are correct." His voice remained calm. "I *was* those things and am deeply remorseful for my actions and for the loss of a practice. I am certain I could have helped many others."

"Yes, thank you." My mouth turned dry. The lines I'd rehearsed on the drive suddenly gone. "Let's talk about the room in your home. It was a child's room."

"Ahh, my hobby." He put on a smile, the sight of it nauseating. "Interior design."

"That's what your lawyers said too. That it was a hobby." I needed something the parole board would question. "If you are truly remorseful for your actions, rehabilitated, then why not tell us the true purpose of that room."

He shook his head and made a tsk-tsk sound, fingers

splaying briefly before he recomposed his hands. "It was interior design. A hobby that I was passionate about and wanted to protect. That is all."

"It was more than a hobby." I looked at Allison when I spoke, a few on the parole board following my gaze.

Another tsk-tsk. "That room was going to be submitted for a national design innovation award, along with some other periodicals."

"I think I saw one of those reality shows on television," a board member commented.

Allison shifted from foot to foot and looked as uncomfortable as I was beginning to feel.

The doctor noticed, his left brow rising. He was finding humor in this. "Detective?"

"Why the locks? The chain and padlocks? The cameras?" I asked, and then waved my hand to rephrase the question. "Did you build that room for someone."

"Of course. I built it for the judges," he answered while looking past me to gauge the parole board. "As for the locks? I wanted to protect my hard work and investment."

"Detective, if there's nothing more?" someone on the parole board asked.

Ignoring the question, I flipped open the folder and held a picture. "Doctor, do you recognize this girl?" There was silence, save for the parole board leaning, chairs creaking, bodies in motion. It was a photograph of Allison at the age of ten or eleven, close enough to when the doctor had first started seeing her regularly. "Wasn't that room built for your patient?"

He gave the picture a look. It was brief, his gaze pivoting to the floor. The parole board couldn't see it, but I could. I moved the photograph closer, a grimace forming on his face. He shifted to the side to see the panel and asked, "May I ask the purpose of this?"

"Detective, this is very irregular—" I heard from behind me.

"Actually, I would like to hear the prisoner answer the question," a panel member interrupted. She was an older woman, her skin made chalky by makeup. Her blouse and skirt told me she was a professional. It was her shoes with the thick, rubbery soles that hinted she might be a medical profession of sorts. A psychiatrist in a hospital perhaps. "This is certainly relevant to the rehabilitation and remorsefulness that's being questioned."

"Again, doctor, could you tell us who this is."

He squirmed, eyes darting from the picture to me and then to Tracy and Allison. He lowered his head, recognizing his old patient, his gaze returning to the picture. His expression was softened by the fonder memories in the face of a child he'd once known. "She was *my* patient."

"Would you want to see this patient again?" I asked, flipping the picture to another. The next one was a recent picture of Allison, older, at eighteen. He shook his head annoyed by the change and reached for the pictures, motioning to the first one. "Doctor?"

"The *other* one," he answered, forgetting where he was, his voice sounding more primal. "Younger *is* better."

"Dr. P.W. Boécemo?" the woman asked. "Could you tell us what you mean—?"

"Enough with this!" the doctor said, voice rising to a shout, his hand raised over his head. Without warning, it came down in a whooshing swing, the folder slapped clear from my hands, the pictures inside scattering across the tiled floor. He squinted angrily and pointed at me, saying, "I know what you are trying to do!"

"Dr. P.W. Boécemo," the panel lead said. There was shock in their voice followed by chair legs screeching. "We'll have no more outbursts—"

"I know you!" the doctor shouted and jumped to his feet, his breath hot on my face. He glared at Tracy and Allison, a guard rushing toward him. Meaty fingers squeezed the doctor's shoulders but went ignored when the doctor saw the picture of Allison again. The one he wanted. The younger one.

"Dr. P.W. Boécemo, please take a seat!"

The doctor wasn't listening. He knelt and picked up the picture, the image of the young child not seen in more than six years. Whatever fascination he'd had once flooded back. The compulsion struck like lightning, his fingers tracing her hair and face. The doctor grunted sharply and clutched the photograph when the guard tried to take it from him.

"What? That's it?" Allison asked me when I returned to them. Tracy stood, the four of us in a huddle clear of the disruption. "I don't have to say anything?"

I shook my head, answering, "I'd say that your presence was enough."

A chair toppled onto its side as the parole board began to leave, half of them already out the door. The guard continued to wrestle with the doctor, the chaos growing with the addition of a second, a third running into the room. The doctor fought for the photograph of Allison, the picture shredded as he desperately tried to save the pieces, his fixation too powerful to deny.

"I don't think we'll be seeing him free anytime soon."

SEVEN

By the time we reached the Outer Banks, the sun was low in the west, the end of the day nearing. Thankfully, the rains were gone. They'd been pushed west by a windy front that had the shorebirds pirouetting where they perched. I opened the station door, a gust lifting my hair with the faint smell of the sea. We were less than a quarter mile from the ocean, and even with the seasonal change, there were beachgoers heading in that direction.

I felt the pull to join them for a late walk before the daylight was gone. There was no better way to unwind from the drive and shed Dr. Boécemo from my mind. But... there's always a but, we had to get back to trying to find Ruby Evans. On our drive south, I'd gotten a text from our station manager Alice. It said to stop in and see her as soon as possible. She knew it would be late and that I'd want nothing more than to get home. A second text said it was urgent and added that Tracy should stick around. When I asked if it was about Ruby Evans, she replied that she couldn't be sure. I was speeding south the last half hour of the drive.

"How did the hearing go?" Alice asked from behind the

counter. She was dressed in full uniform, her graying hair pinned back in a tight bun. She nodded her head fervently, pink cheeks jiggling. "Success?"

I held a thumbs-up. "The board voted no to the doctor's parole."

She clapped her hands together, the slap echoing. "That is wonderful." She embraced me with a quick hug, the top of her hair shoved into my face. "You did good."

"You should have seen that guy cave when Casey started asking questions," Tracy commented, heaving her laptop bag. Alice grabbed Tracy, taking her by surprise with a hug. "Oh okay, we're hugging. I was just there to watch and take notes."

"You watched and you learned," Alice told her and then turned around slow to stare into the station, which was nearly empty, dark shadows lurking with most of the lights off. "It's second shift until eleven. Have to say that for this time of year, it's dead quiet."

"It certainly is." I glanced at the benches, the front of the station used for processing. There was the counter off to the side where she worked, the area where we stood usually filled with arrestees waiting to be processed or walk-ins filing a complaint or some other business. On a busy night, the space would be filled, mostly some drunk and disorderly or pick-pockets who'd been feeding off a school of summer tourists.

A small wooden gate separated the receiving area from our offices and cubicles and conference rooms. There was also a hallway leading to a kitchen area, the usual smell of coffee extinguished by the lack of staff. The interview rooms were in that hall too, along with the holding cells where we kept the arrested who couldn't or wouldn't cooperate.

"Alice, you had something for us? Might have to do with Ruby Evans?"

"This way," she said, her hand on the gate, leading us through. It clapped shut, Tracy taking the lead and ducking into her cubicle. I sat across from Tracy, an evidence bag on the desk, a bottle inside it.

Next to it was an evidence sheet. There was a second evidence bag with a piece of paper rolled loosely inside, the fibers retaining the memory. "This came for you."

"A bottle. A rolled piece of paper." It didn't take much to put one and one together and I let out a light laugh. "Alice, did someone send me a message in a bottle?"

She didn't crack a smile, not even a grin. "We-we couldn't tell if it was real or not."

"Okay, the look on your face says this is serious?" I sat down to take a closer look, legs achy from the drive. There was fine sand sticking to the bottle's bottom and its sides. The glass was mostly clear but had a faint tinge of green like the colors before a storm. There was no label, its thickness and shape leading me to think it might be an antique bottle. There was also a cork like from a wine bottle lying in the bag which had a thin coating of light-yellow wax, some remaining coated on the bottle's neck. "This really *is* a message in a bottle?"

"It is. The person who brought it in, opened it and read the message," Alice answered.

Tracy wheeled her chair toward us until she was next to me. "Why did they bring it here?" she asked. "People throw bottled messages in the ocean all the time. Like it's some kind of ceremony or rite of passage or something."

"That's why I sent the texts." Alice pinched the corner of the evidence bag, lifting it. "Casey, the message inside the bottle was addressed to you."

"What?" I asked, scratching at my jaw. I slid the bottle and evidence bag closer to Tracy.

Tracy's mouth twisted with disbelief. "Addressed to you?"

"Apparently." I picked up the evidence bag, uncertainty building. Or was it concern I was feeling, all humor vanishing? "Is it just me, or does this feel a little creepy?"

"Creepy," Tracy said. "Definitely creepy."

"Heck yeah, I'd say!" Alice agreed with a loud snort. "Detective, you need to read that message."

I slipped on a pair of gloves, handing Tracy the box while asking Alice, "I trust all due diligences are in place? The names and phone numbers, location of the find, that sort of thing. It's been turned in?"

Alice cocked her head, lips disappearing in a bite. She motioned to her head, asking, "Honey, where do you think these gray hairs come from?" When I didn't answer, she added, "The job. As in, I know how to do *the job*."

"Okay, Alice," I said, rearing back. "I was just asking."

She palmed my arm, her fingers warm. "I'm sorry, dear." She glanced over my cubical wall a moment, adding, "Winter is coming. I can feel the cabin fever pressing already."

"We're not quite there yet," I assured her, a shimmer of dust drifting from my gloves. I gave it a puff, clearing the air as I opened the evidence bag. The paper wasn't like any paper I'd used before. There were fibers in the finish, the color of it beige. Not beige, that's the wrong color. It was bone. The color of the paper was like bone. The edges were feathery, torn and not cut. I unfurled the page, words appearing which were written in an ink that was brownish, the letters made tall and swirly and connected in a cursive handwriting. I gleaned what was written, my insides squeezing as a shiver raced up my spine. I forced a breath. "Tracy, get all the information from Alice. We need to investigate this immediately."

"What's it say?" she asked, her voice in my ear as she peered over my shoulder. I couldn't speak, my eyes remaining fixed on where the message addressed me by name. "Casey?"

"You read it." I handed the page to her. I had to get word to the chief and anyone else involved, grabbing my phone as Tracy took the odd paper from me.

"Let's see," she said and carefully lifted the paper into a

blade of bright light. I rolled my chair back, head spinning with possibilities of what I'd just read. "The first line says: *A game for Detective Casey White. Let's see who will win.*"

"No doubting which Casey White they intended," Alice commented.

Tracy's eyes narrowed with a frown as she continued. "*Between the next twenty-four and forty-eight hours, I will take a life. This death is not out of greed or revenge. It is not motivated by jealousy or love or hate. My victim has already been selected and there is no name to share. However, to play the game, I give the following clues.*

"*My victim is first born, a jewel that is both gracious and charitable—*" She stopped reading and looked up from the paper, her face rigid with concern. "Oh shit, is this a joke or real?"

"Ruby," I said, shaking my head. The name made my heart thud and come to a stop. "A jewel that is both gracious and charitable."

"Whoever wrote this is talking about Ruby Evans? Ruby, a jewel?" Tracy questioned. I motioned for her to continue, *a jewel* ringing like a bell in my head. "*—they're older to some and younger to others and have been seen by thousands. I am control. I become power.*"

"It says *twenty-four to forty-eight hours.* The victim was already selected," I commented, repeating parts of the message. It had a time limit, the urgency Alice mentioned understood. I stood up, legs rubbery as Tracy held the page for us both to search for more. I scanned the edges, the corners, but only saw the words addressed to me. "Hold it against the light."

Tracy raised it, the three of us staring into the brightness bleeding through the paper. "There's nothing else."

"Why give us a timeline, but no way to know when it starts?" I braced the desk, worry rising. The bottle was old, I was certain of that. The greenish glass was clear, free of stains, sand littering the creased bottom of the evidence bag. "What beach?"

Alice snorted an answer. "Would you believe it was ours. The one down the street." The station doors opened and shut with a clap, stealing her attention. "I'll be right there."

"Who found it?" Tracy asked. She continued to search the paper, shining a flashlight this time while peering through a magnifying glass.

"It was a couple, looked like local kids from the high school," Alice said, her focus on the station's front. She began to leave, adding, "I'll text you their contact information."

"This has to be about Ruby Evans," Tracy said, a question hanging in her words. She sat, her expression weary. "I mean, it looks legit and all, you know, like it's the real thing."

"But?" Doubts were there, but I wanted to hear her thoughts.

"The timing? We don't know how old it is," she answered, pinching the corner of the paper. She lifted the cork from the evidence bag. The wax which coated the lip was beaten, chipped as if the bottle had tumbled in the surf. "There's a chance it's old and the message meaningless."

"You're thinking it's a coincidence? A jewel, Ruby. How about the words *both gracious and charitable*? She volunteers at the nursing home?" Tracy didn't look convinced. I knew this was real, but we did as we'd been trained. I looked at the physical evidence. "Okay, a closer look at the bottle. Starting with the marks on the cork. They're probably from the couple who found the bottle."

"They opened it, took the message out." She played along, assessing, turning the bottle over and over. "If this was in the ocean, there's no telling how long."

"I don't think this bottle ever touched the sea. It was planted to be found." I raised the bottle into the light like we'd done with the message. There were smudges around the ridges of what could be a fingerprint. On the other side of the bottle, there were more of them, my hopes brief, thinking the author of the message had been reckless in handling the bottle. That was doubtful. "Let's say the message is real, a killer wouldn't chance the game with a bottle in the ocean? They would make sure it got to us. Rather, it got to me."

"Right!" Tracy said, beginning to understand. "Who knows where the tides would have taken it. It could have drifted out to sea and never been found."

"Tracy, I'm as sure of this being about Ruby than any case we've worked," I told her and turned the glass, the light bouncing like it was a disco ball.

She nudged the message, asking, "That means this is from the guy Michael saw?" Without answering, she began to nod, eyes bright with acknowledgment. "He wrote this. He wrote it to you."

I felt my gut flip, revolted by the idea a killer addressed me directly. Why? "How about fingerprints?" I asked. It was a nugget of hope swimming in doubt, but we'd have to check the smudges. "Let's get started on the bottle and then the message, the paper."

She jumped up and paced. "I'll have to get fingerprints from the young couple. You know to exclude them."

"Alice will help."

"Not gonna lie," Tracy began to say, pulling a fingerprint case from beneath her cubical. The clasps clacked open as she continued. "Something this elaborate, I doubt whoever took Ruby Evans would leave a fingerprint behind."

"You're probably right." Deep down I wanted to be wrong. I wanted the kidnapper to have made a simple mistake so we could end this. "Still, we've got to look."

EIGHT

Soft blades of sunlight entered our bedroom, a touch of it warming my face and stirring me awake. I mumbled a quiet curse, having forgotten to lower the window shades the night before. Breaking waves rumbled in the distance, the ocean at high tide. It was the only time we could hear them from our apartment on the beach. A gull called out as it passed our place, its slender shadow crossing the room. I slipped my hand from beneath the covers and lazily tilted my phone to see that it was a little after six in the morning. A sound came from the other bedroom. A stir.

"Babe, they'll be awake soon." I nudged my fiancé, his body warm, inviting. Jericho replied with a grunt, a growing snore following a moment of silence. I tried shutting my eyelids again, promising myself fifteen more minutes. But I'd been stirring restless a while now, the message in the bottle playing over and over like a broken record. Thinking aloud, I mumbled some of the words from the message, "A jewel that is both gracious and charitable?"

"Huh? A jewel. Who?" Jericho answered sloppily, confusion in his voice. "You mean, like a name? Uhm, like the singer, Jewel."

"It is a name," I told him, peeling my eyelids open. "It's the case I'm—" Another snore rose in his chest, sleep finding him in a blink. I could never do that, fall asleep that fast.

I grabbed my phone and texted Tracy, curious if she'd gotten anything from the smudges on the bottle or that strange paper the message was written on. When I hit send, I heard another stir. The pitter-patter of feet came next, a jog outside of our bedroom that rifled down the hallway. The toilet flushed a minute later with the faucet running. It was subtle, almost missed, but there was another pair of feet joining the first. They were trying to be quiet. They weren't. I nudged Jericho, antici-pation building. I leaned over and whispered hoarsely, "Babe, they're coming!"

"Wha—" I nudged again, using my elbow this time. A chor-tled grunt. "Yep, I'm awake!"

"Shh," I said when he rolled onto his side. He draped the sheet over our heads as I reached across his middle, lying face to face. I kissed his forehead, his eyes trying to focus on mine. "Let's wait for them."

"Yeah," he agreed, the corner of his mouth rising. It was quiet for the moment, the anticipation of an attack coming. They were at the door, the steps soft. They couldn't control the breathy giggles though. It was impossible, and contagious, Jericho shushing me when one slipped.

This was my life now, and I wouldn't trade it for anything. I looked deep into his greenish-blue eyes and thought of the first time we met. His name is Jericho Flynn, a ruggedly handsome man who'd once been the sheriff in our small part of the Outer Banks. These days he worked part-time for the Marine Patrol, where he navigated the shores of the barrier islands in the name of safety and security. When he wasn't on a patrol boat, he was home being a foster father to two wonderful children, Thomas and Tabitha. Both had come into our lives recently when we'd saved them from certain death, their parents brutally murdered.

"You nervous?" I asked, my tone turning serious. "About the adoption?"

"It'll work out." He shifted enough to kiss me and answer, "I wish you wouldn't worry."

But I did worry. Our petition to adopt Thomas and Tabitha had been received, processed and reviewed. As of last week, there was a hearing date set in family court. I've sat in a hundred courtrooms and taken the stand countless times. This wasn't like a criminal case. It was family court and the mere thought of standing in front of a judge terrified me. What were they going to ask? What if they asked that one thing? The one thing everyone knew about me. My name was one Google click away from seeing that I was the cop in Philadelphia who'd lost their child to a kidnapping. It happened right in front of me, the fight for her life occurring on the front lawn of our small home. The Internet never forgets. Never. Jericho must have sensed where my thoughts were going, his lips brushing mine, his eyes filling with sympathy.

"What if they say no?"

He shrugged, not knowing how to answer a hard question we'd been avoiding. "If they do, then, they do. And we'll figure out what to do," he said, brow raised as if trying to convince me. When I frowned, he added, "What I'm trying to say is, stop worrying over something you can't control."

"I know—" I began. The sheet collapsed in a blast of laughter. And just like that, our quiet morning was wildly alive in a tangle of little hands, feet, arms, and legs.

Jericho reared up and roared, the sheet covering his head as he bellowed in his best baritone voice, "Who goes there?"

Tabitha shrieked, her hazel eyes enormous with fright. An impossibly high-pitch scream followed. Like her brother, she had pale skin and light-colored hair, the nighttime's sleep shaping it. There were face-pillow creases crossing her left cheek, her pink lips trembling. "Not like it! Too scary."

I clutched the sheet, pulling it off Jericho's head, the seasonal dry air and static making his hair stand up on end. Thomas belted a laugh, pointing his finger. Jericho played it up and stuck the tip of his finger against the dimple in his chin, twisting it. Thomas's laugh grew but his sister only crossed her arms and put on a hard pout. "I'm sorry, baby girl," Jericho told her. He pinched her cheek, asking, "Waffles will make it better?"

"Can't like scary," she answered grumpily. "I feel crunchy."

"Crunchy?" I asked.

"That means, she feels cranky. It's a new word," Jericho answered, smiling proudly. He winked, adding, "Still needs practice."

"It was only in fun," Thomas told his sister, shimmying close to her.

They had a strong bond, a trauma bond. They'd seen their parents murdered and then were stranded at sea. Tabitha wrapped her arms around him, finding comfort in her brother's tight grip. The image reminded me of how we'd found them that day. The memory lifted my heart and put a cramp in it at the same time. They were tiny and shriveled by days adrift on the ocean. We found them with their arms and legs woven together, huddled protectively in the back of a life raft. Thomas dipped his face, their foreheads touching. "It's okay, Tabs."

She sat up, the moment passing in a blink, and asked, "Can make pank-cakes."

"Pancakes it is," Jericho answered. "I mean, pank-cakes."

The bed emptied when he stood. I sat back and watched them follow him to the door. Thomas mimicked Jericho's long strides, trying to make his sister laugh. She did finally smile and ran ahead to take Jericho's hand in hers, looking up, her gaze fixed on him. The moment took my breath and gave me goosebumps. And for the moment I forgot about the adoption hearing later this week. My stare broke with the buzzing from my phone, a text message flying up the screen, Tracy's name with it.

What's a mulberry?

I texted, seeing the word mulberry more than once.

The message in the bottle.

She texted back.

The paper it was written on is called mulberry paper.

I shook my head, texting,

I never heard of that type.

I'm in my lab. When are you coming in?

I'll be there in a few.

I replied, thinking of her finding. Why was the author of the bottled message using mulberry paper? Was there some significance. I relayed the texts to Sherry, telling her,

Find out everything and anything about mulberry paper.

She replied immediately with a thumbs-up.

By the time I reached the station, there'd be a report waiting. And hopefully, I'd find the answers I was looking for.

NINE

The Outer Banks is around two hundred miles long and is made up of islands strung together along North Carolina's south-eastern coast. It's narrow and congested in the warmer months of the year, tourists migrating for the season. There are also those who live here year-round, the population small at around fifty thousand or so. We don't have the police stations like in big cities, and certainly nothing like the ones in Philadelphia where I'd earned my detective shield.

What I'd learned when I moved to the Outer Banks was that crime doesn't know size. It doesn't care if the population is thick with millions or thin at thousands. Crime is crime no matter where you go. With Tracy's recent certification, and another degree under her belt, there was an opportunity to promote her to forensic science technician. I pushed for it, which meant we'd want more than words in a title and a small bump in pay. It meant that we'd want a lab of our own rather than sending evidence across the bay to the mainland.

At one point, I'd been given a nice office that sat adjacent to the station's kitchenette and utility room which housed the building's mechanicals. With a slight modification, a wall opened temporarily, and everything needed to make a crime lab was available. That included water, power, and the means to isolate, vent and drain. I let Tracy design the lab, converting it, organizing the space to best fit the needs of solving crimes faster. When Tracy wasn't at her desk, I'd find her in the lab, a pair of lights above the door telling us when it was safe to enter and when to stay out.

The door to the lab was slightly ajar, the green light shining bright. I peered inside, steam rising from my coffee cup, the taste burning on my tongue. The old office was unrecognizable. There were long black counters like the kind I remembered from high school science class. Half were covered with equipment, some stuffed in the corners, bold print on the fronts with acronyms like UV and PCR and BIO, all meaningless to me without Tracy to explain what they meant. It was the other equipment I recognized though, recalling them from chemistry class. Things like test tubes, beakers, pipets and centrifuges, along with balances and hoods and Bunsen burners.

This morning there were sheets of paper strewn across the lab table, the colors like a faded rainbow. A handful of them were the same pale bone color as the paper the message written to me was on. Its edges were frayed, the fibers producing a light texture.

"Where did you find these?"

"Would you believe they were at a crafts store near my place," Tracy answered, circling the table, stripping a pair of latex gloves from her fingers. There were circles beneath her eyes, the days long, the drive to and from Pennsylvania stealing a lot of hours. It was the bottled message too. I was certain of it. She had that investigator's *must-know* mentality which is what made her good. She saw me looking, and said, "I couldn't sleep and knew I'd seen that paper before."

"It's not even eight in the morning. What craft shop is open this early?"

"A friend of a friend," she answered with a grin and brushed her hair back, urging me closer. Next to the crafts store sheets was the evidence bag with the message, curled in a loose roll, the words hidden. She lined up one of the bone-colored sheets, asking, "See how they match."

The paper's texture was a match, down to the fibers, some of the threads lighter and darker like the pits found in cork or the bark of a tree. "It is the same. But why would they use craft paper?"

Tracy shook her head, an exhaust vent clicking on with an electrical pop. "It's on a timer," she said, glancing over her shoulder. She handed me a sheet, saying, "Feel it."

I pinched the paper and rubbed my fingers against it. "Thicker than I imagined. Sturdy too, like one of those fancy greeting cards."

"It's the same stuff," she said, eyes growing. "That's the stock used in expensive greeting cards. It's also used in fancy menus and book bindings... and messages in a bottle."

"Expensive. Feels like it," I said, thinking of a profile, uncertainty nagging whether any of this was real. I tore the sheet, the fibers separating, edge unraveling like the one with the message. "This is a good find. Anything on the ink?"

She shook her head, asking, "I need permission to test it."

I knew what she meant by that. It meant destroying a part of the message. It was like the bodies in the morgue, the autopsies. We learned by taking them apart. The organs and tissues and bones. The same was true in the lab. By taking it apart, we learned what it was made of.

"I think we'll have to."

Her face grew bright with the idea of what she'd work on this morning. "I promise I won't take too much."

"What about fingerprints?" I asked, lifting the evidence bag with the sheet. When the overhead lights gleamed off the plastic, I sleeved a pair of latex gloves, snapping the fingers into place. Once the sheet was free of the evidence bag, I could hold it against the lab lights like I was searching for hidden figures, a watermark perhaps, like the kind found on paper money. There were no watermarks. There were no smudges or visible fingerprints, stained from ink. "I am thinking that whoever wrote this, probably wore a pair of gloves."

"You'd think so, right?" she answered. "I actually picked up two fingerprints, which was tricky given the paper's texture."

"The paper absorbed enough for you to photograph them using blacklight?" I asked, knowing just enough of the science to make a guess. She nodded as my gaze shifted to the bottle. My heart dipped, the bottle covered in fingerprint dust. "Lemme guess. They were a match to the fingerprints lifted on the bottle."

"That would be a correct guess," Tracy answered. "They belong to the couple who turned in the message."

"Is it hard to find?" I studied the paper, its color, the look of it off-putting. Like it was purposely selected. "I mean the paper in this color?"

"You know," she began and picked up her phone, "I didn't see it at the shop. But mulberry paper is easy enough to get. I bet that color can be found."

"Let's check on that," I told her as Sherry entered the room, her gear in tow. She barely reached my chin and preferred carting her laptop and other equipment, her size a struggle when hoisting it across her shoulders. I'd seen her do it once or twice and thought the weight was going to break her in half. Her brown hair flopped to one side and hung limp, still damp from the looks of it too. She must have rushed to get here, a pang of guilt stirring about the early morning texts. She wore beige slacks and a blouse that was strawberry in color, keeping with a professional look even though we'd explained the dress code a few times already. We dressed for comfort and for supporting field work. I wouldn't have it any other way but appreciated

Sherry's look and found myself wanting to dress more professional.

"Good timing."

"Good?" Sherry questioned, tucking a flop of hair behind one ear. She nudged her chin toward the paper in my hand, asking, "That's the message?"

"That's it," Tracy told her. "I figured out the type of paper. It's mulberry."

"I heard about it this morning. I couldn't sleep and got here as soon as I could," she said with urgency in her voice. She felt the way we all felt. How many hours did we have left to find Ruby? "I got everything I could about mulberry paper and emailed it in a report."

"Excellent, and thank you," I told her. She banged her gear and thumped the lid of the case, opening it to fetch a tablet and laptop. From the body language, we saw that Sherry was not a morning person. I hung my thumb over my shoulder. "There's coffee next door."

"Nah. I never touch the stuff," she commented with a gruff reply.

"Maybe you should," Tracy told her and lifted a cup as if toasting the idea. I tried not to laugh, but the sight was funny. "I mean, it'll help get the gears moving."

"Hmm. Maybe," Sherry said, surprising us. "I'll give it a try."

When she was gone, Tracy leaned close. "She should try a really big cup." I pressed my lips tight, holding in the laugh, Tracy adding, "The biggest one in there." We failed, her laughter ending in a snort.

"Back to this, okay?" I asked, fighting the giddiness. "Please."

"Gawd! That's bitter," Sherry blurted, revolted by the taste. I didn't dare look at Tracy, cheeks aching. "What? What's so funny?"

"Try adding sugar and maybe some cream next time," Tracy told her.

"Guys, let's talk about the ink," I said, steering the conversation. In that message, a murder had been proposed, the weight of it pressing. "Until we figure out where the message came from, and who wrote it, we have to treat it as a threat."

"Understood," Tracy said while placing pens and markers across the lab table. "I didn't get a chance to try anything yet."

"Sherry?" I asked, urging her to join us. "What's your take on the writing?"

"It's cursive, something you don't see often anymore." She gulped her coffee, eyelids fluttering as she shook off the flavor. "I think it's kicking in."

"That's a good thing," I assured her, handing her the box of gloves. "Cursive writing could indicate an age? Someone old enough to have been taught it in school."

She slipped on a pair and moved the message in front of her, lightly tracing one of the letters. *"My victim is first born."*

"Is there something familiar about that line?"

She brought the paper closer to her face, answering, "No, it's not the line I've seen. It's the writing. The typography." She opened her laptop and a text editor and began typing. The sound of her keyboard descended between us. She filled the blank page with the letters as we saw them in the message. After a few sentences and some clicks, the text was highlighted, the fonts menu opened. "Check it out. If I'm right, it's this one."

The screen changed, the characters updated, their shapes matching what was on the mulberry paper. It wasn't an exact match, but very close. Too close to be a coincidence.

"It looks like whoever wrote this may have copied the font," Tracy said, straining as she pawed at the back of her neck. "Why would they try to copy a font?"

I took hold of the lab table and perched an elbow to rest my chin, a magnifier between my eyes and the paper. I examined the letters and Sherry's screen, finding the same stems and tails. Even round letters had the same bowl shape, their sizes matching. I wanted it to be a coincidence. I wanted it to be Sherry finding something that wasn't there. But she was right. Whoever authored the bottled message went out of their way to match a popular font. I looked at the fingerprint smudges on the bottle and the gloves on my hands, an idea coming to mind. "They practiced copying the font to mask their handwriting."

"That way we can't identify it as theirs?" Sherry asked.

Tracy looked unconvinced.

"We've used handwriting as evidence before," I reminded her.

"That's true," she said, warming to the idea. "A message written using a popular cursive font. Written on paper that is a particular type. And whatever ink this is."

"Mulberry Street," I blurted, searching my phone for the address Ruby's mother had given us. "Ruby and her mother live at 98 Mulberry Street."

Tracy spread her fingers and clutched the paper samples. "The mulberry paper! It's a part of the clue?"

"Apparently, yes." There was greater depth in the bottled message. It wasn't only the message. It was the paper used. How about the ink? And what about the way it was torn or rolled? Maybe the bottle is a message too? What about that? "Guys, we've got to look at every part used. There's more here."

"Casey?" Sherry said, voice quiet like a church mouse. "What was that address again?"

"It's 98 Mulberry Street," Tracy answered for me.

"Why?" I asked, heat rising into my face.

She tried to swallow, tongue seeming to stick. "That's how many words there are in the message."

"No way!" Tracy said in a near yell. She dipped her chin, brow raised. "You're sure you counted it right?"

Sherry looked as shaken as I felt inside. Only, I didn't show it, and calmly asked, "Please confirm the count."

She sipped at the coffee, cringing while her finger jabbed the air, counting the words one by one, relying on a finger instead of the computer. I read her lips while the tip of her finger bounced, the feeling of horror coming at us like it was a morbid countdown. Or count-up as the case may be. "It's right. It's ninety-eight words exactly."

"Who the hell is this guy!?" I heard Tracy ask.

I raised my hands as if slowing a race, the pressure of the message suddenly overwhelming. "Every part of what's been found is a clue. Got it."

"Got it," they answered in unison.

"Whoever this is put thought into each part—" I stopped when seeing the look on their faces, their expressions frozen, eyes darting from paper to bottle and back. I sensed they were feeling it too, the large number of facets this one message in a bottle presented. Truth was, I felt we'd underestimated it. "Tracy, we'll work it like anything else. We work all of it. Every part."

"Uh-huh," she answered, flipping on another light to shine onto the mulberry paper.

"Let's try and figure out the ink," I asked, continuing to drive the investigation. "It's got to have some significance too."

"What about the ink?" Sherry asked, setting her laptop aside to join us at the lab table. "Huh, that is different."

I picked up one of the pens Tracy brought and a sample sheet of Tracy's mulberry paper, jotting down her name. "Ballpoint is definitely out." I held up the sheet to show how the pen's impression pushed through to the other side, some letters more than others. "That's with me adjusting and trying to write lightly."

Sherry tapped her keyboard, taking notes. "No to ballpoint pens."

Tracy sniffed a marker, the stink of chemical drifting. "How about one of these?" She wrote down a name in big, loopy letters. We shifted, moving closer to see the possibility of a marker. She frowned, focus narrowing. "I think it's too strong. You know, like there's too much color."

"Yeah, it's bleeding through," I commented when she held the page against the light. "The one used is a lot lighter."

"I think we're on the right track, a felt-tip was used," Tracy said, trading a black marker for a brown one. She scribbled a few words, the ink staining. "Same thing. I think any kind of marker is going to bleed through this paper."

"What about a highlighter?" Sherry suggested. She dug through her bag and handed us a pack of highlighters, the colors electric. She took the most common of them, a bright yellow, and wrote her name. It didn't bleed like the other markers. It didn't look right either, the felt-tip made for highlighting, not writing. "It'd work, but they'd have to shave the felt."

"Let's keep it as a possibility. It's the closest so far."

"Is there a brown?" I heard Tracy ask, my eyes fixing on the message, the letters and the color. "Whatever kind of reddish-brown that is."

"I don't know that I've ever seen a brown highlighter," Sherry replied, the conversation continuing without me.

It was the paper again. The way it looked like bone. In the lab's light, the color of it purposely selected, the message itself had a distinct look. I'd seen it before and felt sick thinking of what it might be. The noise of markers being uncapped and capped and felt scribbled across paper faded. I had to know if I was wrong. From a lab shelf, I grabbed a small bottle of distilled water along with a swabbing kit we'd usually use to collect trace evidence. The girls stopped speaking, their gaze set on what I was doing. I saw that I had their attention and asked, "The message, it looks like it could have been written in a watercolor. Right?"

"That's it! That is what it looks like," Tracy said, mouth slack. "It's why we can see the fibers through the ink in the paper. It's got to be a watercolor."

"Yes, and no," I said and wet the tip of the swab, dabbing it against the corner of an errant drop. It liquefied, the edges of it turning wispy. I rolled the swab, gathering it like we would in the field, the white cotton turning bright red. "Whoever wrote this used blood. Question we have to answer is whether or not this is Ruby's blood."

My heart jumped with the understanding of what we might have. We could lift a sample of blood from the ink and get a type. There was the possibility of DNA too. Present in every cell of our bodies, if the blood was salvageable then we could test for DNA. The moment of elation was brief, the weight of the mulberry paper suddenly too heavy. Why did the killer use blood? It was a message inside the message and I was terrified to find out what it meant.

TEN

A breath. It was weak. A stronger one next, but with a ragged tickle of something sinister inside. Ruby Evans woke with a jolt, recognizing what it was. It was a death rattle deep inside her lungs. She'd heard them before at the nursing home. And it was bad. Her muscles quaked mercilessly when she tried rising, every part of her body aching. A wind raced over her bare skin as she struggled to see. Freezing. She was nearly blind, a sliver of daylight slipping through her eyelids. The lack of sight came with an unusual fright. A surreal sense of already being dead. Maybe she was for a time? She didn't know. Ruby moved a finger. A second. It was enough to pinch what was between them. *Sand?*

But where? she questioned, vaguely sensing the outdoors. A call from a gull answered her, saying they were at the beach. There were other gulls, but their voices were faint and muffled, her ears heavily clogged. There was the low thrum of breaking waves too. The steady rhythm familiar. But in the distance, far from where she lay, there was something else. Something ominous approaching.

A gulp of air reached her lungs but barely took hold. Her

chest tightened with a powerful craving for more. She felt like a vampire in need of blood. *Another sip, please.* Sand slid into the back of her throat which closed tight with an uncontrollable gag. There was more of it in her mouth and nose, the gritty taste of the sea stuck on her tongue. Ruby spat what she could to make room, her muscles frail and weaker than she thought possible.

Cold. A horrific chill wrapped around her like an attack. That's what happened. *I was attacked.* But when was that? *Was it a day? Was it two?*

An arm came free of the sandy restraints, the tips of her fingers awkwardly distant. She reached for freedom and found none, the moment fleeting, the effort overwhelming. Her hand plopped onto her chest as another ragged cough tore inside her. It was like her lungs were made of tissue paper. She tried to feel her other hand, feel her legs and feet and toes but couldn't. What's happening? *Please God! Please let it be from the cold!* Ruby knew there were parts he'd broken in the attack. Parts that would never heal.

He's coming back for you, someone shouted in her head. It was her father's voice. He was speaking sternly to her like she was still a child. *Ruby, you've got to get up now! That man is coming back to make sure you are dead.*

"Okay, Daddy," she tried to say, a cry climbing up from between her trembling lips.

Ruby! he yelled.

"Too sick," she told him, a shiver rushing through her. This was like a fevered dream. That's what it was! She had a fever. A bad one. "I think I'm dying."

Get up!

Ruby heaved. There were bubbles on her mouth, her body rejecting the sea, salty spittle turning foamy. She froze stiff when the vibrations reached her again. It was coming. She could feel the sand shaking beneath her bottom, the mechanized whirring had grown louder with a drumming clop-clop-whoosh.

She felt a memory then, the weight of it crushing like this sandy tomb. In the memory, she was a little girl playing on the beach, her younger brother running around and chasing gulls. He didn't have a care in the world and didn't pay mind to the sand-cleaning machine. That's what her parents called it. A sand-cleaning machine. Ruby had kept her eye on it though. She saw its bristly mouth spinning behind the monster tractor with the tires that seemed as big as their car. The man driving it wore a white and blue baseball cap. He took it off and waved it in the air as the machine crawled to a stop. On that day, he'd seen her and her brother in time. Only, today, Ruby was buried so that even the birds couldn't see her.

Move!

Ruby tugged on her other arm, a shoulder rising. Nothing else moved.

Wiggle your fingers, her father's voice demanded. No movement. Not a single budge. She'd come back to it, the machine's clop-whoosh grinding noise spurring her to dig, to get free.

As she moved, squirming and slithering like a snake, the dankness of wet sand crept into every part of her, every pore. How deep was she? Her heart thumped painfully with a fear of the sand caving and suffocating her. The sand is shallow, she reminded herself. There was the cold bite of an ocean breeze on her fingers, some of it touching her body.

Relief, Ruby swiped with the hand that worked, cleaning it from her chest and middle. Hair, a tangle of it wrapped around her fingers. She shoved her palm against her face, the grit against her skin was like sandpaper, its salty sting driving her to move faster. There was an incessant itch needling beneath her eyelids. She dared to touch, carefully, lightly pressing her finger and the pad of her thumb. Her skin was hot. Too hot.

When she pried open one eyelid, a scream rising weakly,

sunshine struck her pupil, the bright light pouring into her head. There was a dried crust around the edges, the eyelashes gone. The machine was closer, a flutter from seagulls rising above, driven upward to fly away from it.

"Here!" Ruby managed to call out, turning her head and spitting up. She drove her hand into the sky as if planting a flag. A white, surrender flag. She coughed and screamed again, "Please! I'm here!"

Clop-whoosh. Clop-whoosh! She heard as if the machine were speaking. It was in a sense. Its words a warning of what would happen if she didn't move.

"Please don't eat me!" she cried, her mind ripping apart with feverish hysteria. A clamorous clop-whoosh, clop-whoosh called back. It was closer, her heart gushing with terror. She couldn't hear her father's voice anymore. Only the machine. Ruby shook her head, a frenzy taking over. "Don't you eat me! Please no more!"

Clop-whoosh. Clop-whoosh! the machine said.

She reeled back with a blood-curdling scream, throat raw, the clop-whoosh, clop-whoosh nearly on top of her. Ruby saw it. She saw the memory. He'd pulled her over and made her think that he was a cop. He wasn't a cop though. He was a maniac who'd punished her, saying she'd failed to uphold virtues. Whatever that meant. Her mind spun out of control thinking of the bright light which flooded her eyes and that touch of cold metal! Cold metal. Her one functioning pupil expanded suddenly to help her see the truth. He'd threatened her with a saw. A hacksaw. "What did he take?"

Clop-whoosh, clop-whoosh! the machine answered.

ELEVEN

We gloved our hands and slipped booties over our shoes. Tracy stood next to me, the trunk of her car open. Sherry prepared the camera gear, its body and lens new, replacements. The wind blew against us, the muscles in my thighs tightening in a lean. There were waves over fifty yards away, the crest of them foamy white, crashing with a thundery force I could feel in my feet. The waves could have towered with the threat of crushing us. Still, the fear would have felt irrelevant. We were already crushed this morning. I scanned the beach, sunshine gleaming on the wet sand. The seabirds raced along the retreating surf, chasing bubbles with the promise of a tasty morsel. It was a fine setting for anyone visiting the beach today. But we were here for the recovery and investigation of a body. Ruby Evans had been found.

There were families to the north and south of us. Black and yellow crime-scene tape strung from a wall of beach patrol vehicles used to block the area. It'd remain closed most of the day until I gave the okay, which included a sign-off from Samantha Watson, our medical examiner. The ocean was climbing toward a high tide, the distance to it shortened, but it wasn't a threat. I think the killer made certain of it. Ruby's body was placed less than ten yards from the berm that separated the beach from the rest of the Outer Banks. Like the message in the bottle, the killer wanted us to find her, I was certain of it. They wanted a conclusion to the promise made in the message. Whatever sick game was being played, it had us all on edge. I could see its weary toll on the faces of my team too, especially since we had the message and had failed to find Ruby. There was no amount of consoling that would make this right, make us feel better. Dead was dead.

Long shadows stretched west, our gray figures looking like giants. I scanned the gawkers gathering to see who was watching. Who'd come here this morning to see us work the remains that would help us piece together what happened? A few of them craned their necks to see why the beach had been cordoned off, some filling the ears of the patrol standing guard. Watching them was a practice taught to us early in our training. Tracy approached, eyes shielded as we searched the faces to see if anything sparked a second look. It didn't happen often, but some killers were compelled to see their aftermath in real time, the carnage of their work bringing a satisfaction that was impossible to understand.

The medical examiner van pulled onto the scene, and I waited to see if anyone turned their heads to watch. There were a few. An older couple carrying tiny, shaky dogs with bulging eyes. They talked amongst themselves but gave no other indications. There was also a man with a greenish-turquoise jogging suit. He gave Samantha a long look while stretching in place and then turned to continue his run in the opposite direction. Nobody else was staring or showing interest.

"Detective," Samantha said, a hand taking my arm. I offered more of it, supporting her while she prepared for the time we'd spend in the sand. She was petite, small framed, her height barely reaching the top of my chest. Her hair was cut short, dyed jet black, the bangs left long enough to tickle her eyelids. She held up a can of sunblock, spraying it into her hands and lathering it on her skin which was like ivory and burned easily, even in the fall season. I shook my head when she offered some, the heat from the sun warm on my skin. She looked up at me with her pale blue eyes, asking, "Is this the girl in the Amber alert?"

"Unfortunately," I answered, voice cracking. I glanced at the beach-comber with the green and yellow tractor. The municipal worker who'd called it in stood next to the machine, his wiry hair swaying as he worked with a patrol officer to give a statement. "See that guy over there with the cigarette bouncing between his lips?"

Samantha nodded. "He called it in?"

"That's him." I turned to Samantha, adding, "He reported that Ruby Evans was alive when he found her."

"Alive?" she asked, and took to leaning again, sleeving a booty over her other shoe. "I didn't hear about that."

I followed the crime-scene tape to where reporters had gathered, the news spreading fast once the municipal worker called his dispatcher. "We kept that part quiet. I didn't want her mother finding out through a news report."

"Jesus. She was still alive? How long ago?" Samantha asked and began hurrying.

"The beach-comber guy called it in to his dispatch around thirty minutes ago," I told her, working the timeline backward. "We came right from the station and got here while the paramedics were still working on her."

"How long would you say that was?" she asked, gravity in her voice.

Her gaze drifted to the ambulance, its emergency lights doused. Two paramedics sat on the edge of its bay, a patrol officer taking their statements. Samantha was hurrying which alarmed me, a notion of life being possible. We began to rush too, Samantha waving to Derek, her assistant.

"I think we need to get down there and confirm."

"Agreed. It's only been a few minutes," I said, seeing the questions in her expression, the firmness in her eyes. I didn't want to get my hopes up, especially with what was reported. "Do you think they could have made a mistake?"

"No, not a mistake. More like an oversight." She shook her head, the snap of a latex glove sharp. "I've never been to a site where death passed minutes before arriving. I've seen what the human body can endure and want to confirm death... or life."

I walked alongside Samantha, shortening my stride while she tried to keep up. Tracy and Sherry hurried their prep and followed while I continued to give coverage. "The victim was discovered just after daybreak, barely alive, but conscious." We reached the body, Samantha dropping at once, a stethoscope in hand. Nobody moved. If not for the sounds of the ocean and clattering seabirds, you'd never know any of us were there.

"No pulse," she said, peeling the stethoscope from her ears and releasing the victim's wrist. She shifted to the victim's mouth, hair hanging near Ruby's swollen face while she listened for a breath. A moment passed, her saying, "There's no breath either."

"We checked everything," a paramedic called from behind us. Footsteps clopping through sand, the paramedic joined us when seeing Samantha work through the vitals. "Respiratory, cardiac, even her skin. We checked everything."

"Pallor mortis," Samantha exclaimed without looking. She sat back on her heels a moment before glancing up at the paramedics with a squint. "It was the correct call. I had to check with a time of death this recent. You understand?"

"We do," a taller paramedic answered. He hung his thumb over a shoulder, asking me, "Detective, we gave a statement."

"You're good to go. We'll call if we need to follow up on anything."

Sherry held her camera ready to proceed.

I lowered my head near our medical examiner, and asked, "Samantha, can we begin?"

She stood up with my help, the deeper sand making us clumsy. "Yes, let's begin."

"Tracy, would you provide the review for the medical examiner?" I instructed, while Sherry moved to the victim's legs, camera flashing a half dozen times in rapid succession.

Tracy began to circle the victim, speaking from the notes collected, "Ruby Evans, seventeen years of age. She was discovered shortly after sunrise which was at approximately six thirty. She was alive and verbal, and in shock. Shortly after, Ruby Evans died following the paramedics arrival. From the eyewitness account, he'd reported that the victim had been beaten, which was evidenced by injuries around the face and head. Subsequent injuries were discovered in the lower torso, the victim's legs dismembered above the knee."

"Thank you," Samantha said and adjusted her footing to kneel next to the victim's legs. "Death by dismemberment?"

"This poor girl," I said, unable to help myself as I knelt alongside Samantha to investigate the injuries. My stomach turned at the idea of what Ruby had been subjected to. It was perhaps the worst in all the cases I'd ever worked. A flash struck like lightning, Sherry's camera nosing between me and Samantha. It was the incisions, the details of them which might give us a clue, the stark white illuminating them. Samantha saw me studying the injury, spurring the question, "Would it be possible to tell what instrument was used?"

"Um—" she began, blinking slowly, visibly disturbed. "I suppose it'll be one of the first things to figure out."

"How do you do that?" Sherry asked, gulping the sea air.

When we both looked at her, she added, "I didn't mean to speak out of turn. I was just curious."

"It's a very good question," Samantha told her.

Sherry was newer to the team, having worked much of her career on the technology side of an office. When I interviewed her for the position, she said she wanted to mix technology with the practice of crime-scene investigation. Most times, interviews end when enough has been heard to satisfy the job requirements. But I wanted more, and had asked her why she wanted to do that. This wasn't a field you got rich working in. Nothing like other IT jobs out there. There were plenty of those. When I pressed, she'd told me it was her older brother. He'd been murdered five years earlier and she was certain that if the technology they needed then had existed, then her brother's murderer would have been caught. I'd mentioned this to Samantha once, and it piqued her interest enough to work with Sherry, teach her about the human body and what it could tell us. "Join me when we get the victim to the morgue. We've got a camera with a macro lens."

"The close-up photography? It will show us a pattern from the blade?" Sherry asked, jumping ahead. She was right, the both of us nodding.

"Without the close-up, we can see that a finely honed blade was used here." My comment only raised more questions. "Could we determine if the amputations were part of a known procedure?"

Samantha made room for Sherry to continue the photographs while she assessed the injuries. "You want to know if the person who did this had medical training?"

I nodded. "Not just medical training, but if they'd also used the same medical equipment that'd be supplied in a hospital."

"It's possible," she answered, her tone indicating doubt. "They could have watched a video online, maybe ordered the equipment too."

Samantha tucked her fingers beneath one of Ruby's legs, lifting it enough to move. The sight of the separation was surreal and hard to watch. "Is it the bleeding?" I had an idea of what she was looking for. I ran my finger across Ruby's upper thigh where there were creases and bruising in the skin. "These appear to be marks from a rope or belt, tourniquets used."

The camera whirred with a run of clickity-clacks filling our ears, Sherry recording the markings from multiple angles. Tracy showed us her phone, saying, "There's a ton of online sources that show how to do this."

Samantha cringed. "I don't know if I should be shocked knowing that or not?"

"Everything is online," Tracy told her, defending the sources. "I'll see if I can find places to purchase the medical kits to perform an amputation."

"Back to the use of tourniquets," I said, refocusing the questions, and plucking a small sand crab from near Ruby's feet. "Given the bruising around here, the shade of them, I think the procedure took place elsewhere. The killer brought her here and staged the scene."

Samantha dug into the sands, searching. "I don't see any indications of blood loss here. With the sand and distance from the ocean, there would be some, but there's nothing." She moved to the other leg, repeating the slight lift and shift as well as confirming the bruises from a tourniquet. "And from the bruising, I'd estimate the procedure took place twelve or more hours prior to death."

"Do you believe the cause of death to be blood loss?" The question was asked, the remaining injuries to Ruby's body appearing to be defensive, possibly from when she was abducted on Route 12.

"First assessment of a possible cause of death could be hemorrhagic shock," Samantha said, her face bright with sunlight, a worrying look in her eyes. We passed a brief look that was beyond our training. It was a terrible sadness for the victim, an anger for what had been done to her. She motioned to the injuries. "Done incorrectly, amputations cause massive blood loss."

Sherry lowered her camera, jaw clenched, and asked, "Was.... was she awake when that happened?"

"I don't know."

I shut my eyes at the thought of it, a hope stirring for Samantha to tell us that Ruby was sound asleep, that she was completely unaware of the trauma inflicted on her body. Samantha would disappoint, she'd tell us what she was trained to say. She'd tell us the truth.

"It's possible."

"God—" Sherry blurted, eyes glued to the victim's legs, a sand crab appearing between them. When the tiny thing climbed higher, I tore it from the victim's skin, tossing it with the flick of my wrist. It plunked onto the wet sand, a gull swooping down to nab it. This was nature being nature.

Sherry's attention was locked on Ruby Evans, seeing the tragedy the killer made of the girl. This wasn't an act of nature though. It was evil. Sherry began to waver like a flag in a soft breeze, and the little color she had drained from her face. Her knees buckled. "I—"

"Hold on!" Tracy was first to her, an arm saving our newest team member from crumpling into a heap.

Sherry's eyes bulged, the whites of them enormous. "What?"

"Let's get you back to the car," Tracy said, my giving her the okay.

"I got it," Derek said, his thin blond hair fluttering. He was the assistant medical examiner and was big enough to carry just about anything. He took Sherry's arm as Tracy reclaimed the camera gear. "Samantha?"

"Yes, certainly, please," Samantha said, unsure of the words to choose. "Sherry, drink some water and put your feet up."

"This isn't an easy case," I said, gut rolling.

"Small confession off the record," Samantha said, thumbing a recording device, the glow of its red light extinguished. "I've never seen anything like this before."

I looked to Tracy and then the patrol circling. "I don't think any of us have." I moved to Ruby's face, saying, "These injuries. I suspect they occurred during the abduction."

"Horrible what happened." A deep frown set in Samantha's face while she studied the swelling around the eyes, an injury near the bridge of the nose. She gently cradled Ruby's head, fingers probing her scalp and then her face. She sighed and then sat back, saying, "There are multiple contusions and the possibility of a fractured skull."

"Would that mean she could have been unconscious at one point?" Tracy asked, the question picking up where Sherry's had left off.

The waves were cresting with a thundery crash, the placement of the body far enough to remain safe. But it wasn't the tide that had become a disruption. It was nature being nature again. And nature was hungry. Samantha saw the same and gave the cue to Derek for them to continue back at the morgue while I worked with Tracy and Sherry to wrap up the site and give back this part of the Outer Banks. I thought of what Sherry asked, and Tracy's follow-up question and a dark need to know the answer. "Samantha, call me the minute the autopsy is done."

TWELVE

Ruby Evans's remains were carefully removed from the beach, the medical examiner office taking custody. Sherry's color finally returned with a string of apologies and embarrassment, saying something about low blood sugar getting the best of her. I didn't question or make light of it, and instead put her to work. We combed the sands for anything foreign. Anything that shouldn't have been there. Digging through the first layer, the sand loose, some of it lightly stained with Ruby's blood, we found nothing. The small amounts of blood were noted and photographed and sent to Samantha. It told us that the gruesomeness of what had occurred must have taken place elsewhere.

When we hit the next layer, it got harder to dig, the sands packed wet and as cold as ice. That's when we turned it over to a few patrol officers who continued the efforts under Tracy's supervision. If the killer sent a message in a bottle, then they may have placed a second with the victim. There was always the possibility that the killer left something behind too, intentionally or otherwise. We had other priorities—an interview with the person who'd discovered Ruby's body—and left the work to the officer.

His name was Karl Brause, and he was one of the last to see Ruby Evans before she died. Ruby was alive, and according to Karl Brause, she was also conscious. What did she say to him? What were her final words?

The station's air was thick with the smell of vented heat. Alice stood next to a thermostat and tapped the plastic dome. Her attention split when we entered, a gaggle of reporters lining up along the front gate, a low chatter growing among them. We made our way toward the conference room, dodging volleyed questions that went unanswered. Ruby Evans was dead. We knew it and the killer knew it. To the rest of the world, she was still a missing teen who'd been kidnapped. I glanced up at the station monitors which showed the local news, a red and black banner racing along the bottom with breaking news. My insides sank as the letters ran onto the screen with news about a body having been discovered. It was only a matter of time before news of Ruby's murder was splashed across every headline.

Before taking hold of the gate, I gleaned the reporter's faces, knowing most of them while recognizing a few who were newer. I did the same with the camera crews, searching the faces that weren't buried behind their gear. I bumped the gate with my thigh, satisfied with what I saw. There were some killers who were like the arsonist. They couldn't deny the craving. The obsession. And were compelled to watch their fires burn. If the killer was inclined to do the same, they could impersonate a reporter or someone on the crew, allowing them to watch the carnage up close. I turned away, the gate easing shut behind me. The killer wasn't here.

Our conference room was like a fish tank: thick sheets of glass covered the front from floor to ceiling. Anyone walking by got a bird's-eye view of the whiteboard and large screens. Our cubicles did a good job of blocking the view from the front, the layout offering the privacy. At the center of the conference table, Karl Brause sat with his fingers laced, his gaze jumping back and forth. He'd been waiting a few, his body language showing he'd grown restless. An officer waited outside the room, a protective measure in case a reporter slipped by Alice. We dropped our things at our desks, Karl seeing me. He must have seen the badge around my neck and recognized me from the beach when he was giving a statement.

"Coffee?" I offered, mouthing the words with hopes he could read lips. He was slightly older than me, late forties perhaps. He wore hunter-green coveralls and black leather work boots. A lean man, with high cheekbones and a jawline that came to a point, he had a shaggy beard and wore a tattered base-ball cap. His eyes were clear and healthy, which I needed to see. It helped to add credibility to any statements he'd given. He nodded eagerly, my sharing the need for some as well. Before entering the conference room, I grabbed two cups, hot and black, no cream or sugar. Tracy followed, our laptop bags slung from her shoulder. "Mr. Brause."

"Karl, please," he said, taking the coffee and bringing it to his mouth. He puffed at the steam rising over the brim before tasting. "That's good. Thank you."

"First let me say thank you for helping at the scene. The paramedics commented that you'd been a medic and briefed them of Ruby's vitals."

"I seen it before," he said, sipping again. He held up a pair of fingers. "Served two tours as a medic."

"Thank you for your service," I added, air gushing from the seat cushion. "In your words, would you tell us what occurred this morning?"

His expression soured, eyes growing with recollection. "Gosh, I mean, where to start." His fingers trembling, he nodded. "I... I almost run her over you know, driving the sand-cleaner and all."

"Let's start before there," Tracy instructed, a timeline needed. "You were on shift, which started when?"

Karl leaned back, blinking his eyes, thinking back. "Uh... well, I get up in the morning with Ralph. This week was a different time." He picked up his phone, motioning for approval. We gave the okay as he looked at the screen. "Hmm, I was right. An hour difference with the daylight savings thing. Ya know, spring forward and fall back. Sun come up earlier, my alarm was set for it. Ralph woke me up before the alarm went off anyways."

"Ralph? He's your roommate?" I asked, jotting the name down. We'd interview them to corroborate the times given, but only if it was needed.

"Ralph? Yeah, kinda like a roommate. He's my parrot. A macaw," Karl answered with a shallow grin. I scratched a line through the name. "I was on the beach about thirty minutes before sunrise. The glow was just starting in the horizon while the tractor was warming. It takes longer with the colder mornings."

"Yes, it was chilly," Tracy commented. On her laptop screen I saw the sunrise times, the temperature charts, along with the tidal charts—his times checking out. "Do you go when it is still dark? Or do you have to wait?"

"It's important that we got full visibility. Ya know, when them brushes are down for cleaning." He shook his head. "Don't want to run something over or go too close to the water and get stuck."

"Get stuck?" Tracy asked. "It's made for beach cleaning?"

He shook his face heartily. "We keep the John Deere away from the surf. Lost a tractor once. Carlene run it too close to the water and them knobby tires got sucked down by the moving sand. I guess that's why she on the phones now."

"Carlene? Dispatch? That's who you called first?" I wrote her name below the parrot's, feeling more confident we'd be in touch with her.

"That's right. I thought Robbie was on shift. It was Carlene instead." Karl dug into his chin, scratching while he eyed the front of the station. He pointed at the glass as Alice walked past, and asked, "I'm not gonna have to give any kind of statement, am I?"

"Not at all. In fact, it would be preferable if you didn't speak with anyone from the news while the investigation is ongoing," Tracy answered.

"At some point, you were driving along and then stopped. Continue from there."

His focus was fixed on the front of the station, his face shiny. The sight of the news crews was making him nervous. I moved my seat one over, across from him.

"You won't be bothered by anyone."

He made a gulping sound. "They gonna leave me be?"

"We'll do our best to make sure of it," I told him, locking my eyes on his and nodding until he nodded back. "Now, you stopped the tractor?"

"It was them gulls," he answered, voice hollowed, mouth disappearing behind the coffee cup. He cringed, squinting one eye. "I came across some drownings before. Ya know, the bodies getting washed up on the shoreline. The critters and gulls always find them first if you know what I mean."

"I get the picture." I looked over my shoulder a moment to see Sherry working at her desk. "Other than the sea birds, did you happen to notice if anyone else was in the area?"

"Nah. Not there. There was a couple jogging," he answered, scratching at this chin. "They were a few mile back from where I found the girl."

"How about any cars or trucks?" Tracy asked. "Were there any vehicles in the vicinity?"

Karl's mouth turned downward as he continued to shake his head, saying, "No, ma'am. Just them gulls." He tapped the side of the coffee cup, steam hovering. "Was some fog though. Patchy stuff rolling in. That happens this time of year when the ocean temperature is still warm from the summer and the nights get cold."

"It was a thick fog?" I asked.

A nod. There was no fog when we arrived on site.

"What would you say your visibility was?" Tracy asked, fingertips skittering across the keyboard, the observation typed out on her screen. "Was it a mile? More or less?"

"Probably a bit more than a quarter mile. Could be a half mile. That gave me plenty," he answered, gaze lifting to the ceiling as he thought it out. "It was enough to see them gulls. If there was someone, I couldn't see them. They wouldn't see me either if you know what I mean."

"Ground fog and line of sight," Tracy answered. "That's what you mean."

"That's right," he answered.

"The gulls, they alerted you to something being there. Then what happened?" I floated the question, but my thoughts went to the idea that the killer was there with Ruby. That he was still there after placing her on the beach. For the hundreds of yards cordoned by the crime-scene tape, we only identified sandy footprints. Given the amputations, the killer would have made multiple trips or needed equipment to move Ruby's remains. However, there were no tire marks or markings to indicate something was dragged. I had a chat window open on my screen and clicked on Tracy's name, typing,

> I think the killer carried Ruby to that spot. Made more than one trip and then covered their tracks.

"When them gulls shot up the way they do, I hit the brake and clutch. Shifted the tractor into neutral and killed the motor," Karl Brause said, cringing. It was the choice of words used. He looked at Tracy typing, leaned forward and corrected himself, "I turned off the motor."

"Was she conscious?"

Karl slowly blinked, mouth twisting, "Yeah, the girl was awake. Barely though."

"Did she speak with you?" Tracy asked, sitting up.

"Uh-huh." His tough demeanor went soft, his lower lip trembling. "She was asking about her legs."

We don't always find clues in the most obvious places. Sometimes they are hidden beneath the details. "I know this is difficult, but can you recall exactly what she said?"

He finished his coffee, the cup shaking. "She asked me, do I have my arms and legs?" Karl reached up with his right hand, clutching the air, mimicking his actions. "I thought it was shock, ya know from the cold and all. I showed her that I was holding her hand."

"You're right about the shock," I began to say. With his tours as a medic, he was familiar with the injuries. "There was substantial blood loss."

"Yeah. When I seen what was done to her, I didn't know how she was still awake." He drank from his empty cup, disappointment on his face when he plunked it down. My cup had gone untouched and I slid it across the table to him. After a taste, he added, "I've had soldiers lose half their body and still carry on a conversation like we was going out on the town... if you get my meaning."

"I understand," I told him.

"But when they like that, it never last." He took a moment, emotion stealing his words. "Didn't last long with her either."

Tracy lowered the lid of her laptop, the look on her face

showing the difficulty. "Was she aware of what happened to her?"

Karl's eyelids flicked open as he blurted, "When I learned to be a medic, I learned to lie. That's what I done. I lied to her." Even for a soldier who'd served multiple tours, Karl Brause was shaken by what he'd seen this morning. "She asked me about her legs like she knew. I saw what was done to her but told her she was okay. You know, to comfort her. Sometime, in the field just before they die, that's all we get to do."

The emotions took him then, Karl looking away so he could wipe his face. I felt for him but was grateful it was him that had found Ruby. "Did she say anything else to you? Anything at all that we could use?"

He nodded and shook his head at the same time. "There was some gibberishy things, ya know. Nonsensical and all. If you know what I mean." He tapped his forehead, adding, "She was starting to fade."

"Anything could be useful," Tracy told him, dipping her chin to encourage his remembering it. "It could be substantial."

His face cramped with concentration. "It was something like, not the police... might have been, he was not the police." Karl picked up the coffee cup and drained it. "I thought it sounded kinda like a song lyric."

"He was not the police?" Tracy asked, fingers tapping one key at a time.

"That sounds right," Karl answered, telling us something we already knew. "She whispered something else just before she went unconscious... it was a bird."

"Bird?" In my head I saw the message in the bottle. I saw every word, none of which had to do with any birds. "Maybe she heard the seagulls."

"It wasn't a seagull," he said, voice fading as he tried to remember. Leaning closer, he snapped his fingers, saying, "It was a bird. I know that she said something about a bird."

"Pelicans, sandpipers, willets or sanderlings?" Tracy asked, rattling off the common shorebirds. He continued to shake his head, annoyance hinting for her to stop. "Maybe egrets?"

"I'm sorry," Karl shook his head. "She was barely whispering by then. The paramedics were there a minute later, but—"

He didn't finish, the look on his face telling me he'd didn't want to say what we already knew. *Birds?* What did it mean? I handed him my card, and told him, "Don't hesitate to contact me if you recall anything else."

"Should I be afraid?" Brause asked, standing to leave, his height more than a foot above mine. He clenched his jaw repeatedly, his focus fixed on the reporters again. When Tracy followed his gaze, he shook his head saying, "No, not of them. Of the guy who did this to that poor girl."

"It's appropriate to be afraid but I don't believe you are in danger," I told him. I'd never be a hundred percent sure, but Karl Brause came off as reliable, his comments about the fog indicating he was alone with Ruby Evans. That meant the killer didn't know who he was or what he'd done to help the victim. He let out a relieved breath. "Regarding the reporters, I'd ask that you don't speak with them while the investigation is underway."

He scoffed, "You kidding me. Put this mug on the tube?" Brause chuckled and made his way to the door. "The less anyone knows about me, the safer I am."

"The safer you are," I repeated.

Tracy got up, a handful of notes in hand to check Karl Brause's story. We weren't generally suspicious of a witness, but I'd learned to never underestimate what a killer was apt to do or how far they'd go to play their games. Was Karl Brause a suspect? Should he be?

Thinking of the bottled message and questioning how the killer selected Ruby Evans. *He was not the police?* I heard in my head. The killer didn't just happen to come upon Ruby Evans by chance. Not on a dark and rainy night. They could have pulled anyone over on Route 12. They had to have already selected her. Picked her. The killer knew where Ruby Evans was going to be. They must have known her already.

THIRTEEN

It was a bird. I concentrated on what Karl Brause said in his statement about Ruby Evans. I thought so much about it that I started to hear birds flying inside my skull. He may have misheard Ruby, especially with her losing so much blood. But what if it was birds? Was it a clue about her killer? A tattooed arm perhaps? The fact that she spoke to him was a small miracle. If she'd been unconscious, he might not have found her at all.

As sickening as it was, we had the seagulls to thank for cueing him to what was in the path of the tractor. I hate to think of what might have happened if the gulls hadn't shot into the sky when they did. Tracy escorted Karl through the rear of the station. She used a passage and doorway that I often referred to as our secret escape route. In a way, it was too, giving us a path out of the building to avoid the busyness at the front. Later, I'd catch an earful from Alice about using it. Still, it served its purpose today, Karl saying he'd contact me if there was anything more to tell.

It was quiet for the moment. It wouldn't last. For that, I was certain. I glanced up at the station monitors and saw the

breaking news banner racing along the bottom. A breath of
relief slipping from my lips. There was no change. Not yet,
anyway. While the reporters remained gathered, a few of the
crew were missing, those staying behind weren't clamoring or
yelling or doing much of anything. It was a hint that any inside
information a reporter might have gotten had thankfully
remained ungotten. I saw Alice walking by, two patrol officers
with her. I knew the exchange went on. Reporters paying cops
for details. We all knew. That's how the reporters made their
living, and at times, we'd used the same tactic to plant a nugget
in the press, a report that was meant for the killer to read. I
leaned back, my chair groaning. The birds? We could plant a
news story about birds. Nothing too obscure. Just something
with enough bite for the killer to know I was talking to them.
But what would we say?

I made a note of it while looking over the notes from the
meeting. Samantha had Ruby, and by now she had her hands
inside the girl, taking apart what life had put together. In the
anatomy of bones and tissue, Samantha would reveal the truth
of what killed Ruby. This was a criminal homicide case and
required a full autopsy. In a few hours, we'd have the preliminary results. Samantha was good about that. The full report
required more time to support the drug screening and other lab
dependencies. I didn't need the reports though. I tapped my
keyboard, the photograph from the scene bright on my screen.
Leaning closer, I magnified the incisions made to Ruby's thighs.
Those were what killed her.

Incisions. That wasn't the right word and I scratched the
pen across my notepad, a bitter taste rising, *incision* disappearing behind an inky web. When it was gone, I wrote down
another word, *amputations.* The cuts were smooth as though
they'd been performed by a surgeon. I added to the magnification, the pixels getting blocky, a higher resolution needed.
When I reached the limits of the monitor, I panned over Ruby's

legs. There were no tears or slips. There was no awkwardness or deviations. But why?

"Tracy!?" I heard the rustling of chair wheels, the patter of sneakers as she paddled them, rolling from her desk to mine. She joined me with a bump, jostling my hand and forcing me to recenter the frame. On both sides of where the blade made contact, there was a faint blue marking. "Do you see it?"

"Uh-huh," she answered, the smell of her body wash reaching my nose. It was different and she saw that I noticed. "You like?"

I nodded, jokingly saying, "No, not really." She cocked her head and took hold of the mouse, my fingers beneath her palm. I saw where she was going and continued to drive. "Same on the other leg."

When the screen refreshed with the left leg's amputation, the single cut, bisected I think I heard Samantha say, had the same blue line. "It's like they drew where they were going to cut."

From the chat window, I pasted a portion of the screen and sent it to Samantha for confirmation.

> I think our killer would have had medical training to know to do this? Can you confirm what we're seeing in the pictures?

Samantha began to type, the dots bouncing a moment.

> We'll investigate it.

Before I could reply to the chat, Tracy sat straight up and clapped the top of the desk. "Karl Brause has medical training."

An itch raced across the top of my thighs. A phantom of where the amputations took place on Ruby's legs. I grabbed hold and squeezed my legs while regarding Karl Brause as a possible suspect. Crocodile tears was the term that struck first.

I'd seen killers show remorse before, putting on a show for a judge or district attorney. But I didn't get any sense that the municipal worker was a killer, that his statement was a lie. Then again, how many suspected some of the most notorious serial killers? Exploring Tracy's comment, I added, "He does have the medical training. While he didn't say it directly, I believe he performed emergency amputations in the field." I slowly shook my head, unconvinced.

"Casey, he's a good fit. A great fit," Tracy said, enthusiasm rising in her voice. She held up a hand, fingers splayed, and counted down each reason. "He lives by himself. He works by himself. His work happens to be on the beach. Time, he was conveniently the one to discover Ruby's body."

"Karl Brause," I said his name aloud like I was trying to fit him in the mold of a killer. Only, there was no mold. It was evidence we needed. Not speculation based on opportunity such as time alone on the beach. As Tracy's words continued to fill my ears, I saw the possibilities. My focus returned to the picture of Ruby's legs. Her skin had that pale white-blue color that appears soon after death. There was no indication of any lividity yet, which shows that gravity had not found what little blood she had in her system. Karl Brause could have placed her body on the beach while she was still alive. He had the knowledge, knew the medical procedures. And he had the opportunity. Yet, what was the motive? Whatever it might be, it remained a mystery.

"What if everything he said was just some made up story?" she asked. "You know, to mask the truth of what happened."

"Other than his call back to"—I scoured my notes, finding the scratched-out parrot's name, Ralph, the dispatch name beneath—"Carlene. But he could have placed that call to establish a timeline for his story." I lowered my chin, the possibility of his being a suspect growing. We needed to build a timeline and map every minute of Ruby's life, the end of it, along with Karl's statement.

I sat up with another supporting thought. "With a job like his, cleaning the beach early in the morning, he could have placed that message in a bottle too. Partially buried it so that it was safe but visible enough to make sure it was found."

Tracy's eyes bulged, eyelids disappearing. "He staged the message in the bottle, staged the victim. After he called it in, he came here to tell us that bullshit story!" Tracy said adamantly, her voice loud enough to stir chair wheels from a distant cubicle. I motioned for her to quiet down. She spun around to face the small whiteboard on my wall. In big blocky letters, she wrote Karl Brause's name in red marker. We both crinkled our noses at the chemical odor. She circled his name twice, underlining it as well for emphasis. Left alone, I think Tracy would have convicted him without a trial. When she saw that I wasn't entirely convinced, she wrote down the word *motive* and plunked a large question mark next to it. "That's what's got you. Isn't it?"

"The lack of a motive is a definite problem. It's a big problem." I eased back and stared at the name and regarded the exchange in the conference room. I pieced together what we'd worked out, saying, "We have gone to a DA with less. We've also gotten a judge to issue a search warrant with less too."

"Then we get the warrant," Tracy said excitedly, "and search his property? Heck, search the tractor too."

"Whoa. Hold up a second." I stood enough to see the reporters, a station's overhead light glinting from a camera lens. The reporters hadn't moved. With the palm of my hand pressed against the board, Karl Brause's name was removed with a single swipe. "We have to be very careful about this."

"What do you mean careful?" She tilted her head, questioning, "You said it yourself. We've done more with less."

"Tracy, I'm sorry, but we need more, and we need to be

certain of the evidence before taking a leap." What worked on a dry-erase whiteboard, didn't necessarily work on my hand. I peeled open a pack of wet wipes, adding, "If we're wrong and his name gets out prematurely, it won't matter what happens next."

Tracy gestured silence, her index finger perched on her mouth. "Then we keep it quiet."

Elbows perched on my knees, I gave her the nod. "Tell you what. Follow up on everything Brause told us. Every inch of his statement and the timing. When he got up. When he reached the municipal building garage. Even the tractor. It's owned by the township and must have something to log hours of use for tracking depreciative values."

She was gone in a flash, voice carrying, "I'm on it."

The red stain on my palm had turned pink, which was better than before. I peered over at the whiteboard, remnants of Karl's name still showing. Before I could continue with the cleanup, the phone on my desk rang. I'd only used the thing occasionally, the top of it coated with dust. I checked my cell-phone to see if I'd missed a call. I hadn't and picked up the desk phone's receiver, answering, "This is Detective White."

"An inmate of Greensboro Correctional Facility is placing a collect call," an operator spoke, voice wavy and scratchy. I sat back with surprise. "Do you accept the charge?"

"Yes, I guess." When there was silence, I repeated more clearly, "Yes, I accept the charges."

A series of clicks rattled in the phone's speaker, ending with the words, "Bonne journée, Detective." I jerked the phone away from my ear, instincts sending electricity into my arms. I knew the voice. I knew the hint of a French accent too. My gaze fell to the phone's cradle with a fleeting thought of hanging up. It came and went like a shooting star, the tinny sound of his voice asking, "Detective? Detective White? You are there?"

"Doctor Boécemo? How did you get this number?" I

couldn't steady my voice or steady the nerves climbing inside my chest.

"It's amazing what you can get these days with just some-one's name," he answered in that slow and relaxed tone of his, the slight accent hanging on some of the words. There were noises in the background. A yell. A man cussing. The rap of metal on metal. "I won't keep you, Detective White. I'm calling to ask that you come and see me. Soon."

Instinct took over again and I jerked the phone from my ear, wincing at it. When I heard him calling my name, I said, "Thanks for the invitation but I think I'll wait to see you at your next parole hearing."

"Yes, yes. That was quite the show you put on. Wasn't it?" The doctor made wet tsk-tsk sounds, objecting. "Quite unfairly too, I do believe."

My apprehensions went someplace, a grin forming. He was where I needed him to be. Prison. "Doctor, I assure you, fair had nothing to do with—"

"How is your investigation of little Ruby Evans?" he asked. I bolted up in my chair, a frightening chill rifling through me. When I didn't answer, he continued. "Yes. I thought that would get your attention."

"They have television in prison, Doctor?" Of course they did. But I wanted to say the obvious. I glanced up at the station monitor, the news banner the same as it was earlier. "Do the guards allow you to watch the news?"

"Poor Ruby Evans. The girl hasn't got a leg to stand on or a pot to piss in," he said, singing the words like they were part of a nursery rhyme. He was talking in riddles, the prison phone conversations monitored. How could he possibly know about the victim's legs? There was a long silence on the phone line, his finally saying, "Detective White, I do think you will do me the courtesy of a visit."

"Doctor?" I asked, unable to come up with a question.

"Au revoir, Detective Casey White," he said, the phone line clicking.

"Tracy!" Chair wheels in motion. When she reached my desk, I told her, "I don't know how, but Dr. Boécemo knows that Ruby Evans is dead."

Her eyes darted to the station monitors and then to the reporters. "I don't understand. Her death hasn't been released."

"That's not all." I tapped my monitor, finger pressing. "He knew about her legs."

FOURTEEN

How did the doctor fit into any of this? There had to have been a leak. Impossible as it seemed, there had to have been a reporter listening to Karl Brause as he gave his statement at the station. Or it could have been one of the paramedics? I'm sure they'd heard enough about Ruby Evans from Karl Brause during those minutes just after she stopped breathing. Did a reporter release a story that we didn't know about yet? It was his comment about her legs that had me perplexed. It had me terrified! I had no explanation and might not have one until I saw the doctor again, bending to his request to meet with me. But that would have to wait until tomorrow.

For now, I had to concentrate on what Karl Brause told us. We did find a problem with his statement. It was missing time. Not just a minute here or there. It was more than a full hour, possibly as much as two. That could be as much a hundred and twenty minutes lost. We spent the afternoon building a timeline surrounding Ruby Evans's abduction and murder, filling in the gaps with the search of her car, the preliminary medical examiner report, and Michael's statement. When we did the same with Karl's account of the morning, we discovered the time difference. We couldn't reconcile it. There was only one reason I could think of for the discrepancy: Karl Brause was lying. He'd cried when giving his statement, and even made me choke up and feel emotional with him. It wouldn't have been the first time I'd sat across the table from a killer though, taking their statement, believing they were an innocent witness. Any hesitations to officially name Karl a suspect was thrown out the window. He had to be. At least until the questions about Ruby Evans were satisfied.

For now, Karl was home with his parrot named Ralph, and that was where he would stay until we built our case against him. Knowing there was nothing more that could be done until the morning, I was finally home, busy straightening up the apartment, corralling the kids and finishing the last meal of the day. We didn't always have waffles or pancakes for dinner, but when we did, I seemed to be the one to clean it up. Not sure why that was. I guess it just worked out that way. While he was barely tall enough to reach my hip, Thomas had started to chip in and help to clean wherever he could. Jericho even bought him a small wooden stool to use. He climbed the single step to take a plate, the knuckles on his fingers white as he gripped it tight and dried it. When he was done, he lifted his chin and looked for another dish. Sudsy water dripping from my fingers, I swept his light-colored hair to the side, the long strands almost white. Tabitha shared the color, as well as their fair skin and those light hazel eyes that I swore could see my soul.

"You'll be a heartbreaker one day," I told him, handing him another dish.

"A what-breaker?" he asked, the word breaker sounding like braver.

"It's nothing—" His attention shifted to the cartoon noises spilling into the kitchen, Jericho and Tabitha's laughter follow-ing. I nudged him lightly and told him, "You go ahead. I'll finish here."

"Love you," he said with a leap from the stool. He broke into a run without looking back, voice trailing, "What'cha watching?"

A knock at the door had me eyeing the clock on the range. It was seven in the evening already, the days seeming to pass faster and faster. "Casey?" I heard Jericho ask. I imagined him on the floor, his back against the couch, Thomas and Tabitha on each side. I wouldn't want to get up either.

"I'll get it," I told him and dried my hands. A second knock came, annoyance pinching my lips and staying quiet. Hours earlier, I'd been told that I probably shouldn't curse. Thomas was right, his making both me and Jericho promise to do better. That stove was hot though. I can't always control what comes out of my mouth. "A second."

"Casey, it's me," Tracy said, her voice muffled.

"What are you doing?" I asked, opening the door. She had a key and never knocked. I held on to the door, thinking of our earlier conversation. Was it another memory? Did she remember more of what happened after her kidnapping? The door swung open, the smell of autumn rushing in with a scattering of dried leaves. With the rains gone, the ground and trees drying, the fall season was in full swing. I half expected to see pumpkin-spiced lattes in her hands, a favorite we both shared. Her eyes were bright with a grin on her face. She wore denim and a woolly jacket and a colorful red and black plaid scarf that hung loosely around her neck. She looked a million times better than I'd seen her last at the station. "Tracy, what's with the knock—?"

"Because she brought me," a woman said, stepping out from behind an evergreen shrub that needed pruning. It was the evening, a chilly night, and I was only wearing sweatpants and one of Jericho's old concert T-shirts, along with his yellow and green flannel. The bra had been dropped onto the bed a few hours earlier, the girls set free for the evening. I closed the front of the flannel, covering up as heat climbed in a flush.

"I'm sorry for the surprise, Casey. I wasn't sure that you would see me."

I crossed my arms, covering myself some more. "We weren't expecting—" I didn't finish, my gaze struck frozen with hard concentration. Did I know her? The woman was dressed well with long leather boots, a skirt, a blouse and an expensive jacket. She carried a briefcase and wore a cream-colored shawl, the expensive kind that spelled luxury like the rest of her outfit. I knew this woman once, but she looked very different from the detective she'd once been. "Cheryl? Cheryl Smithson?"

She put on a faint smile, a hint of something genuine in it. "Uh-huh. It's me." Cheryl had once been a rising star at our station, the two of us competing. At one point, she'd won a position above me and had her sights to go even higher. I hated to admit it, but her ambitions were far greater than my own. I truly believe we would all be working for her today if a bullet hadn't found her first. It was a case we'd worked together, the two of us beneath a row of boardwalk shops in pursuit of a killer who'd escaped arrest. He had a gun and fired it wildly, the bullet shattering her hip. It was more than flesh and bone though, the lone bullet shattered her career.

"Please," I said, making room for them, immediately feeling uncomfortable. What was she doing here? Cheryl entered first, her body thinner than I'd ever seen. She walked with a cane, leaning on it heavily, her grip tight like a vice on the handle. Gone were the sexy shoes with the tall heels, the lacy, dark stockings and tight clothes she wore to show off her model figure. Even the fiery red hair and lipstick to match were gone too. Her green eyes were still there, still bright and alive. But this was a completely different person. "Cheryl, I'm sorry that I didn't recognize you."

"What's there to recognize?" she joked as she brushed a

hand across her clothes and raised the cane, scoffing at it. She patted the outside of her briefcase, saying, "This is who I am today."

"Coffee? Wine?" I asked, feeling anxious. Cheryl always made me feel that way. Never has there been someone in my life that made me want to compete as much as she did. This wasn't the Cheryl I knew, though. Not anymore. I saw it when I offered her a chair at the kitchen table. She winced and gritted her teeth and carefully lowered herself while blowing out short breaths as though she were in labor. My heart hurt for her. Guilt came too. It could have been me who took that killer's bullet. But it wasn't. And when the operations failed to restore mobility, forcing her to resign, I'd said that I would stay in touch. I didn't.

"Just some water would be great," she answered, beady sweat forming on her upper lip. She swiped at it, her face flush. She saw the concerned look on my face. "Trust me. This is one of my good days."

I was at a loss for words and took her hand. "I am so sorry I didn't stay in touch with you."

Her eyes grew with surprise, a wide grin appearing. "Trust me, you did yourself a favor. I was a real pill."

"I'll get your water," I said as Jericho joined us.

"Cheryl Smithson." He took a seat next to her, the two having some history. Some of it good. Much of it bad. Very bad. She'd gotten personal during a case that had involved Jericho. It was at a time when he was running for mayor. We'd never know for sure, but some words were given to the press, the source of them coming from our station. Jericho lost that election, and I held my breath to see if he'd ask her to leave our home. That's not who he was though. He was made differently than most. You couldn't pay Jericho to carry a grudge. As he'd say it, resentments were for other people. He didn't ask Cheryl to leave and instead gave her a smile, a touch of sympathy in his eyes as he took her hand and said, "It is so good to see you."

"Really?" she asked, looking apologetic. "I didn't think—"

"It's not like that," he interrupted. "Everything happens for a reason, and I'm better for it. We're better for it."

"Hmm," she grunted.

She opened her briefcase and placed a folder on the table. I handed her a bottle of water which she opened quickly, plastic snapping. She chugged it a second, bubbles gurgling. Cheryl lifted her cane and gave it a hard stare before placing it against the wall. "Everything happens for a reason. Maybe you're right, Jericho."

"Cheryl, I didn't mean anything by that," he said, blushing with embarrassment. Tabitha and Thomas marched into the room, eyes filled with curiosity. Jericho opened his arm for them to join him. "Good timing, you two. Cheryl, this is Thomas and Tabitha. This is what I meant."

"I knew what you meant." She smiled like she had a secret. "It's also why I'm here tonight."

"I contacted her," Tracy said from behind us. I'd almost forgotten she was with us. She'd found the dinner leftovers and had made herself a plate at the counter, devouring dry waffles and bacon. Mouth stuffed, she pointed at us, saying, "You guys need Cheryl."

"Need?" I asked with growing confusion. From the cover of the folder I gleaned the names of Thomas and Tabitha's birth parents. Beneath it, I saw their names. Feeling flustered, I pointed at the table, asking, "Cheryl, what is that?"

"It's your petition," she answered. "Family court. You're scheduled for the hearing later this week."

"Tracy?" Jericho asked, motioning to Thomas and Tabitha. "Would you?"

"Oh, right," Tracy answered, picking up her plate and waving for them to follow. "Come on, you two rug-rats."

"It was nice to meet you," Cheryl said.

They waved while following Tracy.

When they were gone, she faced us saying, "They really are beautiful children. They're very lucky to have you both."

"Thank you, Cheryl," Jericho said. His brow narrowed, questions returning. "How do you know about them?"

"Who doesn't? I mean, the *Two Little Souls* news story. Lost at sea and all." Her eyes were wide and bright, almost gleaming. "I was in California when I saw it on the news, and I've been following it ever since."

This wasn't the Cheryl I knew. The old Cheryl only cared about one thing. Herself. There was more here than the spitfire sarcastic and competitive detective I'd known. There was compassion in her voice. This was a person transformed. "Cheryl, I feel like I'm still catching up here? How is it that you can help?"

She opened the folder which had a copy of the petition. There were also copies of Thomas's and Tabitha's birth certificates, as well as their parents' death certificates. "Where did you get those?" Jericho asked.

"Having these is in my job description," she answered.

All at once I had a sinking feeling that Cheryl was involved with the adoption somehow. How else would she have the adoption petition we filed? I traded a look with Jericho and saw that he was questioning it too. The petition had been accepted with a date issued for us to appear at a hearing in family court.

Cheryl saw the concerns and brought her hands together. She dipped her head toward us, saying, "Guys, I am here to help... that is, if you'll let me."

From the briefcase, she fished out a stack of business cards and handed one to each of us, Jericho's lips moved as he read it aloud. "Cheryl Smithson, Family Law." He shook his head, asking, "You're a lawyer now? How did that happen? When did that happen?"

"Well, Casey will remember this, I already had a law degree," she began, a pill bottle in hand. She took two and threw them to the back of her throat and tipped the bottle of water. When she saw my eyes on the bottle, she assured me, "Just aspirin. I never touch the stuff the doctor's push. After I got shot, after the surgeries and the complications, it was clear that any options to return to law enforcement were gone."

"I thought the surgery went well?"

Her eyes sprang open. "Which one?" She used the cane to help her shift, the ten minutes in the chair already growing uncomfortable. "By the third surgery, the complications had me in a wheelchair. I didn't think I'd ever walk again."

"That's terrible. I'm so sorry to hear that," Jericho commented. He nudged the card. "That's when you found your true calling?"

His question eased the pain I saw on her face, a smile forming. "I did. I mean, I really did. I took some refresher classes and studied my ass off for the bar exam. After that, I got my license and discovered family law."

"Amazing." It was a good ending to something tragic. Or would it be a new beginning? Either way, Cheryl had landed on her feet, so to speak, which brought her to our home. "Thomas and Tabitha?"

"After I got my license and set up shop, I needed some pro bono cases. You know, to get my feet wet, get the word out." She lifted another case file from her briefcase, the name on it, Hannah. I froze with surprise, realizing the case she worked. "I took Tracy's case after her identity was discovered. What a messy tangle of government nonsense that was. We had to figure out what legal name she could use. From the government's perspective, you can only have one identity."

"Thank you for working with her," I said, recalling some comments Tracy had made. She didn't involve me in any of it, choosing to work through it with her adopted parents. That stung a little, but I understood. "That's why Tracy brought you."

"Actually, I called her," Cheryl answered. "I was going to show up alone, but I wasn't sure if you'd see me or not."

I took her hand. "We'd see you. Like Jericho said, we're better for it."

"You can help us?" Jericho asked. When Cheryl nodded, he followed up, "What's next?"

"First, hand me a dollar," she answered. When we didn't understand the request, she added, "That way, we can make this legitimate."

"Oh right!" Jericho laughed. "I've seen that in the movies. It's for the client-lawyer confidentiality thing."

She nodded as Jericho unfolded a one-dollar bill and slid it across the table. Cheryl picked it up, and asked, "Now, I need you two to tell me what is it that scares you the most about the hearing. That'll help us start with the preparations."

Jericho already knew what frightened me and let me answer for the both of us. "I'm afraid of what they are going to ask."

"Is there something particular?" Cheryl asked without looking up from a legal pad, the top of her pen twirling as she wrote.

My heart stopped. Seized is a better word, blood stopping cold. I know that's not what really happens, but damn if it didn't feel like I was about to keel over on the spot.

When the silence grew uncomfortable, she looked up. "Casey?"

"It's about my daughter," I answered, looking toward the other room, colors from the television playing on the ceiling. My focus returned as I tried to swallow. But the spit wouldn't come. "It's the questions they'll ask about her kidnapping. How it was my fault she was taken."

Cheryl inhaled deep and tossed the pen onto the legal pad with a blink. "Yeah. That's the one I'm afraid of too."

FIFTEEN

The prison that Dr. P.W. Boécemo called home was the last place I expected to be this morning. Unlike the first trip, I drove this one alone. There was a solid angle to naming Karl Brause as a possible suspect. Tracy was right to push it. Which was why she stayed behind. Her recent promotion meant more than a shift away from the work behind a camera and laptop. It meant going into the field and investigating. By noon, I expected to hear she'd made the rounds, questioning everyone from the garage where Karl Brause's manager worked, along with any of the mechanics, as well as Carlene in Dispatch. She was also working behind the scenes with the assistant district attorney to get a search warrant issuance started.

Poor Ruby Evans. The girl hasn't got a leg to stand on. Those were the doctor's words to me. How was it he knew anything at all? Anything more than what was reported by the news? Shortly after his phone call and the invitation to see him, Samantha texted a message about Ruby Evans's mother. I glanced at the clock on my car radio and felt the ache of loss. By now, Ruby's mother was standing at the table where her daughter lay dead. Samantha would be standing on the opposite side, while Derek stood nearby in the event a hand was needed.

Within the hour, Samantha would have addressed the particulars of Ruby's cause of death, hemorrhagic shock the leading cause. She'd explain the significant assault that had taken place on Ruby's body, resulting in the blood loss contributing to her death. There were no defensive wounds found. However, there were signs that restraints had been used on Ruby's wrists and ankles. The ligature marks were insignificant enough to believe Ruby was not conscious at the time of the injuries made to her legs. We'd meet with Ruby's mother too and ask the questions that needed to be asked. I'd want a list of everyone who'd been in and out of Ruby's life recently. I'd also request permission to search her daughter's bedroom. It was the most painful part of a murder investigation since the timing of it had to take place as soon as possible. Time has a way of changing a memory, the details lost. Tonight perhaps. That'd be best.

The rituals to enter the prison were the same as before, a different guard standing at the outside gate this time. She had a round face and eyes that were set deep. The guard surprised me with a broad smile, along with a, *Have a nice day*. I parked in the same spot and closed my jacket, the air crisp with the smell of fall. The sky was a clear cornflower blue, and somewhere in the distance a fire was burning. It was wood or a pile of raked leaves, the winds encouraging the tree to shed them. Winter was coming and I hurried to the prison's outer steel doors and the second guard station.

My escort took me a different route today, walking us through one of the corridors that sat parallel to a cell block. I could hear the life inside of the prison, the ruckus of men; there were angered shouts and laughter. It was the time they owed that I heard most. Much like the doctor owed and tried to parole. In my gut, I believed the doctor asked me here because of his parole hearing. I believed that to be the case more than the possibility of his having a connection to Ruby Evans's murder, which was surely impossible with him safely behind bars. Still, he knew about her death before the news had reported it. More than that, he knew about her legs.

The guard took me to a room which was large like a cafeteria. The walls were dull and painted with two colors. The bottom was a yellow-green while the other was a cream color that was stained with grime. There were large, capitalized letters stenciled where the colors met, a warning which read, *keep hands in plain view at all times*. The guard motioned for me to follow, entering the room where I saw security cameras high up near the ceilings, one in each corner and pointed down into the sitting area. Round tables were fastened to the concrete floor, four stools attached, the metal surface a brushed stainless steel that was shiny.

"Detective Casey White," the doctor said, his low breathy voice bouncing across the empty room. As I've always seen him, the doctor was clean-shaven, his salt and pepper hair combed back, his expression stuck in a pleasantry I didn't understand. He was thinner. Too thin. Was it an illness? How bad? I expected to see anger on his face but there was none. He looked genuinely happy to see me.

"Doctor," I answered, joining him at one of the tables. He wore the same yellow jumpsuit I'd seen at his parole hearing, his feet together and his hands clasped in front of him. There was a guard near a second entrance, my escort leaving me to join him. That's when I noticed the lack of restraints. The doctor had no shackles or chains to bind his wrists and ankles. It gave me a moment's pause, but I didn't feel the heat of any physical threat. With the doctor, I don't think I ever have. It was the children he was a threat to.

"Detective, I'm glad that you came," he said as I gave him a curt nod and took to one of the stools. Before sitting, his hand stretched across the table to take mine. Like his hair and shaven face and trimmed fingernails, it was a courtesy he held on to from his life outside of prison. That's who the doctor was. He was formal to the point of arrogance. Even incarcerated, he still held himself in a regard higher than others. Maybe it was baked into his nature from childhood. Or possibly from some cellular level in him. He'd lived in France most of his childhood but had family in North Carolina. An old family, as in the founding settlers old. He flinched at clashing metal, gates slamming with a distant yell, a clarifying reminder of who he was now.

"Doctor!" a guard said, the voice urging him to lower his arm. He did.

"Very well," he answered, easing himself slowly onto the round stool before placing his hands on the table, one atop the other. He lifted his chin and sniffed the air, his eyes finding mine. "Detective, I can smell the seasonal change on your clothes. There was a fire, someone burning leaves I think."

"Yeah, seasonal changes and all that." Sitting closer, I looked him over. I did this out of habit to understand if there might be other motivations for the visit. I looked for bruising, swelling, scratches or cuts across his knuckles. Anything that would show his time inside had been made complicated. There was a bruise on his left eye and close to his temple. It was green, days old. His lower lip drooped to the right, a cut on it healing. It was enough for me to keep his motives in check. Rather than pursue, I got right to the point. "How did you know about Ruby Evans?"

"How does anyone inside learn what's happening outside?" he said, answering a question with a question.

I hated that. There were at least a half dozen ways he could have found out about Ruby Evans. It was a sad truth, but someone directly involved with the case could have talked about it. From there, word of her murder spread and eventually reached the doctor. A convict has nothing but time and will burn days if it meant there was something in it for them. That included manipulating my time with the invitation to visit. These were the things I told myself on the drive to the prison, justifying how he knew. But as I took my seat and studied his face, I couldn't be sure. "And how are the plans for your petition to adopt?"

"Wha—?" I began to ask, his question striking me like a punch. It took my breath and shook me. "Come again?"

He cocked his head with a coy smile I'd come to loathe. The doctor placed his hand over his heart as if his feelings were hurt. "Who doesn't know the lovely story about Thomas and Tabitha and how you and Jericho saved them from a horrible demise?"

A hot rock lodged deep in my gut, the wave of surprise leaving me stunned. I cleared my throat, asking, "Your point, Doctor?"

"I mean, the story about them made quite the headlines."

He shook his head and put on a troubled look. "Children can overcome much, but the trauma of witnessing a parent's murder—"

"Ruby Evans!" I interrupted, cringing at his mentioning the children by name. "Your phone call, the comment about her not having a leg to stand on!"

"Now now, Detective, give me something here," he began to say, voice breathy like a whisper. He glanced at the clock over his shoulder, returning to continue. "You've already driven all this way. Tell me about them. Are they adjusting well?"

I felt sick to my stomach as I chewed on what to say. He didn't speak though, my frustrations rising like steam as I finally answered, "They're adjusting fine."

He leaned forward slightly, dark eyes pensive as he waited to hear more. The doctor wasn't going to give me what I came for until I gave him what he wanted. *Be careful.* I knew that I was being manipulated. It felt like the concrete floor had suddenly turned into a slab of thin ice. There was a danger here. A terrible danger. In my head, I heard the warning, *curiosity killed the cat*, but I still had to know. "The petition? How?"

His eyelids lifted with a flutter and then fell. "Come now, I've been involved in at least a hundred hearings. Adoptions, custody, all of them. The foster system is just a temporary solution. It was only natural to assume yours and your darling partner's next step would be to adopt the two little souls."

"Fair," I answered, feeling vulnerable, the ice cracking as I played along. "They are adjusting. They're happy."

"Detective, and how about you?" He lowered his head again, expecting more. I shrugged, unsure of how to respond. "Are you ready to become a mother again?"

"I'm fine," I snapped. His words were sharp with intention, needling on the single point that bothered me most: losing my daughter. "Not that it matters, but I was always a mother. I never stopped."

"That's fair, as you'd say," he replied. "And your beau, Jericho?"

"Who told you about Ruby Evans?" I asked, putting an end to whatever it was he was trying to do.

"Quick to the point. That is very Philadelphia of you, Detective White," he replied without answering my question. "I want to make a deal with you."

"A deal?"

"You made certain that my parole hearing turned into a farce." There was a flicker in his dark eyes, the wrinkles around them disappearing briefly. "So, that left me no option but to have an inquiry opened for a parole decision appeal. It's a process. One that has already begun."

"You didn't answer my question," I said, stating it firmly and purposely ignoring his plans to appeal the parole decision.

"I know what I know. Does it matter how?" he asked, the sly grin returning. My insides turned, but I remained composed.

The grin disappeared abruptly, his voice stern. "I expect the courtesy of a consideration, Detective. You owe me that much since I have something to offer."

"I'm afraid that I am all out of courtesy, Doctor." I made like I was leaving, swinging a leg toward the door behind me.

"All right," he said, his palms facing up. When I settled, he continued. "I've invited you here to tell you what I know about poor Ruby. However, I cannot offer anything without a deal to which you must agree."

"What is it that you are looking for?" I asked, getting this part of haggling out on the table. This wasn't my first time listening to a prisoner's demands. It wouldn't be my last either.

"The parole hearing appeal I mentioned." He cocked his head and paused long enough for me to shift uncomfortably. "You, Detective Casey White. You will appear at it to stand on my behalf and speak to my remorsefulness and my healthy rehabilitation."

Inside, I felt a laugh rise like it was stomach acid. The audacity of his demand! But before scoffing wildly and stampeding from the room, I entertained it. "A deal requires an offer in exchange for something. I know what I have. What do you have, Doctor?"

He raised his hand with his index finger pointed up and answered, "I have a name."

SIXTEEN

My time at the prison was made short once the doctor had voiced his offer. An immediate reaction came from my gut—a howling taunt to ask if he was serious. My response wasn't taken lightly. By the time I sucked in a breath, he grunted that his offer was final and was up from the table and leaving. The idea of speaking to a parole board on his behalf left me wanting to retch onto the prison floor. That's when the rage took hold. It rushed over me with an ache set deep in my bones. If it was left to me, if we were alone, I think I might have vaulted over the steel table and reached down into his sickening throat and yanked the name out of him.

Who was it? Who did the doctor know? An ex-con was the first thought, the name of a prior cellmate. I refused to get my hopes up, having experienced how prisoners boast and tell tall tales to impress. I could almost hear the exchange occurring between them in the quiet of the night when the prison noises rested, and the lights dimmed. Before reaching my car, I stopped dead. *Hasn't got a leg to stand on.* No prisoner would have known about Ruby's legs. Or could they? If there was a leak... I shook it off, the thought feeling unlikely. But what if word about the amputations was out there?

I texted the team with urgency an underlying tone. Messages went flying to both Sherry and Tracy and then back to me. I wanted them to dig into every day of the doctor's incarceration and find the names of anyone he'd shared a cell with. That included going back to his time before the conviction that put him in this place. What if it wasn't a cellmate, but someone else he met inside? The count could be in the hundreds or thousands. I had to start someplace and left the search to any immediate cellmates.

The next thing to do was to literally get the name out of him. There was no way for me to compel the doctor to tell me anything. Not unless I took the legal route. The drive back to the station felt short with all the conference calls. They included the chief, the district attorney and the mayor, and everyone else involved in Ruby Evans's case. At one point, it sounded like half of the Outer Banks had joined me for the drive. There were voices spewing from the sides, from the dash, and even from behind the front seats. I can't recall who it was that talked me into this high-fidelity surround speaker business, but never again.

We debated if the doctor had broken any laws, my sharing that I didn't think he had. Nothing that was substantial enough to use. In my experience working with convicts, they'll often say just about anything if there was a possibility of getting something out of it. Any change of pace from the doldrums of daily prison life was worth it.

The chatter grew in my car, voices spouting legal terms and words rooted in Latin that I had no understanding of. I recognized the district attorney's voice and her mentioning obstruction of justice as a possible charge. She explained that Dr. Boécemo was withholding a name which could have direct bearing on an investigation. Doing that, he was preventing or influencing the outcome.

That was enough for me to ask her, "Can a subpoena be issued?"

"We'll look into it," I heard a voice comment in the background.

"Is it possible to have the doctor appear in a legal proceeding where we request the name? Demand the name?" I didn't wait for another reply and followed up with, "I don't think the doctor is going to risk a contempt of court charge after submitting an appeal to the parole board."

I got crickets with that comment. The silence that filled the car left me slack-jawed. Finally, someone with a poor connection spoke up in a crackling voice, "It's a bit like putting a cart before the horse. We'd need a legal proceeding first, right?"

"This would be a part of the detective's criminal investigation," the district attorney answered them. "It's not too dissimilar from a search warrant to collect evidence used to build a case."

"Can we do that?" I asked, beginning to feel desperate. A long pause. "Hello? Did I lose you guys?"

"Detective, there's some legal loops if we're to get him to forfeit a name," the district attorney began, her tone telling me what I already suspected. They weren't sure how to proceed. "I'll put a team on this immediately. We'll figure out a way to make it happen."

"Why doesn't she just trade up with his offer?" I heard asked. It was the voice with the staticky connection. "She just needs to appear at his parole hearing appeal?"

The earlier rage returned, my answering with a snap, "Because I'm not willing to trade one monster for another monster." I hung up the phone and stomped on the gas pedal.

There was no time for a stop to sit down and eat. My stomach growled and my car's gas gauge bumped the big E, the tank empty like my belly. We both needed fuel. I filled the car's tank and grabbed a sandwich and water at the first rest stop. While in line, the news reports on the televisions showed Ruby's picture from her high school. The screen was split down the middle, the other half showing her classmate Michael Larson and his father talking to reporters. The bread was soggy and the lettuce limp, but it was what I needed to press on to visit Ruby's house. I swung by the station and picked up Tracy. She'd already taken care of some interviews, but I'd insisted she hold back on this one. We needed to see Mrs. Evans together.

"This is the place." I parked the car on the street, the right front tire rubbing the curb. A squeamish look appeared on Tracy's face as I rushed the park job. I knew it was fatigue from the hours of sitting behind the wheel. I was also bothered that the Larsons continued to speak with the reporters. They weren't helping anyone. Was Ruby's mother watching? I hoped not. "Tracy, maybe you wouldn't mind driving us back?"

"I can do that," she answered, taking hold of her backpack, a new one with the department store tag still attached. It was more than just new, every piece of gear she needed was stuffed inside it, the sides bloated and stretched tight. I tugged the tag hard enough for its fishing-line barb to snap, the sound pulling Tracy's attention. "Thought I got them all."

"Tracy, straight ahead," I said and patted her shoulder. In the doorway of a single level brick home, Mrs. Evans stood waiting, the red glow of a cigarette near her mouth. There was a large bay window with white curtains that were sheer and thin enough to see through. My heart sank when I saw the news on the television screen, the same feed of the Larsons talking to reporters. Mrs. Evans straightened when she saw us, wearing sweatpants and a thick wool sweater, the fabric matching the slippers I'd seen when she first came to the station. She flicked the ash from the end of the cigarette, cheeks sinking to show nothing but jawline as she sucked in a heavy drag.

"Detective," she coughed, one eye wincing against a sting of smoke. She glanced at the end of her cigarette, explaining, "I never thought I'd pick this filthy habit up again."

"Ma'am, I am sorry for your loss—" she waved off the words and widened the door's opening. She'd been expecting us. "Now would be a good time?"

Another drag, deeper this time. Her face disappeared behind a puff of smoke as she answered, "There'll never be a good time."

"Understandable." The words were never easy when the circumstances involved a parent and the murder of their child. Mrs. Evans was recently widowed and the quiet of her home, along with the pictures on her walls, told me she was alone.

"We'll try to make this as brief as we can," Tracy said and lowered her chin respectfully.

"It doesn't matter," Mrs. Evans commented, voice melancholy. She tossed the cigarette onto the lawn and followed us inside, the door shutting with a clap. "There's nothing but time now."

She waved at the sofa and love seat for us to take, and dropped onto an orange recliner, springs creaking. I wasn't sure where to begin. This wasn't like our other cases, the murder standing alone. With this one, the message I received told us it was going to happen, and that the killer had already selected Ruby.

"Ma'am, was there anyone who was new in your daughter's life?"

Mrs. Evans raised a bottle of vodka from between the recliner and table. I waited while she poured it into a cup, which I'd thought was coffee or tea. When she was ready, she blinked her eyes lazily, clarification needed.

"Do you think it would have been someone who she didn't

know?"

Mrs. Evans shook her head, the cords on her neck standing out.

"After her father passed"—she stopped and took hold of a gold cross around her neck while looking up at the ceiling with a weepy gaze—"after that, she spent most of the time at the nursing home where she was a volunteer."

"How about there, at the facility? Did Ruby talk about anyone new working there?" Tracy followed up, walking around the room, taking notes. Ruby's mother shook her head, Tracy adding, "Did Ruby mention anything that occurred which would have been out of the ordinary?"

The woman's tired eyes sprang to life a moment, a smile creeping across her face. "There was that news crew that covered her story."

"A news story about Ruby?" I asked.

A brilliant smile appeared, brimming from ear to ear. "Oh yes! It was for her five hundredth shift of volunteering there." The pride faded from her eyes as she drank it away, sadness returning. "That was a big deal."

"When was that?" Tracy asked, noting it.

"A second," she answered, sitting up from the recliner with a struggle. I jumped to my feet to help her and felt the frailty in her arms. "Thank you, I'm good."

Mrs. Evans left us alone. I turned to Tracy, asking, "Let's get the names of any reporters who'd been in contact with Ruby."

"On it," Tracy answered as Ruby's mother returned with a framed newspaper article.

"May I?" I asked.

She ignored my request and dropped back onto the recliner, picking at the rear clips and freeing the article from the frame.

Mrs. Evans handed it to me, saying, "I never liked this frame anyway."

"It's quite the accomplishment." The article was small. The kind that would appear on the fourth or fifth page, its headline reading, *500th Shift by Local Student.* Beneath the headline was the mention about her volunteering at the facility since her first year of high school. "What led her to the nursing home?"

"It was my mother at first," Mrs. Evans answered. She returned to the front door and held it open with her foot while lighting a cigarette. Smoke rose above her in a spiral, the wind catching it as she added, "Ruby's grandmother. She was suffering from dementia."

"Her grandmother is still there?" Tracy asked, taking pictures of the newspaper article and highlighting the name of the photographer.

Mrs. Evans lowered her head and pinched her eyes. "She is... but she isn't, if you catch my meaning."

"The dementia," I said, understanding what she was saying. A nod. Focus returning to the article. "We've got a copy and the name of the reporter to follow up."

"They sold a lot of copies for that one," she commented, gaze fixed outside. "My little girl was famous for a minute. That's more than most can say."

"Was there anything negative from the article?" I asked. Ruby's mother only stared, her lips pinched shut. I looked for a light of recognition in her eyes. A flicker even. But saw none. "Nobody hanging around or calling?"

She seemed mystified by the question. "Uh-uh. It was all such a wonderful thing for her. She was going to use the experience for her college entrance essay."

"Older to some and younger to others," I started to say, lowering my voice for Tracy to hear me. She leaned over, recognizing the words from the killer's message.

"Right. Ruby was going to graduate, she was older than some of her classmates," Tracy said, writing it down. "And she was younger than the folks living in the nursing home."

Mrs. Evans tilted her head, listening. Her interest waned, favoring the outside air and smoking. I grabbed Tracy's arm, urging her closer and pointed to the article. "Been seen by thousands."

The whites of her eyes flashed. "The newspaper article?"

"That has to be it."

A cellphone dinged, its tinny sound steering our gaze to the table next to the recliner. The screen came alive, nabbing Mrs. Evans's attention. She tossed her cigarette and closed the door, alarm in her eyes. "That's not possible."

"What is it?" I asked while the woman picked up her phone, her eyebrows rising as high as they could. "Ma'am?"

"The Find My Phone app, or whatever the thing is called," she answered and slowly shook her head.

Her cellphone dinged again, the sound taking the strength out of the woman. She sat with a drop, clutching the armrest, the phone's speaker continuing to ring. "Ruby and me. We share our locations since we're alone. That way we always know where each of us are."

"Ruby's phone?" I asked, beginning to understand. The victim's phone was nowhere to be found. It wasn't in her car or on site where the abduction took place. "Ma'am, when we issued the Amber alert, Ruby's phone location was searched. The last known position was recorded near her car, a cell tower close to where she was abducted."

She turned her cellphone around to show us a map. At the center of it was a gray bubble, the initial R in the middle. A green glow pulsed around the bubble while it slowly moved a pixel at a time. "That's my daughter's phone."

"I have your phone number," I said, rushing to send her a text. "I need you to share that with me. Share your daughter's cellphone location."

"Yes, of course!" She answered amidst the commotion of us getting up to leave. "Detective, what does it mean?"

"I don't know yet," I said, telling the lie so she'd follow my instructions without question. I felt a buzz from my phone, the vibration rising into my arm. Without hesitation, I shared it with Tracy and Sherry. With the doorknob in my hand, I turned briefly to ask, "If it's okay with you, we'll come back? We have some additional questions and would like to see your daughter's room."

"Yes, of course," Ruby's mother said, the brooding look on her face easing while she clutched her cellphone, the screen reflecting in her glassy eyes. "Go please. Get my daughter. I mean, my daughter's cellphone."

"Thank you."

I closed the door after Tracy, our shoes clopping against the sidewalk. It stung thinking of the hope Ruby's mother was feeling in that moment. It wasn't her daughter we were going to save. Her daughter was already dead. When we were out of earshot, I asked, "Tracy, you and Sherry contacted the cellphone carrier?"

"Sure, of course. Standard practice. It's how we got a cell tower ping," she answered, car door swinging open. "But they said after that last ping, Ruby's cellphone went offline."

"Offline," I repeated and got behind the wheel, fingertips tingling.

"Who do you think has the victim's cellphone and turned it on?" she asked, working her seatbelt, breathing heavy. When she looked up, she added, "It's the killer. Isn't it?"

"I think so!"

My heart raced with huge walloping beats. I revved the motor and thew the car into drive, our bodies lurching. Tracy opened her laptop, pivoting it for me to see the screen. It came alive with a map to show the same glowing bubble: Ruby Evans's cellphone location. It had stopped moving and was staying fixed in one position. "We need to find her phone before the killer switches it off again."

SEVENTEEN

I didn't say a word during the drive, car tires chirping as we cut corners with a sharp spin of the steering wheel. Tracy yelled out the directions, the danger climbing whenever I glanced over at her screen. The sun had long since settled behind a cloudy horizon in the west. But the east was clear with a pale moon shining full and stars specking the sky. No clouds. That was good. We'd need the evening's gray moonlight to help us locate Ruby Evans's cellphone.

"Do we wait for more to arrive?" Tracy asked, sleeving a holster across her shoulders, a firearm harnessed and ready to use. It still looked out of place on her, the sight of a gun surreal. However, it was a part of the advancement in her career. Tracy was a sworn officer now, and as such, she was required to carry a weapon. Jericho had the honor of working with her to complete the weapons training. An area he was proud to call himself an expert in, which was evident in her top scores. She spun around when the flashing blue lights caught up to us, patrol car tires grinding to a stop alongside ours. "I guess that answers my question."

"Where do we go from here?" I asked, shoes sinking into the

loose sands as I walked toward the ocean. The coordinates landed us on a beach that was north of Nags Head and south of Kill Devil Hills. The exact location of Ruby's cellphone was only an estimate, leaving us with no idea of how big a search area we'd cover. "North? South?"

"Looks like we're parallel to it," she answered, pointing east toward the sound of breaking waves. "It's coming from somewhere out there."

"Okay, everyone, listen up," I yelled, hands cupped around my mouth, a stiff breeze lifting my hair. I turned away from the beach to find a stretch of Route 12 occupied by squad cars, the spinning blue lights dizzying. "Let's line up, staggered a few feet between us, flashlights aimed at the sand. You're looking for a cellphone."

"We'll start at the edge of the road and continue forward," Tracy added, her face close to her screen.

"Again, flashlights out and watch where you are stepping." For more than half a football field, the nighttime beach was mottled by the patrol's lights. Spotlights swung back and forth, canvassing the sand, the waves breaking into a foamy surf. "If you come across it, do not pick it up!"

The wind drove across us from the south, bringing a warm air that lifted my hair. My flashlight flicked off, the sands in front of me turning gray in the moon's light. I rapped the side of the tube and jostled the batteries, Tracy shouting, "Casey, we're at the water's edge!" Behind me, the officers had reached the wet sands too, waves chasing the foam near their feet. "I doubt the phone is waterproof."

"Maybe it was thrown in the ocean," I heard an officer say.

"They wouldn't have turned it on, only to toss it," Tracy replied.

"Tracy, do you still see it on the map?" I yelled, a murmur rising from a nearby officer. When Tracy gave a thumbs-up, I strained my voice, exclaiming, "Listen up! It's still here, which means we missed it!"

"We'll backtrack our steps?" Tracy asked.

"Call the number!" With this much beach to cover, the hunt with the flashlights was like finding a needle in a haystack. I joined Tracy at the water's edge. "Call Ruby's cellphone."

Chatter among the patrol was building, the flashlights continuing to swing, the balls of light arching like they were on a pendulum. "Everyone listen for it," Tracy shouted over the waves. "Listen for ringing or buzzing."

She made the call. Almost at once, a rectangular swath of sand lit up beyond our group. It was bizarre to see, but thankfully easy to spot. "There it is!"

We ran to it, the patrol following. It was further north than expected, tensions easing that we were able to see it. "Tracy, keep it ringing."

"Gosh! We were off by almost fifty yards," she said, her arms wide as two dozen shoes circled around the patch of glowing sand. "At least we found it."

When Tracy reached for it, I grabbed her arm. "No, don't touch it."

"Huh? Why?" she asked, her hand remaining above the phone. "I've got gloves on."

"It's not that." I sleeved a pair of latex gloves, snapping the fingers into place. The phone wasn't buried so deep that we couldn't find it, just deep enough to be overlooked when the screen wasn't on. The depth reminded me of how shallow Ruby Evans's grave had been. The phone's placement too. It was identical to Ruby's, the bottom facing due east. I didn't think it was a coincidence.

"The killer placed the phone here intentionally."

"How do you know that?" Tracy asked, following me as I walked toward the ocean, moonshine bouncing off the wet sand.

When Tracy saw it, she answered her own question for the second time this evening, simply stating, "Oh shit."

"Oh shit is right," I agreed and knelt in front of a bottle. "Hit that side with your flashlight, will you?"

"Uh-huh," she answered, kneeling across from me, a beam of light shining into the bottle. "Casey?"

"Yeah, I see it." Inside the thick glass was a rolled-up piece of paper. It stood upright, silhouetted, waiting to be unfurled, its message proposing a new murder. "It was the killer who brought us here. He wanted us to find the message."

"Careful," Tracy commented, fingers stretched out as we cradled a side and shimmied it back and forth.

"What if it's armed?" a patrolman asked, flashlights suddenly stirring as we froze in place.

"I don't see any indication of it," I answered and aimed my light into it, toward the bottom. "There's nothing but sand beneath it and around it."

"Lift?" Tracy asked. I nodded, yanking the bottle from the hole. It made a wet sucking sound and held in place like a tooth that wouldn't give. We finally freed it, sand clinging to the wet glass, Tracy explaining, "Suction was holding it."

"It's been there a few hours." I eased back onto my heels to watch the ocean and gauge the tide. "The killer knew it would be safe though."

With a pocketknife, Tracy motioned to the lip of the bottle, the same wax used to hold the cork in place. "Time to see what it says?"

"It is," I nodded, giving the okay. I motioned to one of the officers, urging her to kneel next to me. "Create two groups and canvass the berm north and south."

"How far?" she asked, catching on that I wanted to ensure we were alone. If not, then who was watching.

"Go until you can't see us anymore."

"I'm on it, Detective," she answered, leather creaking as she stood. Sand sprayed from the tips of their shoes while they rushed back to the patrol vehicles.

The bottle was identical to the first, rounded middle with a short neck. The hope of it being special was squashed when we saw the seams and manufacturing stamp on its bottom. The only thing unique was the oddly green tint that was sometimes blue too. It was the color which could be why it was popular for crafts. This one had a cork and the same thin coating of light-yellow wax, some of it running down the neck. The wax was a pure beeswax, a pound of it probably picked up from a North Carolina farmer's market. I took the liberty of pulling the cork and dropped it into an evidence bag, telling Tracy, "You take the lead."

"Yeah, sure," she said, snapping the lip of her gloves before tipping the bottle. I held my flashlight over her shoulder as she unfurled the paper, which was crisp, hard even. "It's not the mulberry paper like the last one."

"Is that computer paper?" I asked, noting the white and green bars and perforated edges where a printer's teeth bit into it to advance the sheet. "It's green-bar computer paper. We had tons of that at the station in Philly."

"How long ago was that?" Tracy asked, pinching the paper. "I mean, I think this is still used, but not like it was before."

"Not like before," I agreed. "Philly, first years in uniform. That's longer than you've been alive."

"The message is typed too like it came from a printer," Tracy said, holding the paper closer to my flashlight. "Dot-matrix printers?"

"I wouldn't be so sure of that." While the font matched what I remembered about the computer paper, the light's shine was strong enough to show us that this did not come from a printer. "Tracy, I think both of these letters have been written by hand."

"No way!" she commented, lips parting in a shallow gasp.

We were dealing with a killer who was patient and meticulous in their planning. They were using time like a weapon, their seeming to have an abundance of it while we had so little. Tracy raised the computer paper and began to read as I looked over her shoulder.

A game for Detective Casey White,

Here we go again. This is me bringing you message number two.

If you're reading this, it means there is another victim in my sights and the clock is ticking. Who is it? When is it? What will be their demise?

Tick-tock. Tick-tock.

For my next victim, they are a sleuth like you. While they go unseen by most, they can see rather far. They don't see as we see, their fingers driving the way. They follow the shine of a million stars trapped in glass. What is gibberish to others, their mind is trained to decipher, to digest and to surmise and divulge.

When Tracy was finished, we sat back, staring blankly. I shook my head, saying, "We've got to get this back to the station and take it apart."

"Where do we begin?" she asked, her face scrunched, already working the words.

"Tick-tock. Tick-tock," I answered. The creases between her eyes deepened, my response troubling. "The clock is already ticking. We start at the beginning, *they are a sleuth like you*. The killer is after someone like us."

EIGHTEEN

It was a part of the procedures. A part that was stained by tragedy. A part that can sometimes be eye-peeling with horror. And it was always heartbreaking. It was the medical examiner's review of a victim's autopsy. Every detective knows this step in the process and comes to terms with it. For me, that means facing it head-on. There's no training for it. No physical exercises to strengthen your core or to thicken and harden callouses. Not against the ugliness of murder anyway. This morning was Samantha's readout for Ruby Evans. In her search of the nuances that ended the victim's life abruptly, I hoped she found something. It was in the minutia of it all where we sometimes found clues the killer overlooked.

Sherry took the box of gloves and booties from my fingers, a look of worry pasted on her face. This was her second medical examiner readout. Or maybe it was her third. Regardless of the count, she was visibly nervous and I put my best supportive face on with a grin and stayed there until she acknowledged it.

"I'll be okay," she assured me, her voice tiny. As she sleeved her fingers, her eyes were full of disappointment. It was the near fainting she took at the crime scene that bothered her. Word of it had made its way around like gossip. I leaned closer, her posture turning stiff with discomfort. "Truly, Casey, I will."

"I know you will," I told her and caught a glimpse of Tracy rolling her eyes. There was also a smirk rising in the corner of her mouth. Tracy took the box of gloves, thinking nobody noticed. I noticed everything. Sometimes to my detriment. I gave her a quick frown, tilting my head toward Sherry with an urge to help with the encouragement.

Tracy blew a puff of air, inflating one of the gloves and tapping it comically on Sherry's shoulder. "You'll be fine."

"Thank you," Sherry answered, chuckling nervously at the inflated hand.

Tracy rearranged the inflated fingers, showing just the middle one. "That's what you show the ones who are laughing."

"They're laughing?" Sherry asked, red-faced with embarrassment.

"No more so than any of us have been laughed at," I said as quickly as possible. It helped. Some. "Now to why we're here."

I turned toward the thick resin doors, a frosty puff of air curling around the tips of my shoes. Swinging it open, Samantha was already at the autopsy table, Ruby's body in place and seemingly intact, though we all knew better. There was a white sheet covering her torso, the edge of it a few inches drawn close to her knees, far enough to cover what happened to her. Samantha cleared her throat and hit a button on the console above the body. Somewhere in the cloud, as Tracy often said, every digital bit and byte was stored. That included the audio of this readout. "This is the autopsy reading for Ruby Evans, seventeen years of age at the time of her death."

I wanted to start with the most glaring injuries, which were not her legs. It was the terrible swelling and storm-cloud bruising around her eyes. The source of it looked to have been from a deep gash which was caused by a break in her nose. "What can you tell us about this blunt trauma?"

"The victim suffered a break in the nasal bone, just beneath the deep laceration. There was also a fracture to the maxilla, the surrounding bone," she answered and clicked through a series of images until landing on an X-ray of the victim's face. In the fuzzy gray tissue, a calamity of splintered bone showed. Samantha held her hand flat and pointed up straight, motioning a sharp strike. "Could be from striking the edge of a door? I've seen similar injuries during my intern year in an emergency room."

"Like a car door," I answered. "The killer may have used it when subduing the victim."

"It would explain the blood on the pavement," Tracy commented, recalling the faint stain discovered behind Ruby Evans's car. "The rains washed most of it away."

I tapped the side of my head. "Was there a brain injury?"

"Concussed for certain," Samantha answered. "However, this did not contribute to her death."

"Other injuries in the upper torso?" I asked, seeing nothing remarkable. My stomach was tied in knots with anticipation of what waited for us at the end of the autopsy table. With my index finger and thumb, I lifted one of Ruby's fingers, then another, rigor mortis present.

She scrolled to a new image, a circular bruise near the center of the victim's back. "There's also some abrasions around the mouth? Some of it had started to heal," she answered.

In my head, I saw the abduction as if it were taking place in slow motion. "The killer had her pressed down, probably held her with the weight on his knee."

"The seats in the car," Tracy said and clutched the back of Sherry's head, a mortified look appearing on the girl's face. "When the killer had his weight on her, her face was pushed which could have caused the abrasions around her mouth."

"Heads up next time," Sherry asked.

We shifted to her legs, the source of the hemorrhagic shock,

Samantha clearly speaking for the recording. "The cause of death is from complications relating to exsanguination. This was a direct result of loss of blood following the transfemoral amputation of both legs."

"It wasn't shock?" Tracy asked, noting the change in the cause of death.

"We'll cover the cause in finer detail." Samantha's eyes were level with mine, a stepstool aiding her height this morning. She lowered herself enough to turn on the larger wall displays, a full body X-ray appearing. My eyes went directly to where the incisions were made, Ruby's femur bones severed cleanly. "These would have had to been done with medical equipment?"

"With magnification of the area, there's a finer bite which would indicate an amputation kit was used," Samantha answered while tapping a keyboard. With the mouse, she dragged a pixelated lasso around the right femur bone and zoomed in. "What's interesting is how precise the separations are. Entirely uniform and in exactly the same locations."

"How about a field amputation kit?" I was thinking of Karl Brause and his experience. "Like the type issued to medics?"

"It's possible, but the precision applied to both legs is rather surprising," she answered, voice wavering. She returned to the victim and lifted the sheet enough to show the incisions. "That said, in the hands of someone with enough experience and patience, a field kit could have produced these results."

"Was there a paralytic used?" Sherry's gaze jumped with the question. It stayed a moment before returning to a tablet, she continuing to type. "An anesthetic to prevent movement?"

"There's evidence of a single paralytic, known for its rapid onset," Samantha said and looked up at the victim's face. "There was also a high dose of Ketamine present in her blood."

"We'll need a list of the drug names," Tracy said. She looked up, her gaze joining Samantha's. "Was she awake?"

"Yeah. Was she?" Sherry blurted. "I mean, can you tell?"

"The drugs used are measurable for a few days. If we take into account her body weight, then I believe it was enough to render her semi-unconscious," Samantha answered. Her voice and eyes told me she wasn't convinced. She saw that I noticed and bit on her lower lip, adding, "If she was conscious, there's no knowing for how long."

I made my way to the end of the table where I could see all of Ruby, from head to toe. "What else can you tell us?"

"We've already established use of medical tools." Samantha clicked twice, close-up images of the injuries appearing. "However, the only technique applied to control the hemorrhaging was use of the tourniquets. Nothing was done to prevent it though."

Hard as it was to look at the screen, I forced myself. The images gutted me. "You're referring to use of sutures to tie off the severed arteries and veins?"

Samantha nodded as she raised the sheet further and showed the deep scrapes and bruising on the thighs.

"How much total blood loss?"

"She lost more than two-thirds her volume." Her eyes were hidden behind black bangs. She shook them away, adding, "The killer made no attempts at cauterizing or suturing anything."

"The blood used for ink in the message," I said, a thought about it coming to mind. Tracy and Sherry traded a look as they regarded it. "Using the blood must have had meaning too, the same as the mulberry paper."

"Like, the murderer was telling us how he intended to kill her?" Sherry asked, a grimace on her face.

"Exactly. Blood loss and use of the tourniquets to manage the amount." I pointed to the ribbony bruises which had been tightened, and loosened, the process repeated over and over.

Sherry took a picture, the markings appearing prominent in post-mortem. "It's multiple times?"

"With exsanguination as the cause of death, I wanted to

provide you with a time estimate." Samantha opened a window, the screen brightness making us squint. There were medical terms and counts with graphs plotted. "I thought we could understand the blood loss and create a timeline from it."

"We know when she was abducted." There was already a timeline in use which had a beginning, a middle, and an end. It was all the in-betweens we needed to identify. "Next, there's her death, the time of it recorded. That's not something we usually have."

"Having a precise time of death helped." Samantha clicked to show another image, saying, "I found a way to use it by comparing the state of her torso."

I didn't follow her meaning at first. Not immediately. Not until I saw the lividity in the victim's legs and the contrast of coloring compared to her upper body. It was distinguishable, the rivers of purple and blue apparent across her body, but the pooling was more significant in the legs. There was also the nature of the skin and the way it changes following death.

"You used tissue samples and measured the rigor mortis to determine when the amputations occurred?"

Samantha startled slightly, answering, "I didn't think you'd guess that one. But yes, even an amputated limb will show signs of rigor in the same manner as the body."

"That gives us a measurable point in the timeline," Tracy said as she wielded photography gear around her head. Sherry helped with a camera body, fingers trembling. They stood up a second flash, the electronics cycling. The distinctions in Ruby's body were a clue.

Samantha placed her hand on Ruby's left leg and opened another chart, a line sloping from left to right. "Without getting too far into the study of the rigor and putrefaction, the removals took place between twenty-four and thirty-six hours prior to her death."

"What about clotting?" Sherry asked and glanced at the

screens. The stark magnitude was catastrophic. She didn't wait for us to answer. "No, I guess that wouldn't be possible."

"It helps confirm the marks and the contusions." I dragged my fingers gently over the ribbon-thick bruise. "The killer opened and closed the tourniquets. Eventually, the loss of blood caused her death."

"For over twenty-four hours she bled out?" Tracy asked, mouth falling open. "It... it doesn't fit the time?"

"The killer went early? Or maybe the bottle was found after the procedure was performed. We don't know which came first." I was counting in my head and hearing Alice's voice, thinking back to the exact hour, the minute, the second when that first message in a bottle arrived. There was no way for us to map a time, a horrible resignation hitting me like a slap in the mouth. "It doesn't matter what the sequence is."

"Why?" Tracy asked. She shook her head, adding, "We have to figure it out. Don't we?"

"It doesn't matter because the killer has already committed to doing this." It hurt to think it, hurt to know that regardless of the timing, there was no saving Ruby Evans. "Tracy, the moment Ruby was abducted, the killer's plans had already been set."

"We don't really know if there is a countdown," Tracy said. "Do we?"

"If there is, then it's got to be the kidnapping." Like me, she was thinking of the latest message, the clock ticking. We had to hope the killer hadn't taken anyone yet.

"She was like that for over a day," Sherry said, distracted and incensed. "That's what brought the crabs and birds?"

Disgust briefly flashed across Samantha's face as she answered, "I'm afraid so."

Sherry gulped at the air and tucked her head behind a camera to frame the next picture. Though her voice was muffled, I heard her mumble, "Why would they do such a thing?"

"I don't have an answer to that question," Samantha told Sherry. Samantha stepped back onto the stepstool, nudging her head in my direction. "That's what you guys are going to find out."

"It's the control," I answered unexpectedly. In that ugly moment, I felt the strike of a revelation. It was strong enough to cause a shiver. "That's part of the killer's M.O."

Heads turned with a uniform response. "What is?"

"In the message. Rather, at the end, it says, 'I am control. I become power.'"

"The killer wants control?" Tracy asked, writing it down. Her head sprang up with a shrug, "It's got to be control. The use of the tourniquets like that."

"Not just any control." I lowered the sheet draping Ruby Evans's body, covering what was done to her. "This killer wants to control death."

NINETEEN

It was control the killer wanted. With it there came a perception of power to wield over life and death. It was as much of their M.O. as everything else we'd learned so far in the investigation. What we didn't know until Ruby Evans's autopsy was how the killer was using time. The killer plants the message to be found, indicating an abduction will occur. When, or if it had already occurred, remained an unknown. That meant there was no knowing the exact time the next victim would be taken, the killer making a game of it. It made me sick to my stomach. One girl was already dead and there was another in the killer's sights.

The worst part of the case was how utterly alone we were. Dr. Boécemo had a name, its legitimacy in question since he'd only offered it in exchange for my help. How could I help someone like him? Doing so would ensure his freedom, his release back into the world where he posed dangers to everyone. It went against everything I knew to be right, and I wasn't willing to do that. Not yet. I needed the district attorney and her team to come up with something we could use. Something that would put the doctor in a courtroom and in front of a judge where the judicial system could force the name out of him. I think anything that compromised his attempt at another chance with the parole board would work.

The fusty smell of the station was stirred by an ongoing commotion, the stringing of cables, the comings and goings of news crews, along with their reporters. It was more than I'd ever seen, the count doubling since last time, maybe tripling after word of Ruby's murder went public. There'd been a leak too which didn't help. The killer's message was made public.

Was it good reporting? I had mixed feelings about it. While the news brought awareness, it also created a panic in our part of the Outer Banks. Waves of fear and anxiety were breaking like the ocean's surf, the confidence in the investigation eroding like sand. With a public that was panicked and terrified, the mayor called for one hundred percent transparency. That meant everyone was watching. Everyone was waiting. Yet, there was only one person who knew the identity of the next victim. The killer.

The young couple that had first brought the bottle to the station and given it to Alice. We were sure that they were the source of the leak. When they came upon the bottle and the rolled mulberry paper inside it, the couple took pictures. A lot of pictures. Soon after Ruby's murder hit the news, the couple realized the true intention behind the message. That's when we saw them with a local news crew. Their popularity grew more with the podcasters showing interest, along with news stations beyond the Outer Banks.

I glanced up at one of the station's monitors where the couple's faces were made pixely bright, a spotlight shining on the ceiling near Alice's desk. I wanted to tell everyone to take the story outside of the station, but held back. What if there was something helpful that could come from the added coverage? There was the chance that the killer was watching the live broadcast? It wasn't too dissimilar to planting a story in order to stir them into action, a wrong move we could capitalize on.

"Detective White?" I recognized the voice behind me and jumped to my feet.

"Ma'am." There was a reverence in my voice, the mayor standing close enough that I could smell her hairspray. I felt myself leaning onto the balls of my feet, lifting my heels enough to stand eye to eye. She was tall and gorgeous and was dressed for a press conference. A shorter woman with a shaved head followed the mayor's movements, working feverishly to apply makeup, pushing and teasing the mayor's black hair. I motioned toward the couple being interviewed. "Your press conference follows after?"

"I think it'll be a few minutes." She lowered her head, keeping her voice quiet, and asked the woman with the makeup and hairbrushes, "Could you leave us, please?"

As the woman left, I commented, "I'm still waiting for word from the district attorney about Dr. Boécemo." I had no idea where she wanted to start the conversation and picked the area I found most pressing.

She took a step away from me while eyeing my desk and computer screens. "I understand that you can get a name? That is, if you choose to do so?" My jaw tightened at what she might be asking. The mayor must have sensed the disgust of it and continued. "Detective, the doctor will never practice medicine of any kind again. He'll never be in the company of children again. Not without risk of losing his freedoms forever."

My teeth hurt from clenching. "That's the problem. I believe the doctor is willing to risk his freedom." The mayor hadn't considered that part, eyelids fluttering. "Are we going to risk him getting his hands on a child? What he'll do to them, and—"

"Certainly not!" she answered with hushed rebuke. Her scowl was deep and leering as if my words had been taken personally. When it eased, she added, "What if we track him? What if we put a force together to watch his every move?"

She shuffled her feet, the shiny leather on her shoes new and bothering her. I motioned to my desk for her to lean against. "That's a thought, but this is a man who has limitless patience. Could we babysit him forever?"

The mayor's mouth twisted as the idea soured. She went to my whiteboard, the words from the second message listed in parts, our dissecting it. The scowl returned when she glimpsed the front of the station, the reporters and crews. "That damn couple." Her focus returned to me, a glower remaining. Tapping the whiteboard, she said, "You know they're calling this sicko The Message in a Bottle Killer."

"I've heard." It was one of the first things to come across my phone, the sound of it twisting my insides. "There's more to it than the message. That's just a part of what this killer is doing."

"More to it? Which is what?" The mayor returned to leaning. Her gaze followed the message to the bottom of the board, to the words the killer used in the signature. "'I am control. I become power'... who is this guy? Who are we dealing with?"

"I think they are a loner. Someone who lives in isolation," I began.

"Would they have been in the system?" she asked, wanting more.

"It's possible. As a child they may have been abused. A parent or bullied severely. With their need to control, I'm thinking they'd been made to feel powerless and helpless. They could have been bounced from home to home or placed in the foster care system."

"Control and power?" she asked, frown narrowing.

"They're seeking it now. Growing up, they had no control of where or how they lived. When they were older, they may have sought control by abusing small animals which escalated over time." As I spoke, I looked over the words on the whiteboard. These were words authored by a killer, and in my mind I knew who they were. I saw them as a child and felt the heartache for the hate and pain inflicted on what had once been innocent and pure. I saw them as an adolescent when the troubles began to grow, the roots of their childhood made rotten. And then I saw them as the killer they'd become today. "They have a deep-seated need to control what they could never have, what they craved. It's an insatiable appetite and not one that can be sated."

When I looked up, the mayor's eyelids were pressed shut, leaving only the inky black of her mascara. She opened them slowly and fixed a hard look on the whiteboard. "Why the messages? Why make this like it was some kind of cat and mouse game?"

"Because it's his way of controlling the case." The mayor's glare turned in my direction. "And it's his way of controlling us."

There was a long silence as I waited for a reaction. None came, the air between us growing uncomfortably hot. Eventually, the mayor sighed and straightened herself, shoving a finger beneath the strap of her shoe to adjust it. With a wave of her hand, the woman who'd been working the makeup and hair returned, continuing where she left off.

Was it shock? Did I go too far with a profile description? I sometimes did that, my mouth flushing the words from my brain without applying a filter. The mayor reached for me, her arm long and slender like her fingers. She put my hand in hers, squeezing for me to come closer. I did and she whispered, "Get this guy before he kills again."

"Yes, ma'am. I'll do that," I answered.

She was gone then, my skin turning cold where her hand had held mine.

"Whoa," Sherry said, her head slowly rising from behind the cubicle wall. Her eyes were round. Wide. Starlit with surprise. "That was the mayor. Like she was actually here. Ten feet from me."

Tracy wheeled her chair over, chuckling, "Sherry, you do know the mayor is an elected official?"

"Yeah sure," Sherry scoffed. "But she's like a rock star. She's famous."

"How about I introduce you?" I asked, eyeing our conference room. The new lights were bright enough to bounce off the conference room glass. "After they're done?"

"Would you?!" Sherry asked, the star-struck look returning.

"Of course." I nodded while seeking out the district attorney. She arrived to stand next to the mayor and the chief; a calculated decision had been made to keep me removed from the camera's view. It wasn't just that the doctor could be watching. It was the killer too, both of his messages addressed to me.

Damn that young couple. That's what the mayor had said and it was how I felt. We didn't want the press asking about a conflict of interest, questioning if I should continue to work the case. "Let's take a close look at the message."

"I've got some notes to share," Sherry said.

I followed her into the conference room where we had the big table to work from. I also wanted the screens too which had been moved to hide from peering eyes. Mostly, I wanted to cut off the low drone of press conference questions and answers, the distraction of it. Deciphering the next message needed all our attention.

As the glass doors swung closed, Sherry added, "A few ideas too? Just not sure if they are good enough."

"First rule," I told her, turning to face the room. "There are no good ideas or bad ideas. Just ideas. Tracy, what's an unshared idea?"

"An unshared idea is a waste of time," she answered without looking up. "If nobody hears your idea then it doesn't help."

"Say anything?" Sherry asked.

"Say everything," I corrected her.

"This is a place to speak freely," Tracy added. She pointed at the outside. "When we're in here, anything goes. It's our free space. Get it?"

"Got it," Sherry replied, eyes filling with adoration. "This is our free space."

Tracy plugged a video cable into her laptop and tapped the keys, the second message showing on the large display. "Want me to read it?" she asked. "Like before?"

"Sure, you can start us off."

"The top line reads like the first message: *A game for Detective Casey White.* And then the second line, *Here we go again. This is me bringing you message number two—*"

"I made a note of there being a subtle rhyme," Sherry interrupted. "The words *you* and *two.*"

"That one may not have been intentional," Tracy said, a spark in her baby-blue eyes. When Sherry looked back at the screen, Tracy gave me a look. I shrugged just enough for her to see. We did tell Sherry to share everything.

"That was good to note, Sherry." It wasn't significant, but it showed that we were looking. Then again, we'd missed the use of mulberry paper, hadn't we? I wrote down the words, *you* and *two.* "Let's continue."

Tracy read the next line in the message: "*If you are reading this, it means there is another victim in my sights and the clock is ticking.*"

"Hold it there!" I blurted with a hopeful hitch ticking in my throat. "Look at the language he's using. *Another victim in my sights and the clock is ticking.*"

"We don't know exactly when there will be a kidnapping," Sherry said, her eyes on the clock, it's second hand swinging around the twelve. "But it's not like Ruby Evans. It hasn't happened yet."

I raised my hand, pointing out, "I think he was watching to

see when the message was found. That's why he planted Ruby's cellphone. He does want to make this a race."

"Using what we know, that would put us at just under eighteen hours remaining," Tracy said, uncertainty in her voice. I waved her to continue. "Next up in the message doesn't really offer anything. *Who is it? When is it? What will their demise be this time?*"

"*What will their demise be this time?*" I said, repeating. "That tells me the killer isn't planning a repeat. Their approach will be different."

"Oh, thank God!" Sherry blurted. When we looked over, she added, "I mean this is all bad, but that was horrible."

"Murder is horrible." I held up the evidence bag with the second message, the green-bar computer paper a clue like the mulberry paper had been. "Let's put a pin in that line and come back to it."

Tracy nodded, Sherry saying, "That computer paper is called continuous stationery. You know, cause it's made to continuously feed into a dot-matrix printer." She held out her hands as if carrying an imaginary box. "It comes in these really big reams. Has to be something like fifty pounds."

"Find everything you can about the paper." I held it against the ceiling's lights, wishing to see a secret buried in the fibers of green and white, the way pictures can be hidden in money. But there was only the message.

"They still use that stuff in a lot of places," Sherry continued, typing rapidly. "Like school officers and colleges. Even hospitals and government offices."

"*Tick-tock. Tick-tock,*" Tracy said, moving to the next line. Shaking her head. "I got nothing for that except the tease that I think it is."

"Me neither. There is the obvious play on words." We looked toward Sherry who had her head lowered, face close to her laptop. "Sherry?"

"Nothing in my notes," she answered, face appearing briefly.

"*For my next victim, they are a sleuth like you. While they go unseen by most everyone, they can see rather far,*" Tracy read the next line. She leaned back to say, "That one gave me the chills."

"Because you saw who it is they might be referring?" I asked, sharing the goosebumps too. Sherry frowned, unable to see it. "A sleuth like me. The killer is talking about an investigator. But what kind?"

"You mean a cop?" Sherry asked, sounding alarmed.

"There are a lot of investigators out there," Tracy said, throwing a list onto another screen. "I included inspectors too, which really inflated the number of possibilities."

"Huh, never would have thought of journalistic or private detectives or even home inspectors," Sherry commented, reading down the list. She perked up and went to the screen, pointing and saying, "This one. The online sleuthing. That could fit with the next line."

"It could," I said, motioning that I'd take it. "*They don't see as we see, their fingers driving the way.*"

"*Fingers driving the way* could mean typing?" Sherry asked. "And that first part?"

"It could be that they're referring to online investigations." I got up to join Sherry at the screen. "Most people don't understand the underpinnings of the web or dark net. But someone who investigates online knows how it works?"

"That's where I went with it too," Tracy said. "The next line supports it too. *They follow the shine of a million stars trapped in glass. What is gibberish to others, their mind is trained to decipher.*"

"That first part has got to be computer monitors," Sherry exclaimed excitedly and held up her laptop. "Like, the number of pixels and all, each of them being a star, the panel of glass made up of a million pixels?"

She searched our faces for agreement, both of us nodding. "That last part about the gibberish to others and the deciphering part? I'm thinking the killer is picking someone who knows more than just the underpinnings of the web. They know how to code, how to build it."

"Could be a hacker or a cybercrime expert," Tracy said with a firm expression coming over her face. She stood and joined us at the screen, reading the lines from top to bottom. "If we're right with the assessment, that narrows the list. It's a short list."

Sherry stared at me as though she were waiting for me to spit out a single name. I couldn't. I couldn't even breathe. If we were right about this, the list of those who qualified was very short, and it included Tracy.

TWENTY

We didn't have a name yet but we had a profile of who we thought the killer's next victim would be. It was Tracy. Rather, it was a person very much like her. Based on the words in the message, the killer may have selected an online sleuth, a part-time detective who picked up cold cases. Where there was one, there were many, usually working in small groups, collaborating online while remaining isolated. They were a highly technical bunch and could burn through evidence like ants on sugar, each taking a bit of information and piecing it together to solve an old mystery. I knew the type. I'd been the type. I'd become one of them to help find my daughter. If the killer knew me, then they also knew that bit of detail too.

I had to consider Tracy and regard the threat for what it was. She'd seen it first and the fright on her face hammered into my soul. That's why I put a protective order in, insisting she have a patrol outside her place and in her company whenever she wasn't at the station. While Tracy was a good fit for the message, she wasn't the only one.

It was the urgency, the commotion, that put us on the road, taking to the car with a search warrant in hand. It was also the only thing the reporters were not aware of. A thread of hunger wove into the day, forcing us to refuel and eat on the run. The inside of my car smelled of fries and burgers and of the ketchup with hot sauce that Tracy spilled. It was one of our typical fast-food stopovers, eating and driving while we were sinking into the gut of the case. I peered up at the street signs with a squint. The sun seemed to shine bright enough to scare the clouds into tomorrow, the sky light blue, the car's visors angled down to shield us against the midday hour.

This afternoon we were going to the home of Karl Brause. On paper, he looked like the perfect suspect. But to me, he looked like anyone else. He lived in a middle-class home and wore middle-class clothes. He worked early morning shifts and volunteered at the local VA, his being a veteran and serving more than ten years. I dropped my food back into the paper bag, rolling the top, and tossed it in the back seat. I was struggling to bring myself to this fight, to get myself motivated for a search of his property. We were following procedures and crossing the proverbial t's and dotting the i's, but to me, Karl wasn't a fit for this.

However, there was enough probable cause to have a search warrant issued, a judge signing it during the first morning hours. After Karl's interview, we uncovered discrepancies in his story. These had to be reconciled. Karl Brause was alone at the time Ruby Evans went missing. He'd offered no alibi, other than being at his house with Ralph, his pet parrot. There was also his experience as a medic to consider, the military training and the experience during combat where he performed amputations. While he was a man who'd saved lives, I was reminded that it didn't preclude him from taking them. From the Son of Sam killer to the BTK killer, history showed that many serial killers had served in the military.

What had come into question from the interview was Karl's time with the victim before the paramedics arrived on site.

During the interview, he'd given us the hour when he arrived at the municipal building, the location where the tractor and beach cleaning equipment were kept and maintained. During the follow-up investigation, the facilities manager provided us with an equipment logbook as well as access to their time card system. When we reworked the timeline down to the minute, more than ninety were missing. What happened during that hour and a half? It could have been a system error or the recent shift in daylight-saving time contributing to the discrepancy. A deeper accounting was planned, but for now, the call-to-action decision made was to serve a search warrant.

The first thing we saw when turning the street corner was a black truck registered in Karl's name. It was big with knobby tires, the right quarter panel painted a primer gray, a repair from a recent accident perhaps. The truck had an open cab and was parked outside the garage, its height too tall for the small space. I motioned to the boxes lining the floor and walls inside the garage, leaving zero room for a second vehicle. If Karl Brause was the killer, the car used in the Ruby Evans kidnapping wasn't here. We pulled into a gravel driveway, tires biting into the loose stone as we parked behind the truck, a patrol vehicle following us in. The house was older, a small rambler style that was nestled between two newly built behemoth rental properties. The front lawn was sparse with patches of dead grass where the sunlight was replaced by an endless shade.

Karl Brause sat on the front step, one leg over the other, a black leather work boot bouncing. He wore the same hunter-green coveralls as when we'd first interviewed him, the shirt beneath the straps a dingy yellow this time instead of the faded red. He spat black goo into a cup and chewed on a lump jutting from the side of his jaw. His shaggy beard and mustache were gone, clean-shaven with a wad of tissue on his chin. Karl had also ditched the tattered baseball cap, his hair feathered back in a neat manner. When he saw me, he glanced to the nearby street corner where news vans were slowing to park.

Instant regret filled my belly when seeing the disappointment in his eyes. The one thing he'd asked us was to avoid the press. Two vans had followed us from the station, staying far enough behind to go unnoticed. They probably knew about the search warrant too. A woman sat on the steps next to Karl. She was older by two or more decades, her hair silvery white and long enough to reach her shoulders. In her face, I saw Karl's eyes, his chin and mouth. I saw enough of him in her to guess the woman was possibly his mother.

Tracy took the lead and walked ahead, the lawn patchy with some of it covered in fresh soil, grass seed peppering the surface. The home was well kept, the windows clean, the siding maintained. There wasn't anything striking from outside, but that wasn't why we were here. It was the inside we would investigate, along with the cab of his truck. We'd also ask about that morning Ruby Evans was found. We'd asked these questions a few times already, repeating them a strategy. Sometimes in an investigation, it was in the repetition where we'd find the answers.

"Mr. Brause," I said.

He held up his hand to show us a copy of a search warrant, a patrol officer serving it before our arrival.

"Detective," he said with a nod. He waved a hand over his shoulder, saying, "You know, you could have just swung by. I would have given you full access to anything you wanted."

I wanted to tell him that I knew he'd cooperate. Instead, I answered, "It's a formality." Karl didn't introduce the woman next to him, any cordiality lost with our serving the search warrant.

I extended a hand, saying, "Ma'am, I'm Detective Casey White."

"Mm hmm. I know who you are," she answered without

offering a name. She touched my fingertips lightly and motioned behind her, clearly sharing Karl's sentiment about the warrant. "Get on with getting on and do what you come to do."

"My mom, Agatha Brause," Karl said, lips twisting. Bothered as he was, his manners compelled him to make the introduction. He pinched his shaven chin, removing the tissue and said, "Mom is visiting. Come up the afternoon after I found that girl."

"It's nice to meet you, ma'am," I said. Turning toward Tracy, I added, "This is investigator Tracy Fields."

"Mm hmm," the woman said again but kept her hands laced together on her lap. She turned to her son, speaking low, "You really should have a lawyer here. Can't trust them."

"Ma," Karl said, brow bouncing. He waved it off, adding, "She can't help it. Watches a lot of documentaries."

"She makes a good point though," I said, siding with her. "If at any time you feel the need to have a lawyer present, you have that in your right."

"I'll keep it in mind," he said, standing to make room for us. "We'll wait outside."

We made our way into the foyer which was cramped with a rack of coats and jackets along one side, each topped with a different baseball cap. Patrol officers followed us, the room filling fast. A box of gloves was passed around, the snap of them speaking to why we were here. Dust shimmered in a thin blade of sunlight, the touch of it brief while in the noon hour. Before leaving, I expected the inside of Karl's home to be dark, the new vacation homes blocking the light. The search began in the family room while I moved on to an adjacent kitchen. The range and counters were clear save for a napkin holder with tall salt and pepper shakers on each side.

I ran my hand over the top of the kitchen refrigerator, the space between it and a cabinet barely enough to fit my fingers. It was free of any dust. As in, none at all. In the breakfast nook, there was a round table with a glass top, four chairs tucked beneath. On it, a short stack of newspapers were opened, fanned out with articles I recognized at once. These were the papers with the headlines from yesterday and today. I spun around and saw the television was left on, the broadcast the same as what was tuned at the station. That's when I noticed how clean this house was. How very clean. The television. The newspapers. His mother's visit. Karl Brause knew we'd be coming. He might not have known when, but he'd prepared for it, leaving nothing to chance. With a deep sigh, I stopped looking. We weren't going to find a single thing here.

Tracy continued to work in the larger of the two rooms while I checked my phone. Both of us had been reaching out to Sherry without much luck. With the round-the-clock hours, I'd forced a short break after dissecting the second message. Stepping away at times could give the space to show something that had been overlooked. Not sure why it worked like that, but it did. It might have been something we saw or thought of subconsciously. When freeing our minds of the concentration, the blocks were removed. There was no knowing when it would happen though. Vacuuming or cooking, or just bingeing a show. It could come at any time. We'd had no such luck with this short break though.

I texted Alice. She was the busiest of us all, managing the station and the staff, which had tripled.

Have you heard from Sherry? She never arrived at the Brause's residence.

Three dots danced. They bounced and then stopped. Tracy must have seen my face and came over to look at my phone. "I haven't heard from Sherry since last night," she said, swiping her screen to the messages.

I felt my expression pinching, annoyance building. "Maybe she thought the break was longer?"

"I don't think so," Tracy commented.

"I'll try again." I thumbed my screen, sending another text.

"For what it's worth," Tracy began to say, scrolling through recent text messages. "She's been showing up late. A few times now."

"I've mentioned it to her, but it doesn't seem to have helped." Agitation rode on my words. It wasn't intentional or directed at anyone.

"I get it," she replied, abandoning a text and calling Sherry directly. The phone went to voicemail almost immediately. "Sherry, give us a call when you get this."

The bouncing balls returned, Alice texting back:

Call me.

"What's going on?" Tracy asked. I didn't have an answer and put Alice on speaker.

"Alice?" I asked, raising my voice over the pitchy noises. "You there?"

"Yeah, I've got you," she answered, sounding out of breath. "There's a patrol in Sherry's area. I had them stop by to check on her."

"They're there now?" I asked, voice tight.

"They are, but Sherry isn't there," Alice answered, loud clicks interrupting every other word.

"Not home?" I asked, throat dry and pulse racing.

"Casey, the last text message I got from her was after our meeting," Tracy said, confirming a time.

"How about the app we set up to track one another's phones?" I asked, trying to stay calm.

Guilt knifed at my heart though. I was so focused on protecting Tracy that I never considered Sherry. She fit the profile of the killer's second message. I didn't dare leave anything to chance.

"Alice, listen to me! Have the patrol drive from there to the Brause place."

"Already on it," she said, hanging up the phone.

"Anything on that app?" I asked, hopeful to see a blip on Tracy's screen. There was none.

Tracy's face remained unchanged, fingers in motion as she tried different things. She looked at the door, then to me, saying, "I need my computer."

"Let's get back to the station."

We started toward the door, one of the officers giving the nod they'd take charge of the search. Karl and his mother were gone from the front steps, the two standing at the end of the yard where reporters were asking them questions. I supposed he was telling his side of things, getting his face and name out in front. It was smart. It was also a sign of something a killer would do too.

"Let's get some cell tower pings."

"Got it," she answered, opening her laptop, keyboard rattling. When the noise paused, I looked over to see her face cramped and red. Tracy was upset, showing every bit of what I was feeling. She swiped erratically at the hair in her eyes, hands shaky. "Sorry. I'm on this."

"It's okay to be upset," I assured her, the breath feeling like fire, the car's motor roaring to life. "Maybe she's just picking up some lunch for us?"

"I don't think that's it," Tracy said and pointed to a map on her screen. "I just got the update. It says that Sherry was three miles from here. But that was over an hour ago."

"There is another victim in my sights and the clock is ticking," I commented, repeating the last message from the killer. Heart sinking, as I continued, "Tick-tock. Tick-tock. I am control. I become power."

TWENTY-ONE

Sherry was gone. It had been more than five hours since anything was heard from her. That included the morning text messages and the last known location of her phone, which was a few miles from Karl Brause's home. We backtracked and found an intersection where her car was parked along the road, the driver-side window lowered and her computer and cellphone on the passenger seat. Tire tracks were found in the sand behind her car, the impressions photographed and processed. While we didn't have any from the site of Ruby Evans's abduction, we had the blurry picture from Michael Larson. Merging what we knew could tell us the make and model of the vehicle we were looking for. Until then, there was one place I knew had answers. It was the prison, the warden granting me a late meeting with Dr. P.W. Boécemo.

The doctor sat across from me, the wrinkled skin around his eyes stretching whenever he spoke. He ran a hand through his black hair, the salty grays glinting against the prison lights. There were fresh bruises on his face, a puffed lip with blood oozing from a split. A deeper bruise eclipsed one of his eyes, and he winced slightly whenever he breathed. There was no peace for the doctor in prison. Not that I cared. Not tonight. Sherry was missing and presumed to have been abducted. The search of Karl Brause's place turned up nothing. The doctor had a name, and so help me, I was about to reach across the prison table and rip it out of him.

His dark eyes followed mine, staying lockstep with me as I moved to sit across from him. He wasn't one to blink much, not when you were apt to notice it. I'd found that before and thought it was a trait he used as a means of intimidating. If that was his intention, then it was lost on me today. "A name," I said directly, insisting. "You have a name and I need it."

The doctor tilted his head, placing his hands on the table, fingers laced. He pursed his lips and made a tsk-tsk sound like he had at his parole hearing. "You've come all this way tonight, woken me from my sleep, and you've nothing more to offer?"

"I'm not here to entertain you, Doctor." A blink. Just one would help. He didn't though as I stayed composed. In my head, I was imagining the worst for Sherry and felt my training begin to slip away like sand through my fingers. "Be careful, Doctor. You'll want to be very careful."

That coy smile of his showed a moment, his saying, "Come now, Detective. You're not one to make threats."

"Take it however you want."

"Now, now." The expression on his face turned serious with disappointment. "We've always had a repertoire of good standing. I'd expect nothing less in this meeting you've brought."

"A name!" I repeated, his comments ignored.

"You'll accompany me if my appeal to the parole board is accepted?" the doctor asked, unlacing his fingers long enough to dab his busted lip. "That was the deal I presented."

Gritting my teeth, muscles tensing. "Doctor, you know I can't do that."

The doctor leaned back and fluttered his eyelids. He'd finally broken his stare. For a moment, I thought he was going to get up and leave. Instead, he recomposed himself, hands resuming the position on the table promptly. "Detective, that is a disappointment."

"The name, Doctor!" I said again, agitation turning my voice hoarse.

"Perhaps we could trade another way. A tit-for-tat," he said, leaning forward as if it were a secret. The guards took notice of his change in posture. I gave them a slight nod, indicating it was fine. "You could answer a few questions to feed my curiosity?"

"Your curiosity?" I asked, his pale skin looking taut against the bones in his face. Up close, I could see how much weight he was losing. "Curious about what?"

A smile returned. Slight as it might be, I hated seeing it because it meant he had leverage. He knew it too and that made it worse. "Have I told you that I've read every article about you? I also read that book about you and your *dead* husband and your daughter."

"Doctor? What are you getting at?" There was heat on my breath and in my words. Any more of this and I was certain I'd start spitting fire.

"Now now, it's a wonderful tale, but"—the smirk broadened —"it's incomplete."

"It was damn complete to me," I countered, shifting on the stool, a knee bouncing. But he had me curious. "Incomplete how, Doctor?"

He leaned in, his eyes big. "What happened that morning? I mean, what *really* happened to your daughter?"

I played along, telling him what he wanted to hear. It could mean getting the name and saving Sherry. "She was supposed to be in front of the television eating apple slices and watching SpongeBob."

His eyelids peeled back, pleased. This was what he wanted, the details that had never been published anywhere. Remorse turned its ugly head deep inside, the pain of that morning like a fresh burn. A tear stung like a bee and forced me to look away. I couldn't let him see me getting misty-eyed.

"She wasn't there. She wasn't in front of the television."

"You got angry at her for leaving the room?" the doctor asked. He moved to cross his legs, his hands perched on his lap in a tidy ball. He lowered his head until our eyes met. "She'd disobeyed you. A part of you blames her for the kidnapping?"

"What?" I nearly screamed, disgusted. "She was just a child!"

"She was a child who was learning right from wrong," he replied. "Detective, regardless of their age, it's perfectly normal to be resentful of your children. Most parents are, but never realize it."

I'd never considered what he was suggesting. If she had only listened to me and stayed in front of the television, we wouldn't have... I wouldn't have lost her. "Doctor, she was still a baby to me. She was my responsibility."

"Does she know that you resent her?" he asked.

I scoffed, his suggestion like a slap in the face. He was trying to stir trouble, poke a sleeping bear. Only, there was no bear here.

Before I could answer, he asked, "Have you reconciled the past? Or perhaps, it is your daughter? Does she blame you for what happened to her?"

I swiped at my eyes, annoyance drying them fast. "Doctor, I know what you're trying to do. It's not going to work."

"How about the kidnapper?" His fingers moved as he spoke. If not for his yellow jumpsuit, he looked like he was practicing psychiatry again. He wasn't. But I needed the name. For Sherry's sake, I would answer his questions. "In the articles and that book, a ghostwriter I'm sure, it doesn't say what happened to the kidnappers?"

"He died." Short and to the point. The doctor dipped his chin, wanting more. "In prison."

"The woman? His wife?" I frowned impatiently at the question. "Never mind that, I believe she ended up in a mental hospital. The husband, the one who left your daughter to die in front of the hospital. How did it make you feel when you heard he died?"

"What kind of question is that?" Where was he going with this? I thought of Sherry and searched for an answer he'd accept. "I don't know. Relieved, I guess."

The doctor pursed his lips and wagged a finger, saying, "That's a lie. I know when you're lying." I didn't buy that he knew anything. But it didn't matter, I'd have to give him what he wanted. "Detective, did it make you happy?"

"What difference does it make if I was relieved or happy?" I asked. When he didn't reply, I dismissed my question, and pleaded, "The name, Doctor?"

"Weren't you happy when you learned of his death?" he asked, ignoring my plea. "Didn't it bring you delight when learning that he'd been beaten, his skull cracked open like an egg?"

"Yes!" I answered with a growl, wanting him to stop talking. I shut my eyes and saw the man who'd abandoned my daughter to die alone in the pouring rain. I opened my eyes to find the doctor staring at me. There was delight on his face. I cupped my trembling fingers when the doctor noticed them. "Are you satisfied now?"

"Did you resent your daughter?" the doctor asked, repeating the earlier question. I clenched my fists tight enough for my fingernails to bite into my skin.

"You already asked me that," I told him, heat staying in my voice.

His brow rose as his focus narrowed. "You never answered the question." There was a pause, the two of us locked in a stare. The doctor grew impatient and asked, "Do you still carry a resentment? Is it down deep where you think it's hidden from your daughter? How about from yourself?"

"The name!" I demanded, tears racing. I'd heard enough of his questions, my breath short, the beating in my chest heavy. "Doctor, we don't have time for this!"

"Then answer the question," he insisted. "Did you blame your daughter for her kidnapping?!"

"She shouldn't have left the house!" I yelled, the horrible memory raw like an open wound. If my daughter had only listened to me. If she'd stayed in front of the television, then she would never have been taken. The doctor's shoulders slumped as if the release was his to have. I quickly followed my answer, repeating, "She was only a child though. She didn't know any better."

"Child or not, that's not relevant to how you feel," he said quietly. "Detective, it is how you feel and you're letting it define you."

"The name, Doctor? Please!" I begged, ignoring his psychology, raging that he'd drawn out a dark secret like it was an infection. Maybe it was though. Maybe it was defining me. "We're running out of time."

He stood abruptly and motioned to the guard, contented with what I'd shared. I gripped the table, the metal cold. Before leaving, he faced me, saying, "Detective, I know bad people. You are not one of them. But that resentment, if you don't let it go, the bitterness of it will consume you."

"What about the name?" I shouted, voice bouncing as he joined the guard. "Doctor! We had a deal!"

I was on my feet glaring at the back of his head. The doctor looked over his shoulder, hair flopping from behind his ears.

"Detective, the deal was in exchange for your help with my appeal." He turned away with a wave of his hand.

"Doctor!" But before I could say another word, he was gone. My eyes were bugging out of my head, blood rushing strong enough to hear it. I'd been played. The doctor was never going to give me a name.

TWENTY-TWO

Try as I might with Cheryl's help, there was no budging the adoption hearing for Thomas and Tabitha. There was no postponing it either or delaying it until after the message in the bottle case was solved. Did it matter? Wasn't it a moot point? Waiting at the end of every case was the beginning of a new one. It was a cold and sad truth in this ofttimes cruel world, there would always be a homicide to investigate. *Never forget who you are.* That's one of our unwritten rules in law enforcement. Beat cops, station managers, and even detectives are people too. They're not just some robot tasked in life to do a single thing. They have a life which comes with the same ups and downs like anyone else.

A stir of guilt. I pinched my mouth as a pang thumped against my chest. Who was I to even consider a postponement? Thomas and Tabitha were the priority. They deserved better. We'd come so far since finding them alone at sea. I felt the memory of that day. Felt the sea breeze on my face and the sway of the boat beneath my feet. Jericho had spotted the dingy floating adrift and moved us close enough to investigate. There were empty water bottles and a soiled tarp that was lumped into a heap near the transom, the raft appearing abandoned. But there was the sound. It was like the chirp of a baby bird and it was forever fixed in my brain. Beneath the tarp we found Thomas and Tabitha, malnourished and dehydrated, their tiny, shriveled bodies curled up in a shivering ball.

In the marrow of my bones, I knew that adoption was the right thing to do. Jericho knew it too. My stomach fluttered with the excitement of it all, our day in court intended to be a point of celebration. It was there, in front of our family and friends, as well as a judge, our union with Thomas and Tabitha would be made formal. We'd gone through pre-adoption training already, signed and submitted every document, the legal stack tall and sometimes overwhelming. Everything was in place for the big day. Almost everything. We were missing a recommendation.

Not everyone was convinced about our adopting Thomas and Tabitha. With the adoption hearing scheduled, a date and time picked, we'd hoped to have had a recommendation from the one person who'd known Thomas and Tabitha as long as we have. It was Ms. Patricia Welts from North Carolina's Child Services. It was her recommendation the judge would review when making the decision to sign or not sign the adoption decree. Only, it hadn't come yet. There'd been no recommendation. Instead, we received an invitation from Ms. Welts's supervisor. A request for us to appear was a better way of putting it.

The offices for Child Services was about what I'd expected. There were narrow corridors with hunter-green cubicle walls which were nearly as tall as me. We followed our escort, eyes peering up at us as we passed from one path to another, the floor layout like a maze. Jericho walked ahead of me while I stayed close to Cheryl, who was struggling, sweat beading on her upper lip.

"Do you need to stop?" I asked, my voice low amidst the hum of phone conversations. "We can."

She pasted a smile and shook her head, strands of her red

hair pasted to the side of her face. "I'm fine." When she saw that I wasn't convinced, she added, "This is nothing new."

"This way," our escort said, turning down another hall, the back of Jericho disappearing behind them. For the moment I was alone with Cheryl, a wave of doubt washing over me like it was freshly erupted lava.

"What are they going to ask us?" I searched her sweaty face, seeing that she didn't know. There was a calm in her eyes though and I latched on to it. Offering my arm, I said, "Thank you for being here."

A shallow smile flashed briefly, her left brow rising. "Casey, you do know I charge by the hour?"

"Uh-huh." I gripped her arm to take a step, jokingly telling her, "Then I guess you better move faster."

She busted a laugh loud enough to make faces appear from the cubicles. Clapping her hand over her mouth, voice muffled, "Lead the way."

"You're in here," the escort said, leaving us outside a conference room. It was similar to the one in the station. It was a fish tank with glass from the floor to the ceiling and one long table at the center. There were speakerphones in the center, a dozen chairs pushed in, two of them occupied. The welcoming smile I'd been accustomed to seeing on Ms. Welts was gone today, her pinkish complexion absent as well. Her silvery hair was pinned up in a bun and she was dressed for the office with a burgundy blouse, a faint touch of the same color on her lips and brushed onto her plump cheeks.

"Good morning, Patricia—" I began to say, pulling out a chair to sit. On wellness checks when she visited our home, she'd always insisted we call her by her first name. An older woman with high cheekbones and deep-set eyes sat next to Patricia, a case folder opened in front of her. She had golden hair with long white strands throughout, her complexion still carrying a summer tan. It might have been from a bottle, but there was evidence she'd been a sunbather once. Years ago, perhaps. I could see it around her face, hands and arms. Patricia's supervisor looked up from the file, lips firmly pressed, eyes darting from me to Jericho and then to Cheryl. Was she gauging us? "—I mean, Ms. Welts."

"Morning." Jericho followed, holding the seat for me. He took the one to my right after helping Cheryl into the seat to my left. "And good morning, Mrs. Jenkins."

"Heather, please. It's nice to see you again, Jericho," the woman across from us said, eyes warming to Jericho as a smile appeared. Hope sprang and gave my heart a much-needed hug. Patricia's supervisor knew Jericho. *Of course she did.* Their paths had likely crossed during her time in Child Services when he was the sheriff. "Thank you for coming in."

"Ma'am, my name is Casey White." I leaned forward to offer my hand. She accepted it, her fingers delicate and cold.

"Detective," she answered and patted the top of the file. "I'm quite familiar."

"Our attorney, Cheryl Smithson." Cheryl and the women from Child Services exchanged cards, the formalities grating. I wanted to know why we were here. When everyone was settled, I looked at them and asked, "How can we help you this morning."

"First let me start off by saying how wonderful it's been to have had Thomas and Tabitha placed in your home," she said, stopping to drink from a tall travel mug. An Earl Grey tea label dangled from the lip, steam rising. "Patricia has spoken very highly of everything you've done for Thomas and Tabitha."

I felt there was a *but* coming. Or at least a question. My impatience got the better of me and I jumped ahead to ask, "Does that mean we can expect a recommendation for their adoption?"

"That's what we've come together to discuss," she answered without pause. "As I've said, I am familiar with your case. To be honest, I feel like I've known you, that is who you are, and the story of your daughter and what happened in Philadelphia. So tragic."

Was there judgment in her eyes? A question about the kidnapping? I felt terse words clawing up inside me, my mouth shut tight, swallowing them. "That wasn't my fault," I heard myself say, feeling disconnected. It was a reaction instead of a response.

"Oh no. Please, Ms. White, I wasn't implying anything of the sort," the supervisor said and clutched her chest. "The reunion with your daughter was a wonderful thing. A miracle that has inspired."

"That's not why we're here?" Confusion had me narrowing my eyes to try and see what was in the folder. I couldn't.

"Not at all," she answered. Her face drained of any sympathy, mouth returning to the pinched look when we'd first walked in. "This is about today. Who you and Mr. Flynn are now, who you are and can be for Thomas and Tabitha."

That got Jericho's attention. He sat up, elbows perched on the tabletop. "Ms. Welts?"

She shook her head slightly, saying, "I think you are both wonderful and the children adore you. You've been a true gift in their lives at a time when they needed it most."

Short breaths. Fast. Where was this going? Jericho spoke candidly, "Heather, we want Thomas and Tabitha to be a part of our lives forever. Is there a problem?"

There was no pause, my asking Ms. Welts, "What's happened between now and the last time you were over to our place?"

Her supervisor answered for her. "Patricia has some reservations." She sifted through the papers in the folder, pulling one of the sheets and said, "Rightfully so, I have to add."

"May I?" Cheryl asked, curling an index finger, urging the woman to hand her the paper.

"It's the stability that is a concern," the supervisor said. Our gaze followed the sheet as it was passed across the table and handed to Cheryl. "There have been periods of time where both of you are absent from the home."

"I don't know which times you're referring," I tried to explain, sounding defensive. Heat spread across my chest and neck. "I'm sure those were unavoidable circumstances. I assure you the children were never left alone."

"One period in particular, there were multiple hospital stays," the supervisor said, adding details. "Both of you were admitted at different points during the same week."

"I was working a case that had some collaboration with the Marine Patrol," Jericho said, his voice sounding thick. I'd only heard it like that a few times before. He was getting upset and nervous which made me even more so.

"Ma'am, both Mr. Flynn and Ms. White are sworn officers of the law," Cheryl said, her finger on the sheet with the hospital report. She slid it back slowly. "These hospital stays were results of fulfilling their duties."

"Yes, we understand and we thank you both for your continued service and for going above and beyond," the supervisor said, her tone changing.

It felt like I'd swallowed a hot rock, my insides burning with where this discussion was headed.

"Stability?" I said, asking, Cheryl's hand softly touching mine. "You're right. Tabitha and Thomas deserve a stable and loving home. The kind they'd get from parents who have careers that are free of danger."

"There's risk in everyday life and in many professions," Cheryl argued. "From the lineman bringing power to your home to the men and women driving delivery trucks for a living."

"That is quite understandable," the supervisor answered. "We're not prejudice to any profession. But given the children's history, and witnessing their parents' murders, we're taking every precaution."

Jericho sat back, understanding what they were looking for. He scratched at his chin, glancing over at me, and then to the supervisor. His voice soft like a whisper, he asked, "Heather, could we have a moment alone, please?"

"Of course," the supervisor said.

The women from children services stood to leave while glancing at us, my heart sinking. It was their remorseful expressions that got to me. It told me they'd already decided and that this was only a formality they had to fulfill. It meant that we'd go to family court where the judge would deny our decree to adopt Thomas and Tabitha.

"What do we do?" I asked when the doors closed. It was nearly impossible to slow my breathing, hot air passing over my tongue and lips as if it came from a furnace. "Cheryl?"

"I'm not sure what we can do." Her eyes were big and round, the freckles on her nose seeming to stand out. "Listen, it's just a recommendation. Ultimately, the decision is up to the judge."

"Yeah, but the judge's decision is going to be based on their recommendation." I couldn't see the light, the solution that would make us the family we needed to be.

There was one path though. Jericho saw it first and said, "I'm done." We turned in unison, facing him. "That's the answer. I'll announce my full retirement from law enforcement."

"What? Jericho no!" I couldn't let him do that. His life, his career had been in law. "Cheryl, we can appeal, right? Say they were being prejudice or discriminating? Something like that?"

"That could work. But you'd risk them moving the children to another foster family," she answered. It wasn't the answer I expected or wanted. She gave Jericho a nod, warming to the idea. "With one of you home full time, it's exactly the kind of stability they're looking for."

Tears sat in my eyes and blurred Jericho's face. "Babe, it's your career?"

"I choose us," he said warmly. His smile melted my heart as he touched the side of my face. "We're their family."

"We are," I managed to say.

"I've been skating around the idea of full retirement from law enforcement for a while now," he said, running his fingers over his bad arm. "I've given what I've given and I think I've given enough."

"You've given more than enough." I pressed my hand against his chest.

His eyebrows popped excitedly, saying, "There's a few building restoration projects. I can finally exercise some those carpentry skills I haven't touched in a while."

Cheryl was smiling, a plan set. "I don't think they'll find any issues with that," she assured us. She sat up to see if Ms. Welts and the supervisor were nearby. They were. "Shall we?"

"Jericho, are you sure about this?" I had to ask once more, emotions running high.

His chin quivered as he spoke. "I'm surer about this than I've been of anything in my life."

"I love you," I told him, getting up and opening the door. "We're ready."

TWENTY-THREE

A distant shout bounced off the walls. Dr. Boécemo's knees went weak as he braced for another. He heard laughter and a whimper instead. There were five... no, six inmates gathered at the end of the corridor, two turning in time to see him approach. The hairs on the back of his neck stood on end. This wasn't the place to be alone. Then again, he was always alone, and they knew it. He forced himself to look for the doors to the prison's morgue, which were halfway between them and where he stood. His heart thumped painfully as he hastened the pace, the thin soles on his shoes scraping along the concrete floor.

"Please. Oh please," he muttered shakily. His insides seized like a dying engine when a third inmate turned. There was a fourth showing interest now too, another gesturing toward him. Stride growing, footsteps clapping, he broke into a run and ducked inside the morgue. Panting hard, sweat stung his eyes as he flattened himself against the wall to hide. Every stitch of muscle and tendon and bone turned silently still like they were made of stone. Only his ears remained perked as he listened to the approaching shuffle and the low chatter. It was the same gang who'd been at him before. They knew he was alone. They knew he wouldn't fight back either.

The doctor glared at the space beneath the doors, the dark impressions of a shadow arriving. It was someone's shoes. He considered screaming for a guard. They never came though. Not to any of his calls. How many times now? How many more? Thick bangs fell limply in front of his eyes as he waited to see another pair of shoes, the same prison-issued ones he'd forever see in his dreams. His nightmares. He drove his fingers over his mouth and stifled a cry when one of the men whistled a familiar call. They were gathering.

A laugh. A chuckle as one of them razzed the first. Torment ravaged him, a blaze burning inside every cell that told him to run. But run where? He held his head, fingers splayed around his brow as the rush of adrenaline made him light-headed and faint. The shadow feet moved back and forth, a debate growing as a distant bell rang for chow, a guard announcing it. The noon hour had come, the time for the scheduled pickup less than thirty minutes away. His arms fell to his sides when the gang moved on, the shadow feet leaving the door. They were gone then, and the doctor breathed heavily, nearly spitting up. Nothing came and he choked it back, crying, "Oh thank God."

He was safe. For now. He dared to touch the swelling around his mouth. The taste of blood from this morning was still on his tongue, a heartbeat throbbing in his lower lip. They were getting worse. The attacks. The beatings. There'd be more too. Fingers trembling, he reached for his side and winced. It was a bruised rib, maybe broken. They were never going to leave him alone or let him serve his time. How long before they go too far? How long before he was found dead?

The doctor gave the corner of the room a passing look, side-eyeing it carefully so as not to raise any suspicion. A slow smile crept past the swelling when he saw the red light on the security camera was still off. That was good. What was it, two weeks?

Three maybe since he'd disconnected it. Had to be three now, he'd done that business before the parole hearing. Before Detective Casey White made a disaster of it in front of the board. The thought of her name wiped the smile clear from his mouth.

"It's good news," he insisted, thinking of the positive. There'd been nobody in the morgue to fix it. Or had they? Weary, the doctor moved away from the false safety of the wall to stand beneath the camera and search behind it. That's where he'd damaged wires, making it look like mice had been at it, nipping through the sheathing. Shoulders slumped with relief, the cable was as he'd left it. It meant the camera was dead like the rest of the occupants in this part of the prison.

His gaze went to the body refrigerator with thoughts of medical school, the internship and residency, the licensing and his practice. The years of it bringing him to this moment—he was a babysitter for the dead. That's why no one came. How often does a guard need to check on the dead? They weren't going anywhere. Tapping a metal tray with his fingernails, even if the guards came to fix the camera, he'd blame the mice. They'd been here plenty, the smell of decay calling to them.

In death the men were free of their incarceration, but what of their sin? That wasn't a question for him or anyone else to answer. A gentle touch to dab the blood from the corner of his mouth. It was bright red like the rage gnawing in him. This was the detective's doing. By all rights, he was a free man. Gates latching with a metal clamor. It jarred his attention with a reminder. He'd be dead soon if he didn't do something about it. Disappointment clenched his stomach like the meals they shoveled onto his plate. "She'll never let me go free." He could still see her eyes. The smug way she convinced the parole board to deny him. "So be it."

A growl. The doctor clutched his belly and tried to ignore the need to eat. His body was shrinking. It was shrinking faster than he could have hoped. A grumble, his gut seeming to flip and twist and scream for food. But he wouldn't eat just yet. Not until he was out, his backup plan coming together. Arms lifted, the prison-issued clothes hung from them like towels on a bar. When he waved, they moved like window drapes.

A fresh yell bounced from the corridor, his arms and legs feebly bracing the body refrigerator. Frosty air tumbled from his lips as he dared a peek at the morgue's doors and the small plastic windows. They were clear. He was still alone but for how long? They knew he was here and would come back for him soon. Muscles easing, his fingers plopped onto a handle. In his lifetime, it never occurred to him what small prey feel when they're being hunted. He knew it now. And he knew it well.

With a sigh, he opened the first body drawer, a gray sheet covering the genitals of a man they called Fat Pete. They'd also called the man Dump-Truck on account of his abundant size. His skin was the color of ash, his eyes bulging, the rot already strong. He'd never known Fat Pete but remembered the man's enormous figure when he stood guard at the shower room's entrance. That was one of the first times the gang took him, the doctor recalling the dread he felt when Fat Pete wanted in on the shower activities, the morbid terror that it might just break him in half.

"I know it wasn't anything personal," the doctor said and tapped the side of Pete's face hard enough to jostle. Rigor kept the man's head still. And death kept Pete's eyelids fixed in a wide stare, a milky film turning the dark brown eyes into the color of oatmeal. The doctor moved his fingertips slowly, holding them like a farmer with dowsing rods in search of ground water. He stopped when reaching Fat Pete's heart. The prognosis was a heart attack. A massive one, possibly the kind they called a widow maker. To look at Pete as is, he couldn't tell. The dead don't speak. Not without a scalpel. But he was there in the chow hall that day. Pete had grabbed his shoulder and toppled onto a table like a fallen tree. "I guess you got yours, fat boy."

The doctor eased the drawer closed and moved on to the next, feeling a distant sense like he was in a nursery rhyme. He was Goldilocks in search of just the right bed to sleep in tonight. The truck was coming soon for the pickup, and he had to find the one that fit his size. Fingers clasped around the handle, the morgue doors swung open with a clap.

Dr. Boécemo withdrew in a startle, hiding his hands behind his back like he was a child. Two prisoners entered, wheeling a delivery of coffins. His insides warmed at the sight of the wooden boxes, the doctor expecting to see three or more. The morgue filled with the fresh smell of milled pine. It mixed with the ever-present stink of death, the combination common in this part of the prison.

Next to the morgue was the wood shop where they manufactured coffins for the state. A majority of them were made thin and used for the indigent burials. Those were the burials for men whose bodies went unclaimed and became the responsibility of the state for disposal. He held back a chuckle, having worked the detail regularly since his first month of incarceration. There was no burial to speak of. None at all. The coffins were filled with the unclaimed bodies and taken to a field where the earth was scorched, turned black and made crispy. That's where they placed the bodies, lining them up side by side. They added fuel and ignited the pine boxes, the black smoke spiraling upward until there was nothing left but soot and ash.

"What ya up to, *perv*?!" one of the inmates yelled with a snickering laugh. "You in here fucking the dead guys too?"

"Ye-yeah, fu-fucking 'em dead ones," the other inmate stuttered and gyrated his hips vulgarly.

"Put them in the corner over there," the doctor instructed, pasting a smirk, self-deprecating as it was. The comments were beneath him, just as these men were, but safety was first. He turned away, facing the body drawer so the men didn't take his commenting for an invitation to stay. The casters squealed as they rolled the stack next to two gurneys in the corner. The doctor cradled the bruised rib, the bone jutting from beneath his thin skin. From the wall, he took the clipboard, marking the three coffins as delivered. A pickup from the city was scheduled early this afternoon, the dead men on their final journey. Only, it wasn't three bodies leaving the prison. It was going to be four.

Unlike the camera, the clock was still functioning, the time showing it was another fifteen minutes before they'd come for the bodies. When they stopped rolling the coffins, the doctor asked, "If you could, please unstack them. We've got three bodies going out. Leave one and place the others on the empty gurneys."

"Ye-yeah. I-I know what to do," the stuttering man said. The doctor didn't know him. Hadn't seen him in the chow line or in the showers. He was new and no threat to him. Not with his wiry small frame, the acne on his chin and forehead and that stutter painting a picture of who he was. A resolve came over him, knowing what he knows. Not that he cared. Nobody really ever cares. The man couldn't be more than nineteen, too young and too small to be in this place alone. *They'd take him soon. Maybe even take him next, when I'm gone.*

"That's right," the doctor said, the smell of pine growing as they readied the coffins, opening each to receive a body. "I'm going to need help with this one."

The smaller man approached, bouncing on his feet, asking, "Wh-who you got?"

The young man's energy made the doctor smile, his gaze warming. "Help me with him."

"Wh-what! You kidding mmm-me?" the new prisoner asked, eyelids peeled back while assessing Fat Pete's size.

"We can do it," the doctor answered forcefully, the clock ticking. There was no time to wait and he waved the other prisoner over, placing them in the proper positions for a lift and shift into the coffin. "Up!"

Feet shuffling amidst the grunts and groans, the coffin's sides creaking. It held. "We-we did it."

"Just a matter of physics, the use of leverage," the doctor muttered breathlessly, the clock's minute-hand counting down. He knew the other dead prisoners, the unclaimed bodies, saying, "I can get the others."

"I-I could help," the new guy told him. The doctor saw the man, saw the childlike need to please. A faint sense of regret ticked in his heart, but it was fleeting, the doctor's heart more stone than flesh. From his time as a psychiatrist, he recognized the quality, that lovely quality which would only bring misery to the boy. A lot of misery.

"All good," the doctor said, waving to the door.

"Yo-your loss," he answered, leaving while the doctor wheeled the other gurneys into position.

The second body went in without issue, the prisoner dying of old age. As with all the bodies he'd prepared for delivery, the doctor stood over the coffin, his eyes being the last to look on their faces before the flames devoured them. There were no stir-rings or emotional pangs, no religious prayers or last rites to speak. Not even a simple goodbye. The doctor said nothing while lowering the lid into place, the latch a simple mechanism to keep it shut.

The last of the three bodies was of a man who the doctor had watched and studied. In the back of his mind, he knew this man would become his third bear in the Goldilocks's fairy tale. The prisoner was a drunk that died earlier in the week, stabbed to death in the yard. He'd bled out, shanked across the abdomen with a single incision that opened his belly, possibly slicing the aorta. Ironically, it wasn't the pruno that killed the man. It was the unpaid debt for the prison wine that finally did it. And luckily for the doctor, the man drank more than he ate, making it easy for him to lift. It also made him the perfect size to join inside the coffin for the ride out of the prison.

Sweat itched his scalp and ran down the middle of his back as he prepared the lid and shoved a small pack at the bottom. It was a bag he'd set aside for this day, preparing it long before the parole hearing, before Detective Casey White railed it. If there was one person responsible for its use, it was the detective. She'd set this moment into motion. Ever cautious, he checked the bag again, seeing a pair of pants and a shirt that didn't come from the prison. The cash was there too. Just a few dollars to get him moving. Enough to get him food and water and whatever else he'd need.

The fit inside the pine box was getting tight as the doctor lowered himself next to the drunk, whose body was stiff with rigor mortis. It played a morbid tune with each motion. Terror struck when his bum got stuck, the lid resting on his hip. *Just a little more.* That's all he needed to make the lid close. He drove his middle forward, pressing the dead man's body against the far side as he shoehorned himself into place. The lid shut, and at once, death wrapped around him like a blanket. The inside of the coffin warmed with his breath, the stink of decomposition filling the space. The light was nearly gone too, the prison over-heads bleeding through the wood seams.

Dr. Boécemo stared straight into the man's gray eyes, noses nearly touching. How far was the drive? How many miles? The doors swung open and closed with a swish, the sound unmistakable. He sucked in a breath, instinct telling him to hold it. Footsteps quashed all thoughts racing in his head. It was time for the pickup, a hand pressing down on the lid and working the latch. It wasn't fastened. His chest tightened, hoping it remained open. Otherwise there was the risk of being burned alive. His heart stopped when he heard the metal clunk against the side, fingers working the latch.

"Bro? This one is broken," a voice said. The metal thumped

against the wood, the latch staying open. Would the wad of paper he wedged into the groove hold? He wasn't sure it would keep. With resignation, the voice said, "What do we do if the lid doesn't stay shut?"

"What do you mean?" the other man asked.

The lid opened briefly, fright gripping him as it rocked up and down.

"Shit. Hmm."

"See? It's that latch. It doesn't line up or something... I dunno."

"Just leave it," the other voice said. "It's not like it's going to matter anyway."

"I guess it won't," the first one answered. "Not with where these guys are going."

The lid stayed closed then as the doctor felt motion, the coffin bumping the doors when they exited the morgue. It was getting impossible to breathe. How many miles? The question returned like a ghost haunting him, sweat dripping from every part of him. Another bump came. It was followed by a third and fourth, his chest hammering hard enough every time the lid bounced open. When the smell of fresh air seeped into his coffin with a truck roaring to life, he knew he was out of the prison. And he knew, he'd never return there again. Not alive anyway.

TWENTY-FOUR

Bleary-eyed and my head buzzing from a cup of rotgut coffee, a burnt taste coated my tongue. My car brakes chirped when I reached the parking spot behind the prison gates, the commotion around the facility looking like something out of a movie. Blades of light swung up and down the giant stone walls chasing away the shadows, one of them striking my windshield with a blast that hit the back of my skull. I blinked away the spots as voices called out and dogs barked crazily. A pair of guards moved across the front of the car, the dogs stopping at every object to sniff it two and three times, sometimes more.

Dr. Boécemo's prison was the last place I expected to be. Yet, on this muggy autumn night that smelled more like summer than fall, here I was with an escort waiting to take me inside. I was responding to a call from the warden, the name of the prison showing up on my phone. Before hearing the warden's voice, I knew instantly it was a call about the doctor. For a moment, I thought the man I'd put behind bars had been killed. For a convicted pedophile, prison life was a living hell and somewhere in the back of my mind I'd always expected to get the call about his death one day.

The phone call wasn't about the doctor's demise though. Somehow, the medium security prison had lost his whereabouts. More than six hours had passed since the doctor was last seen. How exactly does a prison lose one of its prisoners? That question rifled into my brain like a freight train. It was the thoughts of the dangers he posed that gave me the chills and made me frantic to find him. Prisoners just don't up and vanish into thin air. So what happened to him?

Feet shuffling while I kept up with my escort, the back of my neck teemed with a light sweat like I'd been working out. The commotions inside the prison were equally fervent to what was going on outside. As we made our way through a myriad of corridors, buzzers buzzing and gates slamming shut behind us, the thought of the doctor escaping grew more and more unlikely given the level of video surveillance throughout. We moved deep behind concrete and wire and every ceiling corner had eyes. Somewhere in the data dump of video files there had to be a pixelated image of the doctor's last known location.

We reached the cell block the doctor called home, the warden and guards standing at the center. They'd been joined by a team of US Marshals, their jackets a dark blue with white lettering printed boldly across the back. A woman in the middle of the pack dished instructions and worked a radio simultaneously, the command in her voice telling me she was in charge of the operation. The cells had been emptied, every word echoed like we were in a cathedral. My escort commented that the prisoners had been taken to the cafeteria, where they were being treated to an unscheduled movie night. None of them had been questioned yet and none had come forward either.

I kept my hands close to my body, the doctor's sudden disappearance outside my jurisdiction. That responsibility was given to the woman doling out the commands. She wasn't much older than me, the name on her identification reading, Chancy Smith. She had short blonde hair with a sprinkle of gray highlights. With a round face and somewhat muscular build, she carried herself with authority, her team constantly looking to her for their next instruction.

Listening in, her latest directions included putting up road-blocks, calling out, "If by some miracle the doctor left on foot, he would average between four to six miles per hour. I want road-blocks at no less than twenty-four miles in every direction." Shoes stampeding, a group of marshals took off in a jog. She then instructed another group, "I want teams of two to begin searching every bus terminal and train station in the surrounding areas."

"Thank you for coming," the warden said, looking shaken as he spoke quietly in my ear. I'd met him twice before when orchestrating the visit to the doctor's parole hearing. He'd looked much better then.

"You are?" the marshal asked, turning to face me, sounding annoyed. She looked at my front for an identification badge, which I lifted, her lips moving while reading it. I wasn't put off by the tone of her question, understanding the role she had been tasked with. She turned to the warden, asking, "This one is with you?"

"Marshal, this is Detective Casey White," the warden answered. She seemed to only catch a word of what he said. The warden wiped his brow with a handkerchief, adding, "This is the detective who made the initial arrest which led to Dr. Boécemo's sentencing."

"Uh-huh," the marshal nodded, seeming uninterested. She extended a hand as a courtesy, saying, "United States Deputy Marshal Chancy Smith."

"Ma'am," I acknowledged as she continued to speak into her radio, a squawk replying.

When her attention returned, she nodded toward me, asking the warden, "Jurisdiction aside, how does your being here help me?"

The US Marshal was terse and brusque and demanding. She was a to-the-point and an as-a-matter-of-fact kind of person. There was no question about it, I liked her style almost immediately. Speaking for myself, I answered, "I've had some recent dealings with the doctor regarding a case that involves a kidnapping and murder. It's ongoing and we believe the doctor has information that would be helpful."

She flinched with a fast blink. "Come again?" She pivoted to speak into her radio. When she was done, she asked, "He's involved in a kidnapping and murder? From inside prison?"

"We think the doctor may have the name of a possible suspect. He's withholding it." It was my turn for a distraction, a flurry of text messages from Tracy about the doctor's disappearance. She was safe at home, a squad car parked on the street. "We don't know if the doctor simply had a name or if he was working with someone."

"Is this related to his recent parole?" the marshal asked. "Or the appeal he filed?"

"It is. It's the appeal," I answered, suddenly feeling like I was in the hot seat. She was doing her job though and asking what needed to be asked. She cocked her head, waiting for more. "The doctor is using the name as leverage, as part of an exchange. He's demanding my support for his appeal."

"Okay, I think I got it. The deal didn't go down and the doctor took matters into his own hands," she said dismissively before moving away. A stir of footsteps followed the marshal as she approached the doctor's prison cell. She put the radio down and instructed, "Listen up! We're clearing the cell to search for anything that indicates what the doctor had in mind. If he did escape, there *will* be something."

"There is!" the warden said abruptly, the motions ceasing. "That's why I asked the detective to join us."

"Make room!" the marshal demanded, saddling the radio on

her belt as she followed the warden inside. When I didn't move right away, she insisted, "Detective?"

"Coming," I answered hesitantly, taking a step, fingers wrapping around a bar, the metal smoothed and gleaming from the countless times it'd been held. This prison had the traditional type of doors which were made of bars for direct visibility. I stood at the threshold and peered inside, the walls covered in pictures, some drawn by the doctor, some of them torn from magazines. Near the steel sink and toilet, both made of a single unit, the doctor had amassed a small library, a stack of articles too. I recognized the medical journals and the titles such as *Psychology Today*, and then saw a picture of me with Tracy. I couldn't move. I was frozen with a kind of terror I'd never felt. It was sickening fright, a horrible stew that made my stomach flip. There'd been many pictures of me and Tracy which had been published and circulated. However, there were only a few like this one. It was the two of us from before her kidnapping when she was little and her name was Hannah. I remembered seeing the picture used in a story written about us, the portrait having sat on the hearth of our fireplace back in Philadelphia.

"He had his own cell?"

"Most do on this block," the warden answered. He pinched his belt and lifted, adjusting as we fit inside the tiny space. He tapped the top of a metal bump-out which was used as a desk, saying, "These are why I've asked you here."

The marshal poked around the desk with a pen. "Detective, it looks like the doctor collected articles about you." I saw my face and name beneath the tip of her pen along with another picture of Tracy and me. It was from the same article about our reunion. The marshal's eyes and lips moved as she gleaned the headlines and the opening paragraph, brow rising with a brief understanding of my past. She looked up briefly, saying, "Huh, that's quite the story."

"It would seem as though I got under the doctor's skin," I

commented, feeling lost for words. There were more articles about us, newspaper columns that had been torn from the pages and saved, the edges looking like mice had nibbled them. It wasn't just me and Tracy either. The marshal showed us a magazine with Thomas and Tabitha on the cover. Seeing that the doctor had pictures of the children made me sick inside. Jericho was at home and was aware of what was going on tonight. I couldn't speak, my voice lost to the cruelty of fright.

"Or maybe he was a fan?" the warden questioned.

"I'd say the latter since he left you this," the marshal corrected him. She held open a magazine where a folded note was seated in the binder, the front addressed with my name on it.

"We found the articles and newspaper pictures and thought you'd need to see it," the warden added as a guard whispered into his ear. "If you'll excuse me."

"Let's see what the doc has to say," the marshal said without asking. She opened the folded paper, doing so as part of her investigation. I didn't object. "'Dear Detective White, if you are reading this then it is with much rejoice that I say goodbye to you. I know that deep in your heart you believe you have done well to have put me in this place. I assure you, that is not the case.'"

"I'm sensing some resentment," I commented, expecting nothing less. "Not a surprise."

The marshal lifted the sheet, my nodding for her to continue. "'This prison is a hell on earth that you could never understand. Unless my status changes, I will die in here. Without your cooperation, the appeal to the parole board is futile. Sadly, for me, I know you will never bend. You will never counter your belief that I belong here.

"'Detective White, I need to be free. I need to smell the springtime and see the Sparrows in June. I need to touch the waters on the coast and know that I can walk the sands in the west and the east. And so, I will be free.'"

The marshal looked troubled and stopped reading to flip over the page and search the other side.

"What? What is it?"

"There's only one other sentence, but it doesn't make any sense," she said gazing at the paper. "'Detective, in the company of the dead, the indigent and the unclaimed, I will find my refuge. Goodbye for now.'"

"In the company of the dead? The indigent and the unclaimed?" I questioned, thinking the doctor was playing a game.

"I think I know what that means," a guard said, overhearing the exchange.

"Is it what happens to the prisoners who die here?" I asked. Dr. Boécemo had a medical degree and was a psychologist. I considered all the places someone with his background could work inside a prison. "Just a guess, but did the doctor work in the morgue?"

"That's right," the guard answered, taken aback for a moment. "The doctor worked there to prepare the unclaimed prisoners for disposal."

"Disposal? Of the bodies?" the marshal blurted, the radio squelching alive. "I need eyes in the morgue and a schedule of all transports in and out of there the last eight hours."

"Where do they take the bodies?" I asked, counting the hours backward.

"They get incinerated. It's like a cremation at some state facility," the guard answered, a frown deepening. "It's the same service used by the hospitals and mortuaries."

"The indigent and unclaimed," I repeated, understanding where the doctor was. "We need to go there, now."

It was a field, the state facility where the unclaimed bodies were cremated. Massive floodlights threw brightness on every square inch of dirt and rock and sparse grass, generators humming in the background. At the center of the field there was a small brick and cinder-block building that was the size of a shed, the outside of it still warm from its day of work. It had a mouth with a steel roller conveyor that looked like a tongue sticking out, the steel colored black blue from the heat. Behind the building was a large tank filled with fuel which was used in the process of turning wood and metal and flesh and bone into dust.

I followed the US Marshal around the incinerator, the ground blackened by years of use. We moved to a row of coffins that were lined up on one side, some of them stamped with the prison's name, the lids opened to show men and women who'd died alone in this world. Even in death, there was a line to wait in, the work today having gone unfinished. Two men stood near the oven, both wearing leather and silvery suits, protective gear from the raging temperatures.

We shined lights into each open casket, finding unfamiliar faces. The inspections went further, checking around the bodies to better understand if it was possible the doctor could have fit inside a casket with one of the dead. It was our going theory of how he might have escaped, stowing away inside a pine box.

"You said the doctor looked thin?" the marshal asked, kicking a stone. It skittered toward the cremation oven as she knelt and shined a light over tracks in the loose dirt. It was a path worn by the edge of a casket dragged to the oven. "How thin?"

"At the parole hearing, it looked like he lost a significant amount of weight." I followed the path to the oven where the two men were waiting, one of them checking his watch. When I saw the concern on his face, I told them, "Nobody is in trouble. We're just trying to sort out something."

The marshal was less forgiving, her questions insinuating a

wrongdoing. "Are the coffins inspected before placing them inside there?" The men exchanged a look, both shaking their heads. "Why is that? How can you be certain they're dead?"

"Never had one come through here that was alive," the taller of the two men answered. He pawed at the scruff on his chin, seeking approval from his coworker.

"The smell give it away too," the coworker added. "But we used to it."

"Was anyone else involved in the pickup?" I asked, eyeing the truck used.

Both shook their heads, "Just us," one of them said. The other had a frizzy hair he kept tight beneath a bandana, adding, "Been working together on this shift for about five years."

"Did you hear anything when you drove here?" the marshal asked, tension in her voice. "Anything at all?"

"Like what?" the one with the bandana asked. "They all dead."

"That may not be the case with today's pickup," she answered.

They traded looks, the whites of their eyes bright in the floodlight's glow.

"Naw. There's no way," the one said, pawing at his scruffy chin. "You sure?"

"Was there anything unusual about the pickup?" I looked at their faces for a hint of anything registering. "Anything at all that wouldn't normally happen?"

The worker with the bandana raised his hand, saying, "There was a coffin with a lid that wouldn't latch."

We spun in unison to face the coffins, the marshal asking, "One of them?"

"We cremated it already." The worker with the scruffy chin hung his thumb over his shoulder, answering, "It was the first one we put inside."

"What do you do with the ashes?" I asked. They waved us

to follow them around the cremation oven. We stopped at a large pit, the booties I'd put on my shoes were covered instantly with dusty remains.

"There's a company that comes and does a pickup each week," the worker with the scruff answered. He shook his head, saying, "I don't know what happens to it after."

We stood at the edge of the large hole which was half filled, a fine dust drifting in a beam from the floodlights. "Any remains?"

"No, ma'am," the other worker answered. "The burns are around eighteen hundred degrees Fahrenheit."

"They stay in the burn chamber at least two hours," the other man said as I fixed a hard stare on the pit, wondering if the doctor was in there. "When done, there ain't nothing left."

I pointed at the remaining caskets, the marshal's eyes following. "If the doctor got in one of those with another body—"

"And if he didn't get out in time, if he got stuck or passed out," she said, interrupting. Our gaze returned to the pit, her continuing. "Then the doctor would most certainly be dead. And he took the name of your killer with him."

TWENTY-FIVE

Was justifiable paranoia a thing? Or was it considered reasonable suspicion? Whichever it was, Sherry remained missing and the doctor's escape was a new threat against me and my family. The lack of sleep and buckets of coffee didn't help matters either. I was shaking inside, my heart fluttering as though it'd burst. I'd never felt threatened by Dr. Boécemo. Not directly anyway. After seeing my life laid out in his prison cell, complete with a mini library and pictures plastered on his walls, I didn't know how to feel. By the time we were done turning out his cell, we'd found the doctor collected every article and book there was that had mention of my name. Why was that? We also didn't know if the doctor had escaped or if he'd perished at the cremation site. For now, I had a patrol car parked outside my home to guard Jericho and Thomas and Tabitha.

If the doctor had managed to escape the cremation's fire, what was he planning to do next? And what about the name he was willing to trade? Nobody had said anything directly to me yet, but I sensed there were questions coming my way, especially if we didn't get a break on the case. I squeezed my hands shut and made a fist, tightening them until it hurt, thoughts of Sherry at the forefront of my mind. The questions were already in play, mumblings at the station which ate at me like sands swallowed by the tide. It was a distraction we didn't need and couldn't afford. The truth was, I was doing plenty of second-guessing on my own. I was beginning to hate that I might have blown the investigation by not making a deal with the doctor.

My phone buzzed with a text from Tracy, the latest headlines sweeping across my screen. For the moment, the press seemed to have forgotten about the message in the bottle killer. It was the great escape of Dr. Boécemo that had captured their attention. More than that, it was the mystery of what happened to him afterward that kept the dials tuned to the hourly broadcasts. Beyond the conference room, the reporters and news crews had drained the front of the station.

I found them on the station's televisions, their cameras focusing on US Marshal Chancy Smith, her face made bright by the lights as she provided press coverage outside of the prison. Our theory on how he pulled it off had made the rounds, adding to the mystique and putting a spotlight on the prison. But there was one question that continued to get asked and go unanswered. Was the doctor still alive?

I leaned back into the conference room chair, my sight drifting to one of the station televisions. Tracy waved from the front. She saw how empty the station was, and then saw the press conference around the prison escape, saying as she opened the conference room door, "Guess we know where all the reporters went."

"For now, we do." She handed me a fresh cup of coffee, but I waved it away, my ears still ringing from drinking too much already. "Thanks. I'm sticking to some water for the time being."

"More for me," she said and forced a grin. It didn't last.

Couldn't last. But there was hope in it. Hope that I'd return the gesture. I wasn't feeling it though and went to the conference room monitor. She read through the doctor's handwritten letter, the picture coming from the US Marshal. "Anything about it stand out so far?"

Tracy went to the monitor, reading the doctor's letter aloud. When she was done, she said, "When you mentioned the doctor writing you, I thought that maybe he was behind the messages. But this isn't like those."

"He might not have written them, but the doctor knows something we don't know." I joined her, both of us standing the same, hands on our hips while dissecting the words. When she noticed, she lowered her arms and returned to the table for her cup.

I popped the cap off a whiteboard marker, the chemical odor mixing with coffee. "This part stands out." I began copying the letter, saying, "I need to smell the springtime and see the Sparrows in June."

"What about it bothers you?" Tracy asked, laptop in hand, typing. "Let's see if he copied it from any literature."

"That's possible," I said, tapping the board, seeing something but unsure what. "It's... it doesn't sound like him. And the word sparrows. Why did he capitalize the first letter?"

"It's not the beginning of a sentence," Tracy answered, head tilting like she was assessing a piece of artwork. "Other than starting a sentence, you'd only capitalize it if it's a name."

"That's it!" My voice boomed, Tracy braced, a question forming on her face. "It's a street intersection. June Avenue and Sparrow Lane, June and Sparrow. We pass it all the time."

"Let's see what's there," she said, typing fast, the second monitor coming alive with a map. Tracy drilled into it using a view which made it look like we were driving. "We're on Sparrow and coming up to June."

"Stop there," I demanded, seeing June Avenue end where it intersected with Sparrow Lane. There was a berm and ocean to the right and a strip-mall to the left. I leaned as if we were driving. "Can you turn so we can see those stores?"

"Not seeing much." Her mouth twisted while she followed along, the camera's view turning. "Casey, maybe it's just a coincidence?"

"Hold on a minute." The skin on my hands was washed bright with the screen's colors. I twirled fingers for Tracy to continue moving. With the map, it was like being there in person. The pictures showed trees still thick with summer greenery. They also showed a family suited for a swim, a couple with children crossing the intersection, the beach access on the other side. There was nothing else along the road, but across from the beach there was an office in the strip-mall, along with a computer repair store, a produce market, and a postal shop. The office looked vacant, the windows dingy, the inside hidden by thick, vertical shades, the baby-blue and mauve colors popular at one time. "I know it's a reach, but could you see who owns that property?"

"We could use the lease sign at the curb," she answered, clicking back and zooming out. I saw a grin forming and waited for the snide remark about my missing it. None came, the seriousness on her face deepening. "Pier W. Boécemo."

"The doctor?" I asked, the shock of it brief since he had lived here before his move to Philadelphia. Feeling uncertain of where this was going, I jotted down his name. I also wrote *Sparrow* and *June* to the side of his name. We stared at the whiteboard searching for something to pop out. It didn't. "We'll come back to that. How about his medical licenses? There was the one in Philly. Maybe he had a practice here, a license in North Carolina?"

"I think that's his office," she began to say, waving her

mouse over the dirty window. A moment later, she confirmed, "It is the same address. Casey, why would he send you there?"

"What if it has to do with the name he tried to negotiate?" The question countered who I thought the doctor was. After all, why help us? If he escaped then what was in it for him?

"This doesn't make any sense. Why help?" Tracy asked, shaking her head. I sensed the skepticism but had to explore every option.

I shook my head, thinking aloud, "He gains his freedom with the escape from prison. The name he was holding onto loses any power? Right?"

"Right. It won't help him. But why help us? You'd think criminals would have some kind of code?" Tracy asked, disbelief in her eyes. She flinched with alarm, saying, "What if it's a trap?"

I disagreed and shook my head. "A trap isn't his style—" I stopped mid-sentence, staring hard at the doctor's name on the whiteboard.

"What?" Tracy asked, joining me. "What do you see?"

"I see power."

"Huh? Power?" Tracy replied. "I don't get it."

But it was there. We'd seen it in the killer's messages. It was in the sign-off at the end. In large letters, I wrote it on the whiteboard. "Look at the killer's last line. I BECOME POWER."

"Yeah, *I am control. I become power*," Tracy confirmed, confused.

My legs grew weak with dread, the sinking feeling gaining as I crossed out each letter in the name, Pier W. Boécemo. "Look at what the doctor's name spells?" When I finished rearranging the letters, the words read, I BECOME POWER.

"Oh shit. His name is an anagram?" Tracy asked, the shock sticking as she double-checked my work. "I become power *is* Pier W. Boécemo," Tracy said, returning to her laptop. "Why would the killer write that in their message?"

"The killer probably didn't." With that statement, I felt a chill, recognizing the depth of the doctor's involvement, the name he tried to negotiate. "I think the doctor has been feeding that line to the killer for a long time."

TWENTY-SIX

I become power. It was the killer's sign-off. An anagram for the name, Pier W. Boécemo. The discovery of the wordplay bounced around my skull like a bullet. It ripped through the fabric of every consideration and plan and police procedure that had to be followed. The killer must have had a relationship with the doctor. But what was it? How long did they know each other? Was the killer a past patient? Maybe they were a prisoner? A cellmate who'd recently been released? If that was the case, what terrifying nuggets did the doctor plant in the man's brain? We couldn't answer any of these questions. Not yet.

Sparrow and June. It was a street intersection that was close to my apartment. What looked to have been innocuous dribbling written in the doctor's farewell letter, turned out to be far more. Why not put the name directly in the letter? I guess that would have been too simple. There was nothing about the doctor that was easy. He relished in the complexity of analysis and language, believing himself to be superior. This time, he'd made an exception and buried a clue in his words, leaving it shallow enough for me to find.

I couldn't help but think the doctor added the street intersection as a way of holding up to his side of our tit-for-tat exchange. My stomach rolled at the thought of what was said, a burn rising into the back of my throat. I'd told the doctor things that had never been told to anyone before. Not even to Jericho. These were my secrets. They were my darkest and ugliest secrets I was taking to my grave. It made me sick knowing he was a free man, that he knew them. I hated to admit it, but the doctor was the only person in the world who knew that a part of me had never healed. Perhaps the doctor was living the killer's mantra, *I am control*. Only, I no longer thought of it as the killer's. I think that part of the message was one hundred percent Dr. P.W. Boécemo. *I become power*.

There was a strip-mall at the intersection with a handful of stores and an office. I'd passed it often enough to instantly recall blurred images of tall orange and purple tube men swaying back and forth, their swishy motions powered by giant fans and the breezes spilling off the ocean. I'd see the air dancers at least once a month when one of the stores held a promotion. I didn't know which store it was, and it didn't matter either. The office at the end of the strip was the target of the investigation, promotion or no promotion. Until now, I'd never once given thought to what was behind the dingy glass door and the half-covered window.

The air inside my car was hot, a late season warm front touching the islands with the feel of summer. Stones popped beneath the car's tires, the strip-mall parking lot half full, patrons crossing in front of us. An old couple slowed to a stop, the woman bickering at the man while he pushed a grocery basket. I lowered my sun-visor and hit the flashing lights. Tracy lowered her visor too, the patrol lights installed in both, along with the front grill. Her finger hovered above the button for the siren, but I waved it off when the couple saw us and hurried out of the way.

A patrol car was already on site and parked in front of the

vacant office. Though incarcerated, the doctor continued to own the property and receive monthly rental payments. Life didn't stop entirely once he was sent to prison. Like anyone else, the doctor had to continue paying his bills and even file annual tax returns. For the strip-mall, he had the help of a property management company who took care of the details. That included meeting with us and accepting the search warrant I had in hand. It was the second signed by the judge in as many days, and this one felt right. It had to be right. Sherry's life depended on it.

"Benjamin Nueber. Detective White, is it?" a tall balding man asked. He had brown curly frizz above his ears and wore tight, wrinkled slacks of the same color. His dress shirt was tight as well, the buttons straining. He held out his hand to take mine, the motion made awkward when I shoved the warrant into his fingers. "Yes, of course. Formal and all."

"Yes, formal and all," I answered. "You've been the property manager for how long?"

"Oh—" he began to answer while gleaning the warrant before stuffing it into his shirt pocket. Leaning back to glance at the strip-mall, he continued. "Gotta be going on five years now."

"This corner office has never been occupied?" I pressed a hand against the office window while the property manager searched his phone. With the shades and the build-up of grime, it was impossible to see inside. "None?"

"Correct," he answered. "No occupancy since the property owner was arrested."

"Keys?" I asked, eager to enter. We had it within our rights to break open the door but didn't. As the property manager moved to insert a key, I saw the bottom of the door move. Instincts took over, my arm raised and guarding him against touching the door. "Seems we don't need the keys after all."

"There shouldn't be anyone inside," he said and shook his head, sunlight seeming to find the bald spot and glint a bright smile. Stammering, he continued. "The owner gave very specific instructions that this office was never to be rented or entered."

"Could be squatters," a patrol officer said, voice like a grunt. He had a hard expression, unfazed by the unlocked door. "We see it all the time."

"Well... well, you sh-should do something about that!" the property manager said, face turning red, eyes bugging.

"Sir, we'll take it from here," I assured him, motioning for him to return to his car. "We'll handle it."

"Yes, handle it." He stepped onto the pavement, peering over his shoulder, saying, "Thank you."

A snap, the safety on my holster released, my palm cradling the butt of my gun. Tracy did the same, the patrol officer asking, "You guys expecting more than squatters?"

A nod. "We are," I answered, the ease in his expression drained as another patrol car lined up behind his. We stood motionless until the additional patrol took to standing with us, a rallying of a small team ready to wage war with whatever was inside. "Eyes and ears open, let's enter single file and fan out."

"Yes, ma'am," the group said with hushed voices, the door opening toward us. The floor was carpeted beige, the fringes gray with dirt. A receiving counter lined the right side and had a desk with a chair tucked beneath, all of it covered in thick dust. There was an old computer on the desk along with a calendar mat which was dated more than six years ago. The room behind the counter must have been a waiting room, the kind you'd see at a doctor or dentist office. From the history, we knew the doctor had a practice here, but moved it to Philadelphia. Another doctor must have held their practice here as well, keeping the same setup.

"I remember these," Tracy commented as we entered the waiting area. Magazines were strewn across a table which was surrounded by chairs and couches, the furniture cheap. She picked up a *Highlights* magazine with the bold red and cartoony cover. Her eyes met mine, the moment of nostalgia vanishing. She lowered the magazine, muttering, "Got it."

"You guys check that room," I said, eyeing the magazines and pictures on the walls. Whatever office this was, it was intended for children. As I took to one of two corridors, a sneeze threatened, the stale air stirred. "I've got two rooms back here."

"Utility closet on this side," an officer said, relaying it to the other. In the dull silence, I heard the first adding, "Clear."

I flipped a wall switch, a blue spark popping, the overhead lights flicking on as I faced a closed door. "Tracy, do you hear that?"

"Is that buzzing?" she asked, our ears near the closed door. "Something in there is humming."

"Cover me." I didn't hesitate and drew my gun, palm sweaty and my chest tight. The door opened inward, my foot kicking the bottom when the doorknob's latch was free of the cam. It was cheap like the office furniture and rattled loose as it opened.

"Casey!" Tracy said in a near shout, the two of us running into the room. There was a table in the center, the body of a half-naked woman strapped down. Her face was partially covered, but not enough to hide the injuries, the swelling and black and blue marks. A powder blue sheet covered her lower body, her chest and face and arms naked, save for the medical tape and tubes. An old-fashioned steel hanger was stretched out of shape and used to hang a plastic bag from the drop ceiling, the liquid funneling into a tube buried in the woman's arm. Tape covered her eyes and stitched her mouth closed in a criss-cross, but the black hair and the style worn told us we'd found her. We'd found Sherry.

Tracy holstered her gun, trading it for her cellphone. She dialed it quickly, saying, "I need an ambulance at Sparrow and June, the corner office. The door is unlocked."

"Help me with these," I told Tracy and pinched the corner

of the medical tape as the officers filled the doorframe. I turned enough to ask, "See if there's a rear door!"

They were gone in a blink. Tracy was misty-eyed, her teary gaze fixed on the blue sheet, the possibility of a nightmare lying beneath it. "Casey?"

"I don't know," I answered, a cold tip of terror deep in the question of what was hidden. A stir. Sherry opened her swollen eyelids, remnants of the tape leaving a mark over them. She whimpered and moaned painfully as her eyes swam lazily while trying to focus. Half-lidded and confused, she'd been dosed heavily with a sedative.

"It's the IV! She's sedated." Tracy reached for the tube burrowed into Sherry's arm and pinched it off. But before she could remove it, I stopped her and looked at Sherry's legs, explaining, "We can't. Not yet. Not until we know."

"We need to look," she said, the color gone from her face. We turned briefly at the sound of a siren, the paramedics arriving soon.

"There was a rear door, it's been secured," a voice said from the room's doorframe. It had filled again with the officers, more of them joining now. The one with the hard expression nodded toward me, saying, "The office is clear. We're looking at the remaining stores."

"Show the paramedics in," Tracy pleaded, faint red and blue flashes shining on the officer's faces. They were gone, her attention returning to the IV tube and sheet. "Casey?"

I held my breath and bit down onto my lower lip and lifted the end of the sheet. All of Sherry's clothes had been removed. She'd been catheterized, another tube with fluid leading to a bag suspended beneath the table. In the back of my mind, I heard a prayer that she'd been asleep for the procedure, for all of it. I lifted some more, following her smooth skin from her middle to her thighs. "There's no tourniquets." Hopes rising, I whisked the sheet to the side with a flick of my wrist. Sherry's legs were intact. They were unharmed. Tracy saw it and removed the IV, blood pooling where the needle had been, a red pearl forming. I handed her a square patch of gauze from a nearby table. "Apply pressure—" Emotions took hold of me, and I couldn't finish. But Tracy knew what to do, and I went to Sherry, fingers caressing the side of her face. She was my responsibility, someone from my team. Dare I say, she was like one of my kids and I hurt that she was hurt.

"Sherry, we're here. You'll be okay."

TWENTY-SEVEN

The stink of hospital antiseptic made me cringe. But it was nothing compared to the sight of Sherry's face, the injuries she'd endured. It broke my heart. I felt her agony and hurt with a maddening anger. A contusion saddled the bridge of her nose, her nostrils stuffed with white cottony swabs that were tinged with blood. It was a break in the bone which was going to require surgery to fix. The injury blackened her eyes, causing them to swell severely. Another contusion was discovered on the back of her head, which was believed to have been the source of the attack. Nothing was found at the site of her vehicle. Nothing that could fill in the blanks of what happened to her three miles from the station. If Sherry was knocked unconscious, it's likely that her short-term memory of the attack was lost. I couldn't help but wonder if not being able to create the memory was a good thing. I think it was.

The paramedics wasted no time getting Sherry into the ambulance and to the hospital. I stayed with her, leaving behind a sizable team that was led by Tracy. The doctor's old office was a crime scene that had to be processed. It was where the killer had taken Ruby Evans before burying her at the beach. With

Tracy running the crime scene, every inch of that place was going to be inspected, a full forensic collection made. My leg vibrated with the updates being delivered to my phone every couple minutes.

Sherry's heart rate pinged steadily, a monitor showing the numbers of beats per minute. There was concern when we first arrived, her heart beating less than thirty times a minute. It was too low. The hospital doctors gave her something to counter the sedative, the effects of it finally showing results with a steady climb. It was up to forty-four beats per minute now. Although she wasn't out of the woods yet, the sedative that had been trickling into her body the last twenty-four hours was finally wearing off.

Her fingers were like icicles, and I couldn't help but cup her tiny hand in mine, rubbing as I blew a warm breath. I didn't know if it was going to help. And I knew she wasn't aware of it. Or aware of anything. I did it anyway, the gesture making me feel like I was doing something. Her eyes hadn't moved again since we found her. She'd closed them soon after and that's where they remained. The emergency room doctors said it could be a few hours, possibly another day or two before she was awake and alert.

Another buzz rifled over my thigh with new messages from my phone. A quick look at the screen showed one from Jericho, his asking how Sherry was doing. He asked how I was holding up as well, never missing a beat. I replied a thumbs-up and a heart emoji before moving to the second text which was from Tracy. There'd been no fingerprints found yet, and none of the doctor's patient files were found either. I thanked Tracy with a reply and opened a folder that was delivered to the hospital. Sherry stirred as though sensing the help I needed. I know her reaction was an unconscious one, but the folder contained pictures of five prisoners who'd recently been released from the prison where Dr. Boécemo was serving time. I think it was one of them who'd attacked her.

Two of the men were ruled out immediately. They were older and had been moved to a nursing facility on compassionate release. The other three prisoners were all released as part of a parole, two of them living in a halfway house, their records showing times at work, their leaving and arriving in their rooms. The last of the prisoners was Geoffrey Dolans, and after leaving prison, he returned to live with his parents. He'd also violated parole recently when pulled over in a traffic violation, traveling without permission from his parole officer. The matter was resolved, the infraction considered minor.

I glanced at the clock, the time stirring me to get ready to leave. There was a meeting scheduled at the station with a prison guard who'd spent time working on the doctor's cell block. He might be able to offer us some insights about the prisoners, particularly Geoffrey Dolans. There was an idea, an inkling of one that hadn't been shared yet. It first started with the US Marshal, what she said the day the doctor had escaped. What if all of this was part of the doctor's contingency plan to gain leverage?

The timing was right. Ruby Evans was abducted before the doctor's parole hearing. When his freedom was denied, the first message arrived to set up her murder. It pained me terribly to think it, but would Ruby Evans be alive today if I hadn't destroyed the doctor's parole hearing? Had I underestimated who he was? That it was in him to orchestrate a plan with such depth and deviousness? These were the questions that would haunt me. And these were the questions I might never get answered.

Leverage was a powerful negotiator. There was a state-wide panic, the press and public all believing we had a killer selecting victims and executing them. What if it was staged to look like a serial killer so the doctor could offer me a name in exchange for my cooperation? When that didn't work, he went through with his escape. Call it his contingency plan to an original contingency plan which went into motion when he saw that I'd never cooperate in the appeal.

Sherry stirred and groaned painfully. I pinched her fingers, my legs trembling as I hovered close enough for her to see my face. One eyelid opened. It was a mere slit, the brightness making her shut it again. "Hang on, let me turn off the lights." I jumped to where the light switch was and smacked it.

"Thank you," she said, voice a groggy whisper. "My head hurts."

"I know it does." I held her hand again and felt the pain for her in my chest. "It's going to hurt for a little while."

"Wha-what happened?" she asked, raising her arms and eyeing the tubes attached to her. Tears rolled down the side of her face as she gently touched one cheek. She jerked her hand back, unable to recognize herself. "Casey?"

"You were attacked," I said, speaking directly. "You were on your way to the station—"

"I got pulled over," she interrupted. There was shock and awe in her voice. "It wasn't a police car though. It was unmarked."

"We believe it was the same person who abducted Ruby Evans."

With mention of the name, Sherry jolted sideways, her head rolling as she gagged and heaved. It was a reaction to the drugs, the doctor warning us. A nurse joined to help, Sherry clutching a bag and pressing it against her mouth. "My legs?" she managed to ask. She looked deep into my eyes, the fright on her face like a nightmare. "Casey?"

I gripped her hand in mine, assuring her, "Sherry, you're okay."

She half nodded, eyes drifting again. I thought she was going to fall back and close them to sleep the drugs out of her system, but she didn't. Instead, Sherry reached for the picture of a prisoner, pinching the corner of it and dragging it across the hospital sheet. "I know him."

"How do you know him, Sherry?" I asked, voice rigid as I texted Tracy, telling her to meet me at the station. "Did you see this man when you were pulled over?"

She nodded. "Uh-huh." Sherry carefully touched her arm where the IV had been. She imagined it there and looked up at a homemade IV bag which wasn't there. "He was talking to himself. He kept saying stuff over and over."

"What did he say?"

"He kept talking about the doctor's work. Kind of reciting it —" When her voice wavered, the nurse gave me a look that I knew. I held up my hand, mouthing, *a minute more please* while Sherry continued. "It sounded like medical stuff. Instructions."

"He was saying the instructions?" I repeated. The nurse motioned to the door, the sliver of eye contact I'd made with Sherry fading. She was asleep again. "Sherry, get some rest."

TWENTY-EIGHT

The station was filling with reporters again. Long camera lenses aimed, lights on, and fluffy-covered microphones swaying on the ends of long poles. With Sherry's abduction and rescue, the news crews shifted away from the doctor's prison escape to follow the latest story. The reporters didn't know my theory about the doctor yet. That he was the proverbial OZ pulling strings to create a serial killer and build a heart-stopping panic. All to ensure winning a negotiation. Only problem, I wasn't willing to negotiate and now he was a fugitive.

I had no proof of any of this, but it was the strongest hunch I'd ever had. The station's front gate clapped shut as Sherry's name and face flashed on the station monitors. It was a picture of her I didn't recognize. In it, her black hair was longer and nearly reached her shoulders. She wore a nose piercing I'd never seen and had heavier makeup around her eyes, thick mascara, a noir black color. From the clothes, I thought it might be a school picture, maybe from college.

The press questions were ignored, the voices urging me to move faster. I brushed aside the normal courtesies as I made my way to the conference room. Alice hurried alongside me, her shorter legs swishing while she tried to keep up. From the corner of my eye, I saw the worry on her face. I stopped at my desk to put an arm across her shoulders and turned her away from prying eyes. "She's going to be okay."

"Oh thank God!" she cried, her head dipping forward while she grabbed her chest. Tears slid down her round cheeks. Her lips quivered as she tried to continue. "I was so afraid—"

"We got her in time," I assured Alice, trying to bring comfort. But there was no comfort to bring. This was an attack on one of our own and the impact of it was going to be significant. Alice inched closer, the top of her head beneath my chin, arms circling my middle in a hug. I reciprocated with a squeeze, saying, "We got her."

When she was ready, Alice dried her eyes and tilted her head toward the conference room. "The prison guard. I made sure he came dressed in plain clothes."

I peered through the conference room window to see the man sitting at the table, steam rising from a cup of coffee. He had a dark complexion and wore bland-colored business casual clothes, the pants and shirt giving him a look like someone who could have worked here. The press never took notice. "Thank you, Alice."

"That's the guard from the prison?" Tracy asked, breathless, racing to unpack her gear.

"It is," I replied, motioning to the reporters, urging Alice to return.

Alice nodded, leaving us. "I'll make sure they're not a bother."

When she was gone, I asked Tracy, "Tell me you guys found something at the office."

She lowered her head, not wanting to disappoint. "Some fingerprints and hairs." Lips stretched tight, she added, "They appear to be from Sherry and the first victim though."

"Process them quick. Could be a partial print that the killer overlooked?"

"Already on it," she replied. "Other than those, there wasn't anything definitive."

"How about the supplies?" I asked, referring to the instruments used. The medical equipment.

"On that too," she answered with a hesitation. "But it looks to be all over the counter. Like the killer pieced the stuff together."

"Well, stay on it," I told her. Holding up the folder with the recent prison release. "Join me?"

"Sure thing," she said, following. "Sherry?"

"She's better. Her parents are with her." I opened the conference room door, a cushion of air passing over my face. "They said that once she's more alert, she'll be able to go home."

Tracy sighed with relief. "I'm going to see her first chance."

The guard stood to greet us, his shoulders broad, his build substantial. "Ma'am," he said, wiping the palms of his hands against his pants. His eyes darted nervously between me and Tracy. "Name is Chet Williams, the prison guard you spoke to."

"Detective Casey White." I extended my hand, his fingers covering my hand like an oven mitt. I wasn't a small person but felt tiny in the guard's presence. He towered over us, his hulking stature hidden when sitting. Looking up, I said, "Call me Casey. And this is Tracy Fields."

"Sir," she said, eyes huge. "Guess none of the prisoners ever bothered you, huh."

He chuckled with a suave grin, answering, "You'd be surprised how many try. It's like a game to them."

"They do like to play games, don't they?" I invited him to sit as we took to the chairs on the opposite side of him. "When you've got nothing to do except burn time, I guess you'll try just about anything."

"Don't I know it," he replied. "Got fifteen years of battle scars to show for it too."

"The doctor." With the mention of his name, the casual talk exited the room like a stiff wind. I opened the folder and took an eight by ten glossy from it, placing it face up. It was the doctor's mugshot, the guard leaning onto his elbows. Next to it, I placed the mugshots of the recently released prisoners, setting the two older men aside. "These two have been moved to a nursing facility."

"I helped with their move," he said, tapping the picture closest to him. He pressed the corner, the photograph scraping the table as he dragged it closer. He took the second picture next, saying, "Both of them were lifers, older than old by the time I was on their block. They were a few cells away from the doctor, but I never seen them pay him any mind."

"How about these three?" I asked, showing him the last of the recently released. "They were all on the same cell block too."

The corner of his mouth rose as he regarded each of the pictures, doubt forming in a scowl. He glanced up at us briefly, saying, "The doctor mostly kept to himself. Ya know."

I could feel the disappointment like it was a weight around my neck. It lifted subtly when I saw recognition on his face. "This one." The guard spun one of the pictures around, a thick finger covering most of the face. "Geoffrey something."

"What do you recall about—" I began to say, flipping the picture over where we'd added the profiles. "Geoffrey Dolans."

"He was an odd cat. But most of them are," he said, scratching at his jaw. "I mean if they're in that place, they ain't right if you catch my drift."

"I catch your drift," I said agreeably, nudging the picture, needing more.

"A few months before he was going to be released, I'd seen him coming and going from the doctor's cell. It wasn't uncommon though. Prisoners got their own social thing that goes on if you get what I'm saying. We mostly look away since it helps keep the peace."

"Did the doctor keep company with any other prisoners?" Tracy asked.

"Hmm." The guard mulled over the questions, his gaze lifting to stare above us. "None like that. It could be why I was noticing it."

"How long ago did the visits to the doctor's cell begin?" I asked, texting Alice to help get the status of the APB we'd issued. Sherry had identified Geoffrey Dolans earlier, which was all we needed. When the guard didn't answer, I added, "A ballpark? Six months? A year?"

"Got to be more than six months," he finally said. "Not much more though."

"And you've no idea what they were doing in the doctor's cell?" Tracy asked, typing, her laptop lid shaking. "Sex? Talking?"

The guard shook his head again and reached to scratch at his chin, the habit a nervous one. "Job was mostly about keeping the peace. If it was quiet, it was good."

Alice replied she was on it. I put my phone down, asking, "An odd cat? What was it about Geoffrey Dolans that stood out?"

The guard thought over my question, a smiling frown forming. "Cat was always talking to himself. Nonstop, you know? The other prisoners got to calling him Mumbles on account it was all the time."

"Mumbles," I said to Tracy. "Sherry said the man who took her kept reciting something she thought sounded like instructions."

"Instructions?" Tracy asked.

"What if they included medical terms?" I said, suggesting an idea. I flipped over the picture of Geoffrey Dolans which listed his priors of theft and assault. It was the assault of a store owner that landed him in prison for six years, a robbery gone wrong. "This isn't the profile of a killer."

"Detective, with all due respect, prison changes a person," the guard warned, his voice edgy. He sat up and re-turned the picture to show Geoffrey Dolans's face. "I've seen a man who was sentenced for cybercrimes bite another man's ear clean off. I think they were fighting over a pudding cup."

"That's fair," I commented, my mind fixing on what took place in the doctor's cell. I slid my card across the table, telling the guard, "Thank you for coming in. If you can think of anything else, don't hesitate to call me."

His brow bounced with surprise, chair wheels squealing when he stood. "Yes, ma'am, of course."

We walked him out of the conference room, Tracy taking him through the kitchenette to the small hallway where there was a utility and storage closet. It was the rear door that led to the other side of the station. The guard caught on, the commotion with the reporters continuing.

Where was Geoffrey Dolans? With Sherry's identifying him and the guard having seen the prisoner with the doctor, he'd quickly become the only person we wanted to speak to. A text message buzzed against my leg, Tracy returning to enter my cubicle and take a lean against my desk. "Got something?" she asked, nudging her chin toward my phone.

"It's Sherry. I mean, it's from her mother." The strength in me vanished like the smell of flowers in a stiff breeze. Gone. I took hold of my chair and dropped into it. "Sherry's mom says they're taking her home today."

Tracy's face was cramped with concern, relief easing the hard look. She grabbed her heart, saying, "Oh, it's good news. For a moment I thought something bad happened."

I hoisted my phone higher, its weight feeling like a mountain. "That was the first text message."

Concern returned with a grimace, Tracy asking, "What's the second one?"

"It's a text direct from Sherry." My insides felt unsteady, nose stinging as I fought the emotion. I cleared my throat, telling Tracy, "It's her resignation. She's going home with her parents and won't be coming back."

TWENTY-NINE

We had a sighting. The APB turning up the location of Geoffrey Dolans. It was daybreak when the ex-convict's shift supervisor called the station to tell us Dolans had clocked in for the morning shift. Sunlight bled into our eyes as we followed a patrol, Tracy tending to the collection of paperwork which was finalized, a warrant for the man's arrest signed and delivered. Sherry's account of who took her was more than enough. I rammed the shifter into park, hands itching to put things into motion. Tracy exited the car, joining me as we both sleeved our arms with bulletproof vests and jackets, patrol officers joining.

The parking lot was made of stone and gravel, parts of it bare, some filled with muddy puddles. The building where Geoffrey Dolans worked was a rusty, pale blue with a tin roof and large doors that were open, six trucks backed into it. I pinched my nose, our suspect's workplace a seafood processing plant, the time of year busy with fresh catches delivered daily. A row of green and brown dumpsters lined the edge of the property, some filled, the tops slick, a stink clinging. Men and women wandered back and forth, dressed in rubber aprons, hands and feet covered with the same thick material.

I knew the shift supervisor immediately. Not just because he was the one approaching. But because he was the only one who didn't have a drop of blood on him. While he wore thick rubber boots, the rest of his clothes were meant for work behind a desk. He tipped his head, greeting me, pointing toward the rear of the building. "I've got Dolans working in the back where they do the cleaning."

"Toward the back," I repeated, motioning for him to remain outside. One by one, we directed workers to leave the plant as we ascended, trading places with them. All had the same white coveralls, rubber squelching. They had caps on their heads, protective eyewear, their sleeves a clear-blue plastic from wrist to elbow. It was the glint of light against a blade that tipped the fire in my gut, setting it aflame. This was a fish processing plant after all, and in their thickly gloved hands, they carried sharp knives that could cut us down with a single swing. When a woman looked at my sidearm, hand cradling the butt of it, I tipped my head at the exit, "Everyone outside."

"Salida," Tracy said to one of the workers. They were speaking in Spanish, Tracy translating. "Salida!"

We walked from the front to the back, shoulder to shoulder, no more than a few arms lengths from one another. From me to Tracy to the officers, we covered the width of the plant, passing the tables and conveyor belts, the smell of fish gaining as we moved deeper. I heard the unmistakable sound of metal on stone, a blade being sharpened as the suspect came into view. I raised my gun, Tracy and the officers doing the same. "Geoffrey Dolans, you are under the arrest for the abduction and assault of Sherry Levin."

"Wha—" he began to ask, a pair of green eyes locking on mine. He looked at Tracy next, and then the officers surrounding the area.

Geoffrey Dolans was a short man with blond hair poking out from beneath a white cap. The rubber clothes hung slack from his thin frame, shoulders narrow. Every inch of him was soiled by the work he'd been doing. The clear shield protecting his face was littered with specks of blood and pieces of fish, some of it glistening.

"Geoffrey Dolans!" I demanded, seeing that he wasn't listening. Our focus was trained on the eight-inch filet knife in his right hand. I widened my stance, pivoting weight to my back foot, and braced for the worst with the tip of the barrel solidly aimed. Geoffrey was left-handed and swirled the knife, a beam of light rushing over Tracy and the officers. His right hand was covered in a protective glove, the yarn made of steel. When he moved abruptly, I saw an officer flinch, the motion making me grit my teeth. "Geoffrey! Put down the knife before anyone gets hurt."

He shook his face, lips moving. I couldn't hear what he was saying, his words swallowed by the low whir of machinery. Geoffrey's gaze shifted to the fish in front of him, blood oozing where he'd been working. The filet glove dropped from his hand and landed with a plunk. He dipped the tip of his finger into the running water, disrupting a thread of wispy blood, his lips moving nonstop. He raised the protective shield enough for us to see his face, speaking in an endless mumble. His words remained a mystery, but I heard the tone of his voice change and it told me all I needed to know. I knew it wasn't us who were in danger. Geoffrey was a danger to himself.

Light flashed against the knife, the blade rising and twisting inward. I dove, my free arm stretching across his front to block the attempt he was making on his own life. We collapsed against the floor, metal clanking against the concrete. Tracy was next to me, her foot on Geoffrey's wrist while she wrestled the knife out of his fingers. I remained straddled on top of him, breathing heavy while I holstered my gun. When my focus returned to mirandize him, there were bloody drops on his pale skin, blooming like flowers. Thick and bright, I searched his neck and chest and face, finding no injuries. The bleeding continued, his eyes fixing on my arm, the backside of it peeled open. Just how sharp are those knives? I never felt a thing.

"You know what that means?" I asked as Tracy tied off the bleeding and officers took the suspect into custody. Tracy helped me up, both of us staring at the table of fish and guts.

She shook her face, grimacing. "No, I don't know what that means."

"Tetanus shots. Painful things." I squeezed my arm like there was no tomorrow. Pain rifled into my fingers, and I stomped the floor, blood and water splashing. "Shit that really hurts."

"Let's get that cleaned," Tracy said, painting on a smile. It lacked heart, the disgust of fish guts bothering her. She followed my stare as officers removed the suspect. Sensing what I really wanted to do, Tracy added, "He'll be at the station when you're bandaged up."

"Make sure!" I told her, holding my arm, blood seeping through my fingers. "Reach out to Alice for me, I want him in a holding—"

"Casey!" Tracy said, eyes huge. I was rambling from the adrenaline and apprehension and injury, the three together making a marvelous stew. "I got it handled. Right now, I need to handle you."

"Fair enough," I told her and let her take over. By midday, we'd have Geoffrey Dolans in an interview room, my brain full of questions. I leaned over, face near Tracy's. "Thank you."

It was a few hours before I was face to face with Geoffrey Dolans again. The stitches in my arm beginning to throb where a filet knife had given me a kiss. On paper, it was an assault, but it hadn't been intentional. The suspect was aiming for his own throat when I lunged, my arm reaching to block him just in time.

The station's interview room was roasting with heat, the door left open but guarded. Tracy sat next to me, both of us across from Geoffrey Dolans, who looked completely different than he had earlier at the fish processing place. His eyes were sunken deep, cheekbones high, teeth yellowing, the gaunt look making me wonder if he'd been eating. Or was it something else? Did the doctor plant a thought of death in the man's head? Brainwashing him to commit these acts and then die?

"You like to put messages in bottles?" I asked him, finding a place to start. There were so many to choose from. He moved, rattling the chains attached to his ankles and wrists. We'd secured him to the interview room table, looping the links to the metal surface before reattaching it to his handcuffs. He wasn't going anywhere for the moment. He also wasn't going to be a threat to himself or to us. When we were done, Geoffrey Dolans would be reprimanded to a psychiatric facility for evaluation. "Geoffrey? Can you hear me?"

"Messages," he answered. It was a single spoken word while his lips continued to move, his breathing stuttered by a continuous whispering. He stopped muttering, confidence appearing on his face as his eyes locked with mine. More than that, it was a coherence we hadn't seen yet. "Yes. I put the messages in the bottles."

I opened his file, his unblinking gaze unnerving. "Geoffrey, you're a seasoned thief. Been around a minute and all," I began to say, becoming annoyed by the stare as he continued saying a lot of nothing. I put a picture of a convenience store in front of him. It was the place he'd robbed which led to his sentencing and incarceration. Next to it, I put a picture of Ruby Evans, one of the crime-scene photographs showing her legs amputated. At best, he had a ninth-grade education. How was he able to perform a surgical procedure and keep the victim alive? His eyes remained unfocused, and his lips kept moving. "Explain to us when you graduated from robbery to murder?"

The muttering stopped, the confidence returning. This time, there was a grin. A subtle sneer. "It was a release." He shook his head, adding, "It's not murder if I'm helping them."

"Helping them?" Tracy said, asking aloud as she wrote down his response.

His eyes shifted to her, his lips continuing to move without sound. I couldn't read lips but began to think that Geoffrey was reciting something. But what?

"A couple more questions," I said, urging him to return his focus to me.

Next to the picture with the amputations, I added a photograph of the doctor. Geoffrey Dolans froze. He stopped mumbling. He stopped blinking. He may have even stopped breathing.

"Do you recognize this man?"

"Pier," Geoffrey answered, jaw hanging open. He shut it long enough to look at me and say, "I can hear him, you know."

"Hear him?" Tracy questioned. "How so?"

Chains moving, Geoffrey craned his neck enough to tap his fingers against his skull. "Inside my head. That's where he tells me things. Tells me what to do."

"Is he speaking to you now?" I asked, staying with the line of questions. I didn't want to lose the momentum. Geoffrey began to nod, his jaw hanging loose again. The confidence I'd seen moments before seemed to vanish. It was replaced by someone who was more vulnerable, less coherent. "Geoffrey, can you tell me what he's saying to you?"

"Pier is telling me I should be at work when I'm not doing the other stuff," he replied, gaze drifting. "It's what I'm here to do. It's my mission to release them."

"Mission to release them?" Tracy asked. "The do— I mean, Pier gave you the mission?"

"Work and therapy," he answered her. He lifted his left hand, pointing his index finger. "Just Pier's therapy though."

"Was Ruby Evans Pier's therapy?" The interview room was setup to record everything. Faces. Voices. It might have even been setup to record our heart rates and how fast we were breathing. Both of those were climbing fast, sweat building as we gained ground and closed in on some answers.

"The messages," he said with a nod, the green in his eyes deep. "The messages were for you, Detective."

"I know." The confidence returned to his voice as if to frighten me. I didn't scare easily though and leaned forward, my middle pressing against the table. "Were they from him? Were they from Pier?"

"Uh-uh." He flinched slightly at the question and frowned. "They were from the doctor."

Confusion, my knee bouncing beneath the table. I nudged the picture of the doctor, asking, "Who is this?"

"That's Pier," Geoffrey answered, annoyed. "I told you that already."

"Geoffrey? What does the doctor look like?" Tracy asked. She added two more pictures of the doctor. One from when he was a practicing psychiatrist. Another was from his most recent mugshot. "Do these men look familiar?"

"They're both Pier," Geoffrey answered, agitation building. "Why are you asking me these things?"

The itch of worry climbed up my spine. To Geoffrey Dolans, it was like the doctor and Pier were different people. We'd rattled him with the question, any confidences washing away. There were tears in his eyes, his demeanor returning to someone who was easily led, someone impressionable. What went on in the doctor's cell? "Geoffrey, do you know what the doctor looks like?"

"No! Never!" Geoffrey answered in a near shout. "The doctor only talks to me when I can't see him."

"When you can't see him?" Tracy asked, the confusion shared.

Geoffrey worked against the chains, moving closer as if he were telling a secret. "The doctor makes the drawings appear."

"What kind of drawings?" I asked him, thinking through the inventory of the doctor's cell. We'd found no drawings. Not a single one. Geoffrey lowered his head like a shy boy who'd been blown a kiss. He lifted his head, lips moving fast again. Did we lose him? I clapped the top of the steel. "Geoffrey?"

"I can show you," he answered. When he lifted his arms, dragging the chains, he added, "But not with these."

"Officers," I requested, two of them entering. They went to Geoffrey's side. "Remove the chains."

"Detective?" One of them asked as Geoffrey stood. He barely reached the nape of the officer's neck. "Yes, ma'am."

When the chains fell to the floor, Geoffrey lowered his pants and lifted his shirt. The move was swift and was made without warning, his gaze drifting toward the ceiling while we stared in shock. He wore nothing beneath the light brown jumpsuit, his groin and legs and belly completely shaved. Geoffrey Dolans was bone-skinny, his skin stretched tightly around a skeleton. And on the surface of his skin, we saw the drawings he referred to. Hundreds, maybe thousands of tiny cuts were made, thinly drawn figures with words grouped to make up sentences. All of it was upside down and backward so he could read them. Words stood prominently above the drawings, the letters carved boldly and broad. It read, I AM CONTROL. I BECOME POWER. What exactly happened inside the doctor's cell?

"Casey?" Tracy said with a gasp. "That's called a skin carving. It's a kind of tattooing."

"Only, instead of ink, the art is made with thin cuts." I moved around the table and was unable to take my eyes from what he was showing us.

"It's the medical procedure to perform an amputation,"

Tracy said. She had a camera in one hand and handed one of the officers a piece of paper. The officer understood and covered the suspect's genitals, Tracy snapping more pictures. "I think it's what he's been saying to himself over and over."

"Instructions," I commented.

Geoffrey's gaze was fixed on the ceiling lights, a sickening grin on his face. It was like he was showing off the work. Showing it proudly.

"Geoffrey, who did this to you?"

Slowly, he lowered his head until his focus returned to us. "The doctor did this for me. He made it. That way, I could never forget."

EPILOGUE

While the killer's motive remained unclear, what was clear was that Geoffrey Dolans was impressionable and had been influenced by the doctor. By now, the mayor and chief and district attorney were aware of my theory, that the doctor was the mastermind behind it all. To the finest of details in selecting the victims, the bottles and writing the messages, it came from the doctor and was directed at me. Why? Because I put him in prison, and I'd kept him there. Little did I know, I'd only been a piece in his game, a pawn he moved around the board to help gain his freedom. There was no serial killer. There never was. Not like the press had portrayed. It was all the doctor's doing, but I had only my theory and nothing else to back it up. To the Outer Banks, they had their killer in custody, the threat of additional murders ceasing.

There might never be a trial though. No courtrooms. No attorneys. No jury of twelve men and women to listen to our testimony and deliver a verdict of guilt. The district attorney had everything needed to file charges against Geoffrey Dolans. That included the murder of Ruby Evans and the abduction and assault on Sherry Levin. After we interviewed him, Geoffrey Dolans was turned over to the state for psychological evaluation. It was the skin carvings, the medical instructions made permanent on his body. These were only the tip of the iceberg in terms of what a trial might look like. From the district attorney, she knew exactly how a defendant's lawyer would tackle the charges. They'd put Geoffrey Dolans on the stand and ask about Dr. P.W. Boécemo. They'd ask about the man Geoffrey knew as Pier and who the doctor was. Next, they'd paint a picture of how Geoffrey Dolans was an instrument and nothing more. They'd paint a picture that showed the doctor as being the true killer. And as much as I hated to admit it, it was exactly what I believed happened. Convincing a jury could be impossible.

Was it a disappointment? Absolutely. One hundred percent. The gut-wrenching kind that left me feeling sick. Ruby Evans was dead, and her mother would never see justice for her daughter's senseless murder. We'd also lost one of our own. Sherry was gone. The only good news in all this was that we could breathe again. That was true for all the Outer Banks. With Geoffrey Dolans in custody, there were no more bottles washing up on shore. No messages inside them with cryptic riddles to decipher. Our station emptied. The mayor and the chief were satisfied. And there was even a contented look returning to Alice's face.

I'd kept tabs on Sherry's recovery which wasn't going that well. From her mother, I'd learned Sherry was physically well enough to leave the house and take short walks, and even drive some. While the physical damages were healing and would have no lasting impact on her life, it was the mental anguish that was lasting. Geoffrey Dolans broke something in her mind. There were nightmares and moments of confusion, her mother describing how Sherry would startle at the smallest of sounds. Time takes time. It heals. But sadly, it might never heal all things.

Shortly after Geoffrey Dolans's custody was transferred, I reached out to Sherry. I wasn't sure of what I'd hoped to accomplish but I wanted to talk. Question was, would she even listen to me after what she'd gone through? My heart leapt when she took the call, her mother answering initially. When I heard Sherry's voice, I melted a little, a flutter of nerves making the call a difficult one. The conversation was mostly one-sided though. The kind where I did all the talking and heard the occasional *uh-huh* and *I understand*. I gave her my best speech about the good we could do together as a team, and how the team needed her. Before she hung up the phone, Sherry thanked me for the call as I said goodbye. I sat alone with my thoughts a moment, the sound of her voice still in my head. I'd no idea what the future of our team looked like, but sadly, I didn't think Sherry was going to be a part of it.

As for futures, there was a courtroom in mine. Not just mine. It was in Jericho's and Thomas's and Tabitha's too.

"Please rise," I heard the court bailiff begin to say. The shuffle of bodies standing mixed with his words as he went on to say, "The court is now in session for the Honorable Judge, Darcy Walsh."

"Here we go," Jericho said, leaning close to my ear. He smelled as good as he looked, the suit and his cleanly shaven face a good distraction. Cheryl Smithson was dressed for court, looking as professional as I'd ever seen her. I offered a hand which she politely brushed aside, proudly standing with the help of her cane. All eyes shifted to the judge as she made her way to her seat. An older woman with heavy makeup and red hair spun into a bun atop her head. Her hands were filled with paperwork, her eyes fixed on her chair as her black robe hugged the floor with each step. She glanced out at us once, eyes remaining cold and distant until she saw the children. There was a flicker, a twinkle that turned into a smile as she gave them a wave. They had that way with people, the judge's face remaining warm.

"You may be seated," the bailiff announced, bodies shuffling, benches groaning.

I'd had butterflies before, but nothing like this. Nervous sweat threatened while my fingers and toes were like ice. If I had to open my mouth and speak, I was certain my jaw would erupt in a loud chatter. Jericho gently gripped the small of my back, his body sliding as he moved closer. "You okay?"

"A little scared," I whispered, glancing at him, and then looking again. I wasn't used to the look, his hair swept back and his skin smooth. There wasn't a whisker to be found, his rugged styled Indiana Jones look was gone.

"Aren't you?" I asked, lightly poking his side.

His brow furrowed, answering, "Of course I am." He glanced over at Ms. Welts, adding, "A little birdie told me there'll only be a few questions. A formality."

"A little birdie?" I asked, his having an endless list of contacts in the Outer Banks and some of the mainland. He reached for Tabitha's head, playfully flicking one of her ponytails. She made a funny face at him and swatted the back of his hand. "Am I going to have to separate you two?"

"Never," Jericho answered. And it was the right answer. This was the family court date we'd been waiting for.

"Agreed," I told him, heart ready to burst. "Never."

Behind me, I found Tracy and Samantha, along with Derek. They had smiles pasted on their faces, Tracy's dimples deep. She reached out to take my hand, tears gliding down her cheeks as I squeezed her fingers. Sherry was nowhere to be seen.

Ms. Welts was with us today too and wearing a happy grin which took me by surprise. It was a stark contrast from the meeting we'd had with her just days earlier. I guess we made a positive enough impact to win her favor, a late email telling us that she'd forwarded her foster adoption recommendation. I suppose if she hadn't put in the recommendation, she wouldn't have been here today. Near the back of the courtroom, the rows were filled with the faces from the station, the sight of them warming me. I saw patrol officers and the station's office staff. The chief and district attorney were there as well, standing alongside the mayor who gave us a thumbs-up while working her phone. There were so many joining us that when I saw Alice's smiling face, it left me wondering who was working at the station. I don't think it mattered. The station could wait.

In a row of chairs nearest us, I saw a lanky reporter with a puff of red-frizzy hair. He sat with a camera technician, the two documenting the proceeding, which was open to the public. I recognized the reporter from my first year in the Outer Banks. Back then, he looked like he was still in school. He'd grown a lot since and had moved on from reporting to being a documentarian and host of a popular podcast. One was about the children's rescue at sea and about our fostering them. It was the *Two Lost Souls* story which had gone viral, much of the nation knowing us briefly. The fostering and adoption were going to be his follow-up, a conclusion, an epilogue to a fairy-tale story that would see us become a family.

"Raise your right hands," the bailiff asked. We stood up alone in the court, all eyes on us as Thomas and Tabitha stood too. The bailiff instructed each of us to follow his lead; a burly man, he came over to show Thomas and Tabitha what to do, the judge smiling at the interaction. When we were ready, he recited the words to finish being sworn in. "You may be seated."

I remained standing with Jericho, Cheryl urging me to speak. "Casey White, your honor," I said, introducing myself to the court and the judge.

Jericho took a deep breath and said without hesitation, "Jericho Flynn, your honor."

"Ms. White and Mr. Flynn are here today to petition the court in the foster adoption of Thomas and Tabitha Roth,"

Cheryl said, voice booming. She shuffled a sheet of paper over another, turning to face us, and asked, "Ms. White and Mr. Flynn, for the court, would you confirm your intention to give Thomas and Tabitha Roth a loving home."

My nose stung as I fought tears, Jericho clutching my hand, his eyes wet too. We brought Thomas and Tabitha to stand with us and together, we replied, "It is."

Cheryl continued to speak on our behalf, answering the judge's questions, having us answer as well. These were short and simple and a formality for the judge to complete the adoption, yet, they were monumental, our lives changing forever. We did as Cheryl had instructed, which was to limit what we said, and to speak only when spoken to. It was hard keeping quiet at times, but I just kept looking at Jericho and Thomas and Tabitha, my appetite for them seemingly insatiable. The air in the courtroom was electric, charged with anticipation, the hairs on my arms rising as each question was asked and answered. There was nothing contentious or argumentative. Nothing at all like the meeting we had with children services.

Maybe it wasn't nerves that I'd been feeling at all. I think it was a buzz of happiness. That's the look I saw on Jericho's face too. Happiness. There was a touch of something magical about it all too. I held my breath when the judge lifted her pen, the tip of it hovering above the decree of adoption signature line. When I saw the end of the pen go into motion, my insides just about burst. I had to sit, no, fall was more like it, my knees striking the floor while I wrapped my arms around Thomas and Tabitha. I felt their little souls touch my heart and melt every concern and reservation that I'd ever had. This was our family.

As she continued signing, the judge declared, "With such a large audience, it's the opinion of this court to be diligent and proceed in granting the joint adoption of Thomas and Tabitha Roth to Casey White and Jericho Flynn."

We were a family, and the emotion of it filled my soul. I

couldn't stop hugging Thomas and Tabitha, the two of them
laughing giddily, joining in the cheers. I had to tear myself away
from them and plant a kiss on Jericho's lips, his arms and large
hands lifting me off my feet briefly before he picked up the children. The judge joined us, her eyes weepy as she squeezed Jericho's arm, saying, "I'm so very happy for you." Of course, she
knew him. Jericho knew everyone. She took hold of my hand
next, "And you too, the both of you."

"Pictures! Pictures!" I heard Tracy yelling, shoes stomping
as she ran to join us. She stopped abruptly, her eyes huge with
shock. "Oh wow! I just realized, I've got a baby brother and
sister."

"An instant babysitter," the judge laughed.

White light streaked across the front of the courtroom and
put green and yellow blobs in my view, the rush of footsteps
joining us as the first dozen of a million photographs were
taken. But throughout the celebratory mayhem, I saw the face. I
saw it staring back at me. It was the doctor. He was dressed in
all black, from the hat on his head to the shoes on his feet. Only
the pale skin of his face showed in contrast, the weight loss
appearing to be ending, his cheeks filling out.

"Jericho!" I said and gripped his arm hard enough to make
his smile disappear. "The doctor!"

"What's that?" he asked, moving closer, his ear near my
mouth. I looked back to find the courtroom doors closed, the
doctor just an afterimage like a ghost. But in my head, I was
certain there'd been a swift motion, a blur of him glancing back
and tipping his hat with that sinister grin of his appearing
beneath his cold eyes. "Where?"

"Over there!" I answered. But it was too late and I wasn't
certain if was him that I saw. Whoever it was that I saw was
already gone. For a second, I thought to ditch my heels and take
chase, but even if it was him, he would have thought of every
move like it was a game of chess. In my gut, I knew that by the

time I got to the doors, there'd be no sign of the doctor. "Never mind."

"You okay?" Jericho asked.

"Yeah, sure, I'm great," I assured him and rejoined the celebration. After all, we were two minutes into beginning a new life together. But down deep, I knew that we wouldn't be starting it alone.

A LETTER FROM B.R. SPANGLER

Thank you so much for reading *Her Last Hour*, Detective Casey White book 11. If you did enjoy it, and want to keep up to date with all my latest releases, just sign up at the following link. Your email address will never be shared and you can unsubscribe at any time.

www.bookouture.com/br-spangler

Thank you to the amazing team at Bookouture and to the readers who have supported the series. What happens after book 11? What mystery will Casey and the team tackle next? What's next for Tracy?

Want to help with the Detective Casey White series and book 11? I would be very grateful if you could write a review, and it also makes such a difference helping new readers to discover one of my books for the first time.

Do you have a question or comment? I'd be happy to answer. You can reach me on my website or through social media.

Happy Reading,

B.R. Spangler

KEEP IN TOUCH WITH B.R. SPANGLER

www.brspangler.com

 facebook.com/authorbrianspangler
x.com/BR_Spangler

PUBLISHING TEAM

Turning a manuscript into a book requires the efforts of many people. The publishing team at Bookouture would like to acknowledge everyone who contributed to this publication.

Audio
Alba Proko
Sinead O'Connor
Melissa Tran

Commercial
Lauren Morrissette
Jil Thielen
Imogen Allport

Data and analysis
Mark Alder
Mohamed Bussuri

Cover design
Head Design Ltd.

Editorial
Claire Simmonds
Jen Shannon

Copyeditor
Janette Currie

Proofreader
Shirley Khan

Marketing
Alex Crow
Melanie Price
Occy Carr
Cíara Rosney

Operations and distribution
Marina Valles
Stephanie Straub

Production
Hannah Snetsinger
Mandy Kullar

Publicity
Kim Nash
Noelle Holten
Myrto Kalavrezou
Jess Readett
Sarah Hardy

Rights and contracts
Peta Nightingale
Richard King
Saidah Graham

Made in United States
Orlando, FL
06 March 2024

44424814R00150